GLIDEPATH

A MAX FEND THRILLER

ANDREW WATTS

POINT WHISKEY PUBLISHING

The Cold War may be 'over' for the West. For the Soviets it has entered a new, active and promising phase.

— ANATOLIY GOLITSYN, KGB DEFECTOR

1

Gibraltar

"Have you met Mr. Morozov before?"

"No. But I know the type," Sergei said, sweat on his brow, shielding his eyes from the bright sunlight shining off the Mediterranean.

Sergei was a midlevel manager in one of the most powerful Russian mafia organizations on the planet. Born in Moscow, he had come to France a decade earlier to run his family's business dealings there.

Mikhail and Sergei sat on a small porch overlooking the marina, ten floors up. Below, tourists lined up for ferry rides and deep-sea fishing trips. Seagulls glided in the air, searching for discarded food.

"When you speak with him, make sure you are respectful and to the point. Mr. Morozov does not normally meet with men like you."

Sergei waved his hand dismissively. "Maybe I don't normally meet with men like *him*."

Mikhail took a final drag from his cigarette and then

pressed it into the glass ashtray on the porch table. *If that's how this arrogant little prick wants to play it, fine.*

He'll soon learn.

Mikhail had seen enough of this new generation. The ex-Spetsnaz soldier was getting older, but he still was a foreboding presence. He had cut his teeth in Afghanistan as a member of the Red Army. Mikhail didn't care for men like Sergei. He would just as soon have snapped his skinny little neck for disregarding his advice like that—but working for Morozov required total discipline.

And Morozov wanted to talk to Sergei.

"Can you shut that thing up?"

Sergei's terrier was yapping at Mikhail's feet. The dog hadn't stopped barking in the five minutes since he'd entered. An earsplitting, high-pitched yelp. Over and over and over.

"He likes you. He's a friendly dog."

Mikhail glared at the animal, then looked down at his buzzing phone.

"He's coming up."

Sergei shrugged. He glanced down at the gun holstered on Mikhail's right side.

"You like that piece? I can get you something better."

Mikhail ignored him.

Minutes later, Pavel Morozov entered with two security guards in tow. Mikhail's men. They were younger, but well trained. They closed and locked the door behind them and remained near the entrance of the small vacation condo.

Morozov stepped out onto the patio and took a seat. He was fit for a man of his age—nearing sixty-five. And his tanned skin hinted at a comfortable life in the sun. His expression was stoic. But behind his eyes was the distinct look of a man who had experienced decades of power. The look of an oligarch who expected nothing less than pure obedience. Behind those confident eyes was a master spy—one who had seized power through treachery and violence after the collapse of the Soviet Union.

Sergei hadn't stood as he'd entered. And the tiny dog only intensified its bark—now aimed at Morozov.

Sergei made a clicking sound and the dog hopped up on his lap, now emitting a low growl at the guests.

Morozov looked at Mikhail with one eyebrow raised and then gave a thin smile. Mikhail pulled out a chair for his boss and positioned himself behind Morozov without saying a word.

"Glad you could make it," offered Sergei.

"Tell me what I came to hear."

Sergei said, "I have information that you will be most interested in. My associates and I would like to provide you with the first bid."

"What are you offering?"

"Access. Access to the Fend Aerospace data center. Every document they have. Their designs for aircraft. Their software. Their classified military programs. I can get you into their system."

"How?"

Sergei leaned back and smiled, looking satisfied.

Morozov glanced back at Mikhail and then said to Sergei, "Fend Aerospace is a multibillion-dollar American corporation. They will have very good IT security systems in place. I find it unlikely that a man in your position would come into something like this without outside assistance. So...who is getting you into their system?"

"Max Fend." Sergei petted his dog and stared into the eyes of Pavel Morozov.

"Max Fend? Charles Fend's son?"

"Yes."

"How do you know him?"

"We have done business together."

"What kind of business?"

Sergei ignored the question. "Mr. Morozov, as I understand it, you have been interested in Fend Aerospace for some time. Word is that you have been fishing for a way into their network. I can give it to you. For a price."

The tiny dog was showing its teeth at Pavel Morozov. Sergei made a shushing sound to quiet it down.

Morozov rubbed his chin. "Why?"

"Excuse me?"

"Why would you offer this to me?"

"I was told that you would be interested. And with your work...you would be the best person to help monetize this. My family doesn't normally deal in this area, as you know."

"Yes. Your family deals with prostitutes and drugs." Morozov looked as if he was contemplating something.

"Only the best prostitutes, and the highest-margin drugs." Sergei chuckled.

"Tell me, Sergei, why am I hearing about this from *you*?"

Sergei shifted in his seat. "What the hell does that mean?" The dog began growling again.

Morozov took the tone of a school principal speaking to an unruly student. "Why not one of your cousins in Moscow? I've dealt with them personally in the past. I have a relationship with them. Do they know about this?"

Sergei swallowed.

"Look, if you are not interested, I can go—"

"Oh, no. I *am* interested."

"Then what is the problem?"

Morozov said, "Tell me, who would the buyer be? In your most experienced and professional opinion."

Sergei shrugged. "If you are worried about the liquidity, don't. You wouldn't have to sell this stuff to a big aerospace company. I would think that you could sell the different pieces separately. Any technology company would be interested in the technology. Fend Aerospace is a treasure trove. You are familiar with their new automated flight program?"

"I am."

"My sources tell me that the right person could make billions with this."

Morozov crossed his legs, looking out over the Mediterranean Sea.

"Sergei, are you familiar with the significance of my namesake?"

Sergei rolled his eyes. "I am not here to talk about your name."

Morozov shot the young Russian a look.

Sergei winced. "I'm sorry, Mr. Morozov. I just...what does this have to do with what we are here to discuss? I want to talk about a business proposition. You—"

"I don't care what you want. When I tell you something, you listen." Morozov snapped his fingers.

Mikhail walked over and gripped Sergei's neck in one hand, twisting his left wrist behind his back until Sergei let out a squeal of pain and pressed his head down firmly against the overhang. Sergei was now bent over, his smushed face looking towards Morozov, partially protruding over the edge. The street was ten floors down.

The little dog barked furiously and then grabbed onto Mikhail's pant leg, pulling.

Morozov uncrossed his legs and stood. He grabbed the tiny animal by its neck.

"What are you doing? Let me go. You know who my family is. This is not the way we do business—"

Mikhail punched Sergei in the kidney. With the size of Mikhail's arms, it was quite painful. "Be quiet and listen—or you get more."

Sergei shut up, his eyes wide. The dog kept barking, suspended in air by Morozov's left hand.

With his free hand, Morozov took out a knife from his pocket. He flicked it open and rammed it twice into the dog's throat. A quick, sickening squeaking sound emanated from the dog's mouth. Morozov released his grip and the animal fell to the ground with a thud.

Morozov's hands were covered in blood. One of the guards came over with a damp towel, and Morozov began cleaning himself. He left the dog's carcass on the ground.

Sergei's mouth was open, releasing a slow, painful gasp. His eyes were moist with anger and fear. Spittle dribbled from his lips.

Morozov moved his deck chair closer to the edge, so that his face was mere inches from Sergei's own.

"Let's try again. The name Pavel Morozov—my name—are you familiar with its story in Russian history?"

Sergei's voice was strained. "Yes. Of course."

"The more commonly known name is Pavlik. Pavlik Morozov. A Soviet boy. What is he known for, Sergei?"

Sergei's eyes were looking down over the ledge, ten stories below. He then looked back at Morozov. "He turned his parents in. To...to the Communists."

"Yes. Pavlik Morozov was thirteen when he did that. A peasant. Born in a small village in the country. He was a good Communist. But his father was not. His father had broken the law, forging documents and selling them to criminals. So Pavlik did what any good Soviet boy should have done—he turned his father in to the political police. What happened next?"

Sergei had stopped fighting but was still being forced down at an awkward angle.

"The boy was killed—by his relatives."

"Something like that. Pavlik Morozov turned his father in. His father was sentenced to ten years in a labor camp and then executed. But then Pavlik's family took their revenge. They did not appreciate disloyalty. Little Pavlik's uncle, grandfather, grandmother, and cousin murdered him in cold blood. And they killed his younger brother too, for good measure."

Sergei winced in pain. Mikhail's thick fingers still dug into his neck, Sergei's forehead scraping against the plastered overhang.

Morozov whispered, "Then the Soviet political police— found out about the horrific murders. So they went into town, rounded up the perpetrators, lined them up, and executed all of them by firing squad.

"The people of the Soviet Union were aghast at what happened. Pavlik became a martyr. A symbol. Statues went up. Songs and poems were written. Poor young Pavlik's school became a memorial where children all over the Soviet Union were sent to pay tribute to his great sacrifice."

Morozov looked up at Mikhail and nodded. Mikhail placed Sergei back on his chair but remained standing behind him. Sergei was bleeding from his forehead, where it had ground into the rough stone wall.

Morozov said, "So my parents named me after this great example of Communist bravery. What do you think, Sergei? What do you think of my name?"

Sergei said, "I don't know...I think it is good, I guess."

"Do you know what I think?"

Sergei shook his head, looking down at the floor.

"I think it is all propaganda bullshit. The Communists

fabricated that story. It was the most perfect Russian tragedy you could imagine. And my poor parents bought it. Now I have to walk around with this goddamned lie of a name."

Sergei just stared back, eyes lowered.

"But you know what, Sergei? The story does have a good lesson. But it is not the lesson that the Soviets wanted us to take away. Do you know what I am talking about?"

Sergei shook his head rapidly.

Morozov got in his face, speaking through gritted teeth.

"Family members are often a great source of vulnerability. They are blind spots. Take Max Fend. Max Fend might be his father's undoing. And what about you, Sergei? Are you the weak link in your family?"

Fear shone in Sergei's eyes.

"Like I said, Sergei, I am used to dealing with your family. *Not you*. So when you called, guess what I did? I called your uncles. And I told them something that they did not know. Your uncles don't want to have a rat in the family. That is a problem for them. A problem that they would very much like to go away."

Mikhail came back into Sergei's view again. He was twisting a silencer onto the barrel of his gun, his eyes on Sergei.

Morozov smiled. "I make problems go away, Sergei. I'm very good at it."

"Mr. Morozov, please just—"

"I want you to tell me everything you know about Max Fend. And then I want you to tell me exactly how you propose to gain access to the Fend network."

"You are going to shoot me." Sergei's voice sounded defeated.

A thin-lipped smile. "Tell me what I want to know, and I promise you that I won't shoot you."

* * *

Twenty minutes later, the sounds of the marina were interrupted by screams. The screams began ten stories up and changed pitch as the source hurtled downward, ending in an abrupt smack as Sergei's body smashed onto the pavement.

2

National Air and Space Museum
Washington, D.C.
Five Days Before the Fend 100 Flight

Charles shook his head. "How did they get through our firewall?"

"I just spoke with our IT security team. They still don't know."

"And you're sure that they weren't able to access the Fend 100 software?"

"It appears that way, but they have the aircraft design, including the wing. If the investors find out..."

"They're going to find out, Maria, there's no way around that. The best thing we can hope for now is to manage the message. You've notified the authorities?"

"Yes, Charles. We did that when it happened. But we're just now learning how serious this was."

"I'll have to fly to New York and speak to some of the investors. The NextGen contract isn't complete yet. They'll be nervous."

Maria Blount nodded in agreement. She was one of Charles Fend's top executives and head of the Fend 100 autonomous flight program. She had just broken the news that a cyberattack had penetrated many of their most precious company files. They had known about the breach for several weeks. But until today, the Fend Aerospace leadership had been under the impression that their cybersecurity had prevented any important data from being stolen. This was bad news at a critical juncture in the company's schedule.

"The *Today Show* is ready for you, Mr. Fend."

The camera crew was setting up right under the National Air and Space Museum's exhibit on commercial aviation. A DC-3 was suspended in the air overhead, and the giant front end of a Boeing 747 protruded from the wall.

"Excuse me, we will have to discuss this more later," Charles said and walked onto the set.

The production team hooked a microphone to his shirt and handed him an earpiece. Bright lights illuminated the area. The crowd of museum tourists that had gathered around him hushed, seeing that *the* Charles Fend was about to go on live TV.

Charles could hear "the talent" in his ear, carrying on with their morning news update. Then came the voice he assumed belonged to the producer, instructing them to cut to Washington for Charles Fend.

The large black camera rolled up in front of him, keeping the museum's aircraft in the frame. A tiny TV screen next to the camera showed the host saying, "We're now joined by the illustrious Charles Fend—aviation pioneer and owner of Fend Aerospace. He's coming to us live from the National Air and Space Museum in Washington, D.C. Charles, would you care to tell everyone watching how the Fend 100 project is going so far?"

Charles smiled, his white teeth and gray hair recognizable to the viewers from many years of wide publicity.

"It's going great, thank you for asking. In five more days, the Fend 100 will be airborne, and I wanted to thank you for having me on your show to talk about it."

"Can you tell our audience what to expect during the flight next week?"

"Sure thing. The Fend 100 will fly its first passenger flight just like any other commercial airliner, with one key difference. The Fend 100 Artificial Intelligence Pilot System will be doing all the work. The computers will completely take over for the pilots. The Fend 100 will fly up and down the Florida coast for a few hours, allowing our passengers to experience what real airborne luxury can be like, and then the Fend 100 will return for a safe landing back at our headquarters near Jacksonville."

Charles looked around the room, beaming. "I can't tell you all how proud I am of the men and women on the Fend 100 project team. They have each put a great deal of hard work into this. Decades of research and development have led to this moment. It is truly the dawn of a new era in aviation."

The TV host said, "Mr. Fend, what do you say to those that are worried about flying on pilotless aircraft?"

Charles nodded and smiled. "You know, there was a day not too long ago in our history when people rode on elevators, and they couldn't imagine the possibility of not having a bellboy there to expertly control it for them."

The crowd around him gave a muffled laugh.

"Today," Charles continued, "we think nothing of walking into an elevator and pressing that little button. That button sends you traveling through the air, thanks to a bunch of computers and electronics. There was a time when pilots used to control aircraft mechanically, through yokes attached to cables. You needed muscle power to move the elevators and ailerons. To manipulate the surface of the wing, which would move the aircraft into a turn. Aviators needed a wealth of knowledge to navigate and solve problems while flying. But those days are long past. We have computers in our phones that are exponentially more powerful than anything we had in the early days of aviation."

The TV show host said, "So you're saying that computers can do it all now?"

"Let me ask you a question. Have you gone on an airplane in the past few months?"

The TV host smiled. "Yes, Mr. Fend."

"How long was your flight? Probably a few hours, right? And do you know that the pilots on your commercial airliner were probably only touching the flight controls for about two minutes out of the entire flight? Aircraft can *already* do everything by themselves. On a foggy day, they even land themselves. Why? Because computers make fewer mistakes than people. In truth, mankind has been ready to take this step for quite some time. And, despite what the newspapers say about me, I'm a human being...not a computer."

The crowd around him laughed again. Louder this time. That was good. Keep them happy. People needed to believe in this.

"I... believe it or not, I understand the unease that some might feel at the thought of a pilotless aircraft flying them around the world. But science and statistics prove it... computers *are* safer. The majority of advancements in aviation over the past few decades have been incremental intro-ductions of automated flight. Airspeed control. Altitude hold. Different computerized functions that most of you laymen would simply lump into the term 'autopilot.' But each one of these improvements was another step towards allowing a computer to more fully control the airplane. It is worth mentioning that these improvements have saved countless lives. Now, with artificial intelligence, we have machines that can learn, just like a pilot. And that is really the ground-breaking technology that we're going to provide. We want to make flying even safer and more efficient than it is today."

The TV host said, "Will you still have pilots as a backup? In case anything goes wrong?"

Charles Fend looked over at Maria and then back at the camera. She had told him to be ready for that question.

"We have built in that capability. And we will continue to work with the FAA and other regulatory agencies on best practices as we look to integrate this into the commercial aviation industry. Fend Aerospace has meshed the latest in AI capability with autopilot software. This creates a propri-etary feature that enables safe and effective pilotless commercial flight. It's really quite extraordinary—and it will make flying both safer and cheaper."

"Mr. Fend, I think we can all agree that those are both two improvements to look forward to." The host thanked him and transitioned to the next segment.

Cheers and claps from the crowd around him.

* * *

Brunch was at Sequoia, a restaurant on the shores of the Potomac. White tablecloths and a glitzy atmosphere.

"Are you excited?" Max said.

"Thrilled," his father answered, although he didn't sound it. Max and Charles Fend sat across from each other at an outside table. "This automated flight program has been more than ten years in the making. It will be nice to see it through before my retirement." He took a drink. "So your classes start in a few weeks?"

"Orientation. It's just a weekend. The classes start in August. I think I'll be the old man of my cohort."

His father shook his head. "I can't believe you're going to Georgetown. It hurts my heart. You know you don't need it for a resume. I'll give you the job anyway. That's a privilege of owning your own company."

Max smiled. His father had gone to Boston College, a rival Jesuit institution, for his undergrad degree back in the day.

Max had decided to get his MBA at Georgetown prior to starting his new career. His twelve years of prior work experience would qualify him for an elite subset of jobs, but those jobs were unrelated to managing an aerospace company.

"Well, we'll have to start betting on the sports games," his father said.

"Deal."

Max forked another bite of his "Chesapeake eggs Benedict"—a delicious hollandaise sauce dribbled over lump crab meat, a poached egg, and an English muffin. His father sipped on his bloody mary, looking up at the dreary gray sky.

"So you're sure about the retirement, then?" Max asked as he chewed.

"Mr. Fend, good morning!"

A woman strolled along the walkway near the restaurant's outdoor seating area.

"Maria. You can't get away from me, it seems. How are you, my dear? Care to join us?"

"Oh no, I couldn't."

Max realized Maria must have been in the group of executives that had flown on the corporate jet up from Jacksonville the day before. They were doing a full court press publicity tour in the run-up to the Fend 100 flight. Max's father had been on TV more often in the last few weeks than in the past decade. And for a man as in the spotlight as he was, that was saying a lot.

"Are you sure? We don't mind," said Max's father.

Maria came up to their table, sliding awkwardly through a large set of potted frond leaves.

"No, thank you, though. I was just doing a little shopping before we head back." She smiled at Max. "Max, I'm surprised your father didn't send you on the *Today Show* in his place yesterday. Now that you'll be joining the company and all."

Max gave a humble grin. "I hope he has more common sense than that. After spending the past few weeks with you all in Jacksonville, I've realized just how much I still have to learn."

Maria pushed a lock of her red hair back over her shoulder. "Max, you will do just fine." She smiled widely and looked back at Max's father. "Every time he comes down to Jacksonville, he's always asking such good questions."

"Well, I've always been interested in flying. Just need to learn more about the business, I suppose."

"Oh yes. I recently heard that you're a pilot. Is that right, Max?"

"Just for fun. I have my private pilot's license."

"What aircraft do you fly?"

"I've flown a few of them, but I'm partial to the Cirrus aircraft. I keep telling my father that Fend Aerospace needs to get into the general aviation market."

Charles laughed. "Maria, this is the part that worries me. If I give him too much of a leash, he'll turn the company into his own hobby center."

Maria smiled politely. "That's the sign of a good executive, Charles. Someone who's already interested in the work."

"Excellent," Charles said. "Well, you don't need to waste time on us. Anything more on that thing we were discussing yesterday?"

"No, I'm afraid not."

"Very well. I'll see you later today."

"Max, it was a pleasure as always. Charles, I'll see you on the plane."

Maria departed and walked away, along the brick walkway next to the Potomac River.

When she was out of earshot, Charles said, "A lovely woman. She has exceeded my expectations. You'll do well to shadow her when you join us full-time."

Maria had been hired by Charles Fend personally a few years ago, out of London. Max had gotten to know her relatively well, as she was one of the few people he interacted with when he would visit his father. She was one of Charles Fend's most trusted advisors.

Max lowered his voice. "So you were saying you think you're ready to scale back a bit?"

His father looked at him and nodded. "Yes. It's time. I'll still keep involved. I'm staying on as chairman of the board. I can step in if I see anything out of sorts. But all the day-to-day decision-making will be handled by a new CEO."

"And who will that be?"

Charles shook his head. "That's months away. I need to get us through this Fend 100 project first. Once we get that finished, my real work will be complete. The Fend 100 program will set Fend Aerospace up for the next few decades."

Max raised an eyebrow. "I don't mean to be selfish, but your retirement does make me curious about how I might be affected."

His father smiled. "That doesn't make you selfish, just human. Nothing will change for you. I'll see to that. You'll be employed with the company, as long as that's what you still want. You can finish your master's program here at George-town and then start working full-time after that."

Max sat back in his chair, mulling it over. His whole life, he'd been running from his wealth. His father had a control-ling interest in one of the largest aerospace companies in the world. Everyone had heard of Fend Aerospace. When Max was growing up, most people that he met assumed that he was some spoiled rich prep school kid. And he *had* gone to all the best schools. They'd never been short of money. His father had taken him around the world on fabulous vacations.

But he'd always had a chip on his shoulder. Max wanted to forge his own path. He hadn't gone on to work on Wall Street or as an investment banker, like many of his class-mates at Princeton. Instead, he had chosen to take a job that allowed him to see the world, live an exciting life, and do something fulfilling.

It just wasn't the type of occupation that he could talk to people about. In that field, talking about your work was the quickest way to ending up dead in a ditch.

But he was no longer *in* that line of work, he had to keep

reminding himself. Whether he wanted to or not, now it was time for him to move on and try something new. Time to learn his family trade—and in doing so, accept an opportunity that few received.

The family business was worth close to twenty billion dollars. Fend was one of the largest airplane manufacturers on the planet. For years, Max and his father had an ongoing joke about how Max would one day take over as CEO. At least, it *had* been a joke. Until that walk on the French Riviera, when Max had asked his father if he might be able to come to work for Fend Aerospace.

Max said, "I don't feel like I've earned it."

His father took a bite of his bagel, a smear of cream cheese and smoked salmon on top.

"You *haven't* earned it. But *I* have. That's capitalism, son. To the victor go the spoils. One of mine is being able to name whomever the hell I want as my successor. And another is being able to place my son in management, if I so desire."

"I don't like getting handouts."

"It isn't one. You'll work your tail off, won't you?"

"Yes."

"I know how smart you are." He hesitated. "Your mother would have been proud of the man you've become, Max. I mean that."

Max flushed. "Thank you." He had trouble looking his father in the eye after that one. Compliments were sometimes hard for him. He changed the subject. "So what's next for the Fend 100?"

His father's face lit up. Max knew that he could talk all day about his work. "The FAA is going to evaluate the first passenger flight the week after next."

"And they don't mind that you're going to have a big show about it?"

"The FAA has all but granted us the contract as the sole supplier of autonomous flight technology for the NextGen program. They want us to succeed, and to generate enthusiasm among the public."

"And you don't have any reservations about it? Safety-wise, I mean."

"No, of course not. We've tested everything a million times. This is a dog-and-pony show. For the investors, for the trade, and for Washington. The FAA and those who are making the decisions with NextGen want to see consumer confidence in the product before they grant us final approval for the contract."

"So you'll have this first passenger flight..."

Charles said, "Yes."

"And that will get you the contract?"

His voice lowered. "Essentially, yes. That's what I'm being told. After that, the FAA will approve Fend Aerospace as the contractor for all US autonomous commercial flight software and networking. And then...I'll be looking at taking more vacations."

Max didn't respond. He was distracted by a young couple sitting at an umbrella table on the far end of the restaurant patio. They weren't talking. They both had sunglasses on. And Max was almost positive that they were conducting surveillance on him.

Why would anyone be surveilling him now? He hadn't been in Europe for a few months. And who were *they*?

Max tried to keep up his conversation with his father without appearing distracted. "Any thoughts on where you'd travel to first?"

"I liked Japan very much the last time I was there. There

are some great spots in the mountains. Peaceful spas. Great food. Friendly, respectful people. I very much like the Japanese culture."

"That certainly sounds nice."

He spotted two more inside the restaurant. Max guessed that they were probably US federal law enforcement. They each wore a very small, almost imperceptible earpiece. And they looked nervous, like they were trying too hard to play it cool. Definitely not interested in what they were ordering, or in talking to each other.

For a moment, he thought that they might be there for someone else. Perhaps even his father, the way the man was obviously glancing in their direction.

No. They appeared to be watching *him*.

They never looked at him *directly*. Their glances were always at someone or something *near* him. Just like they were trained, Max knew. Just like *he* had been trained.

Max's mind kicked into high gear. He began thinking about an exit strategy. Vehicles. Doors. Weapons. No— weapons were out of the question. Better to just roll with it and trust that his father's lawyer would be able to handle whatever misunderstanding there might be.

But what if he was wrong? What if they *weren't* US law enforcement? What if they were some less talented foreign intelligence service? (The talented ones wouldn't be so obvious.) What if they were contractors? Lawyers might not matter to those types.

Max spotted a dark SUV with tinted windows in the street. The door opened only for a second, but it was enough for him to see a dark blue jacket—just like the raid jackets that federal agents wore.

He wracked his brain to think of what this might be

about. His father was still speaking. He had moved the conversation on to Max's new corporate training plan.

"Come to think of it, I may have Maria schedule some time to go over the company's priorities for the next fiscal year. It would be good for you to get a head start of sorts. To learn about the company's big bets and priorities while you're still in school. You'll have a steep enough learning curve as it is."

Max tried to remain in the conversation. "Alright. Anything else I should do to prepare?"

His father took another bite of his bagel and washed it down with ice water. "Yes, actually. I think it's about damned time you learned how to fly."

"I *know* how to fly, Dad."

"I'm talking about one of these bigger aircraft. You can't very well be expected to lead a company that makes jet airliners and not have any idea how to pilot them."

"You mean get my multiengine or jet rating? Sure. I can do that. Maybe I can schedule some lessons up at BWI? There's got to be a multiengine instructor there."

"Max, we have our own school. It's top-notch. We can train you. You'll just need to find the time."

Another SUV pulled up and parked just in back of the first. What were they doing, bringing in the whole agency? He was one man, and unarmed. He wasn't going to fight them. Not to mention that *he hadn't done anything wrong.*

The couple at the far table both cocked their heads at the same time and looked at each other. Someone had just given them a command via their earpieces.

The man rose from his seat. Then the woman.

They began walking toward Max, hands down near their waists. The two at the table inside were headed his way as well now, walking through the restaurant exit and out onto the patio.

"Dad."

"Yes?"

"I think I may need you to call your lawyer."

3

The agents were actually quite polite. They asked Max if he would voluntarily accompany them. He wasn't under arrest; they just had some questions. Max was amenable. His father was not.

"This is ridiculous, disturbing us here like this," his father said.

"We're sorry, Mr. Fend, but this is an urgent matter that we need to resolve."

Max tried to calm his father down, but that proved to be a tall order. After arguing with the agents and threatening to sue, Charles was on the phone with his lawyer. Max wasn't sure what his father would sue for, since he was voluntarily following his FBI escorts. But he knew that his father was just embarrassed and maybe a bit scared. He was always overly protective of Max.

Still, Max knew this wasn't normal, the FBI showing up like this. He tried to think of why they might have done it. Something time-sensitive, perhaps.

Or maybe they wanted to catch him off guard. Before he had the chance to lawyer up. If Max was running this little op, he would want to get as much out of the guy as he could, as soon as he could.

The FBI probably realized that as soon as one of Max's father's high-powered attorneys came into play, he wouldn't be saying a thing. Max wondered if they knew about his background. *No. That's not possible.* If anything, they knew about his cover. Now *that* could be a problem. Maybe that was it, then.

Max reverted back to his training. In the US, federal agents would need probable cause to arrest him. They could detain him no more than about twenty minutes without placing him under arrest. But if he voluntarily went with them...that changed the dynamics of the relationship. Still, it would be hard for them to use anything in court if they didn't play it by the book.

The FBI was all about what they could prove in a court system. That wasn't an issue for men like Max. In his former occupation, they only cared about getting accurate information, no matter how it came out.

Max and his FBI escorts walked up to a line of dark government SUVs parked on the curb of Rock Creek Parkway. The doors opened, and a few men stepped out of the cars, "FBI" emblazoned in bright yellow on both sides of their blue raid jackets. People on the street stared. It must have looked like a scene out of a movie.

"Mr. Fend, my name is Special Agent Jake Flynn. We'd like to speak with you for a few moments, please."

Max looked at the group, a grin on his face. "All of you?"

"Could you come with us, please, sir?"

Max said, "Sure thing."

A few moments later, Max sat in the middle seat of the Suburban. Two big FBI agents on either side. The vehicle drove fast through the streets of D.C.

The SUV stopped at a townhouse on Eighth Street in Northeast.

Max gave the FBI agents an odd look. "What's this?"

"It's an off-site residence that we use sometimes. It's easier than taking you all the way down to the D.C. field office in Manassas. Unless you'd rather be stuck on I-95 for three hours today. If you can answer all our questions, we might be out of here in under an hour."

"I'll do my best."

An agent at the door collected his phone on the way in. "You'll get it back once we're done. Security."

They walked up to the second floor. Max kept going over things in his head. With this many agents here, Max figured that whatever they were working on must have been pretty high-profile. Maybe that was just because his father was Charles Fend. Maybe it was something else.

"Have a seat." Special Agent Flynn extended his hand to a simple white desk, surrounded by a few chairs. Max sat.

"Can I get you anything to drink?"

"No, thanks," Max said.

"Do you know of any reason why we might want to speak with you today?"

Max shook his head. "I don't."

Agent Flynn stared back at him for a moment, letting the question hang.

"Can you tell me where you were on the fifteenth of last month?"

Max thought about it. "I was in Jacksonville, Florida."

"Where exactly?"

"I was with my father. Touring the Fend Aerospace plant and headquarters."

"Touring the Fend Aerospace plant and headquarters?"

"That's right."

"Did you access the computer network at the Fend head-quarters?"

"Can I ask you something? Do I need a lawyer?"

"Not if you didn't do anything wrong."

"I didn't."

"Then we can keep this informal, if you want. It'll be quicker. Did you access the computer network at the Fend headquarters?" His voice was melodic. Casual.

Max didn't have a good feeling about this. Why were they concerned about the Fend computer network? He thought about his former line of work. If the right person had access, they could have done a lot of things with corporate network access like Max had.

Max said, "I think I might have used one of the company computers. Maybe to type a few emails. That sort of thing. But that was several weeks ago. It's hard to remember."

"It was three weeks ago."

"Okay, it was three weeks ago."

"So you had access to the Fend network?"

"Yes. I'm becoming an employee there. They've granted me access."

"What type of employee?"

"Excuse me?"

"What will your job title be, if you don't mind my asking?"

"My father owns the company. He's training me for a managerial position."

A few of the agents raised their eyebrows, smiling. "Must be nice," one of them said. Max reddened.

Flynn said, "While you were there, did you email anyone who resides outside of the country?"

Max frowned. "I don't know. I doubt it."

"You doubt it, or you did *not*?"

"I don't remember."

"You don't remember?"

"It was almost a month ago. Do you remember everyone you emailed exactly one month ago?"

"Did you email anyone in Syria or Iraq?"

Max frowned. "No."

"Have you ever had contact with a foreign government, its establishment, or its representatives—whether inside or outside the US?"

"I worked for a European consulting firm. We did a lot of business with a variety of clients. Some of them were foreign governments."

"Any from any of those countries that I mentioned? Syria or Iraq?"

"I don't think so, no."

"Have you worked with any government or nongovernment organizations that were involved in criminal or terrorist activity?"

"No, of course not."

"Were you involved with any nongovernment organizations from any of the countries I previously mentioned? Or maybe somewhere else in the Middle East?"

"Probably not."

"*Probably* not?"

"What do those countries have to do with anything?"

"Could you please answer the question?"

"I thought we were having a friendly discussion."

"We are." Flynn gave a forced smile. "See?"

"Some of our clients were from Saudi Arabia, I believe. And I think at least one was Syrian. But I worked with businessmen from just about every other country in the world. So it's not like I was just working with Syrians and Saudis the whole time. Although last time I checked, Saudi Arabia was a pretty staunch ally."

Flynn frowned. "Did you communicate with any of those clients from the Fend network on the fifteenth?"

"What clients?"

"The *Syrians*."

Max shook his head. "No. I do not have a continuing relationship with any of my *former* clients. I don't send any of them emails. I'm changing fields."

"Are you aware of a Fend network security breach last month?"

"No."

"Did you know that a foreign entity attempted to steal information from Fend Aerospace?"

"No, I didn't know that."

"Do you know how much someone would pay to access the Fend Aerospace servers?"

"I wouldn't know."

"Don't you find it interesting that this security breach happened on the fifteenth, right when you were there?"

Max stayed quiet. Was the FBI agent telling the truth? He certainly looked like it. So how was it that Max *didn't* know about this, if it was true? Why would his father have kept it from him? Perhaps the agent was misinformed? Or maybe it was a minor incident, and they were blowing it out of proportion. If it was something routine, Max could see his father not telling him about it. Would the FBI be questioning him if it were a minor incident? Unlikely...

Flynn waited for a response but got none. Then he said, "Mr. Fend, you will understand when I tell you that this security breach has raised some very serious questions. Fend Aerospace has some pretty big government contracts in the works. Some of them are defense-related. Some of them aren't, but still affect the safety and well-being of many Americans."

The agents were watching him closely.

"How can I help you with this Agent Flynn?"

Flynn said, "We have reason to believe that on the day of the incident, someone provided an external source—likely originating from one of the countries that I mentioned—with access to the Fend computer network."

Max moved in his seat. "That is concerning."

"It *is*."

No one spoke. A dog barked outside. An ambulance siren was going off in the distance.

"You understand why I'm asking you about your foreign connections now, don't you?"

Max said, "I think I see where you're going, yes."

"My team of specialists think it's possible that someone from the inside granted access to this hacker group. The hacker group then attempted to steal highly confidential corporate secrets from Fend Aerospace."

"That's incredibly disturbing," Max said.

"Yes, it is. And do you know what *else* is disturbing?"

"What?"

"The hacker group had connections to one of your former business associates in Europe."

"Well, I wasn't—"

"And the account that granted them access was *yours*."

* * *

They continued to question him for almost an hour. The longer it went on, the more uncomfortable Max got. There was definitely a trail of evidence that pointed to Max.

Multiple cyberintrusions on the Fend network over a

two-day period. Each through Max's account. Each from some group that was supposedly connected to someone Max knew in Europe. They wouldn't say who.

"Are you sure there isn't more that you'd like to tell us?" Flynn said. "Because to me, it looks like you could be connected to a cybercrime. You know people that were likely involved, and you were at the location of a crime at or about the time it occurred."

"Special Agent Flynn, respectfully—I can assure you that I had no knowledge of any hacking that went on at my father's company."

"And?"

"And you must agree that I have no obvious motive. You have a few bits of information that are implicating me, but the obvious hole is this: why would I want to harm my father's company? I have a good relationship with my father. And I would never want to harm him, his company, or our country. Look, I'm happy to continue to answer any questions you might have—I will cooperate fully. But please know that I didn't do anything wrong."

The room was silent. One of the agents glanced at Flynn, who looked uncertain.

The doorbell rang. Max could hear one of the agents as he marched down the stairs and spoke to someone at the door.

"Flynn?"

"What?"

"The father's lawyer is here."

Flynn whispered. "You gotta be shitting me. How'd he know where we were?"

The agent shrugged. "What do you want me to do?"

Max tried not to appear pleased.

Flynn said, "Let him in, of course."

A tall, thin black man wearing a suit jacket walked up to the floor where Max was being questioned.

The lawyer scanned the room in silence. He seemed completely comfortable as he looked each one of the agents in the face. His gaze landed on Flynn.

The lawyer said, "What in the *world* are you doing?"

"He voluntarily came with us. He—"

"Do you have PC?" *Probable cause.*

Flynn clenched his jaw. "Not at this time."

"Then he doesn't need to answer questions. Let's go, Max."

Max stood. The lawyer began walking out.

Agent Flynn cleared his throat. "We aren't *finished*. We really could use about twenty more minutes of your time, if you'll give it to us, Mr. Fend."

Max looked at the lawyer questioningly. He guessed that the lawyer would say no, but Max didn't want to appear as anything other than cooperative. Let the lawyer be the bad guy.

Max said, "If it will help clear up this mess..."

The lawyer stopped and turned, hands folded across his chest. He sighed. "If Mr. Fend wants to continue to answer your questions, we can finish this at my office. *Tomorrow*. I need time to confer with my client."

The FBI men looked at each other. One walked away with his phone to his ear, whispering into it.

"Fine," Flynn said. "We'll finish up tomorrow."

Max could see the other agent on the phone in the kitchen area. He was making eye contact with Flynn. He held up two fingers.

Two minutes.

Special Agent Flynn nodded back to him.

What was happening in two minutes?

Max got up and the group of agents escorted him down the stairs. Flynn said, "Give him back his phone and personal items."

One of the agents leaned in close to Flynn. Max tried to read his lips but couldn't. It looked like he uttered the phrase "press charges." As in, "*Do you want to press charges?*" Max knew that if one of the agents was asking that, then they were probably close to that threshold of evidence they needed to place him under arrest.

They *couldn't* have that. Not unless there was something they weren't telling him.

He didn't hear Flynn's reply. But he saw Flynn looking right back at him, shaking his head. The group continued to walk outside the building.

A maroon Lexus sedan was parked on the curb. The lawyer opened the door for Max. "We'll be in touch," he told the FBI agents.

Once Max was inside with the doors closed, the lawyer looked Max in the eyes. His expression changed.

Max heard some commotion outside the vehicle. The FBI agent that had been on the phone was running down the front steps of the townhouse. Holding up his hand, calling something out to Special Agent Flynn.

In the side mirror, Max could see them talking. Flynn turned and looked at the sedan. He held out his hand and yelled, "Hold up!"

The doors in the sedan locked and Max looked at the lawyer in confusion. The lawyer placed his hand on Max's shoulder. "Listen to me." His eyes were deadly serious. "I'm not a lawyer. And I've never worked for your father."

A sinking feeling grew in the pit of Max's stomach.

The driver said, "Someone set you up. That's why the FBI is questioning you. And it won't get any better."

A knock at Max's window. Flynn stood there, giving him a signal to roll down the window. His voice sounded muffled from outside. "Max, please step out of the vehicle."

Max looked up at him. A group of agents were behind him. One was going around the driver's side. Flynn's hand began reaching down toward his holster.

The lawyer said, "Max, whatever information they just received, it's *false*. But it's something that could lock you up for years, and place your father and his company in peril. You need to get out now, while you can."

"Right. Question—can you go back to the part where you—"

"Max, I need your consent. This will be your only chance. Come with me now, and I can give you a shot at freedom. You'll have a chance to find out who set you up, and stop them. But you need to tell me now that you're in. Otherwise, my orders are to release you back to the FBI."

Max looked into the face of Agent Flynn. He didn't look happy.

Max said, "Let's go."

"Strap in. We're going to try and lose them."

"Oh, hell."

The lawyer slammed on the gas and peeled out, his Lexus tearing down the road. They left the FBI agents open-mouthed and panicked.

4

A t first, Special Agent Flynn had thought the lawyer was just a pompous ass. Coming in like he owned the place, happy to throw his weight around and force the FBI to play by the rules.

Flynn had been stuck between a rock and a hard place. He had taken a risk, asking Max to voluntarily come in to answer questions before the second arrest warrant was issued. The first warrant had been recalled as they were moving in to arrest him.

The Cyber Division had sent them evidence that morning, and his team had a location on Max Fend. A judge issued the warrant, and they began moving.

The evidence was obvious enough at first glance. Fend looked dirty. The Syrian hacker group on the other end certainly was. The electronic forensics data connected Max to the cyber intrusion. The Cyber Division had cross-checked it with their partners at the NSA, who in turn had shown it to the DNI's office as a courtesy.

That's when the trouble started. After the warrant was issued, the lawyers from DNI and the NSA had informed the Justice Department of some irregularities in the data. Flynn had seen this show before. The judge would recall the warrant. But by that time, his team was walking toward Max Fend and had likely been spotted. Pulling them back meant that they would be alerting Fend that they were on to him, and giving him a chance to flee.

Sure enough, the judge decided to cancel the warrant. Flynn's team was already moving in on Max. He had to think fast. So he told them to see if Fend would come in voluntarily.

But Flynn needed corroborating evidence. So he reached out to the DST—the French domestic intelligence agency. They had responded to a request for information on Fend earlier. The French had records of Max taking meetings with men connected to the suspected hackers. Flynn needed those documents sent to the judge.

Flynn's team received the evidence from the French and were taking it up the chain. They would have an arrest warrant within the hour. In the meantime, Flynn would ask Max Fend a few questions. If they were lucky, he might get spooked. Maybe he would admit allowing the hackers into the Fend computer network. If not, the French evidence would provide what they needed to place Fend under arrest before they had to let him go. That was the plan.

The Fend lawyer had changed everything.

Once he entered the picture, Flynn began to worry that any case he had would be thrown out because of procedural mistakes. He had stuck his neck out, and now his head was about to get chopped off. Flynn had attempted to take down wealthy guys like this Fend character before. Their lawyers always got them off on technicalities. That's what the money paid for. Greatest judicial system in the world.

So Flynn went along with the lawyer's suggestion to meet down at his office tomorrow. Better to play it by the book at this point and live another day. If the lawyer wasn't going to raise a stink about taking Fend to the safe house for questioning, that was a good thing. The judge's office was due to call back any minute.

Special Agent Flynn didn't know what would make someone like Max Fend get involved with organized crime rings out of Eastern Bloc nations. But that's what his file said. Fend had taken meetings with people who were involved in arms dealing, drugs, and human trafficking. He had close ties to some less-than-reputable Middle Eastern businessmen. Some were even on terrorist watch lists.

He was also plugged in to the young elite European crowd. Wealthy twenty- and thirty-somethings not unlike himself. Lots of flashy cars and pretty girls. Fend liked to have a good time, apparently. He worked as some type of high-end consultant—wheeling and dealing and living the high life in the South of France. Why he cavorted with criminals, Flynn didn't know.

When the FBI asked Special Agent Flynn to investigate the potential hacking incident at Fend Aerospace last week, he would never have guessed that it would lead back to Charles Fend's own son. But that's what the evidence was telling him. The Cyber Division was dependable. They could really work some magic with their computers. And the more Flynn read up on Max Fend, the more it all fit into place.

Flynn had come so close to arresting him.

But now, as the brand-new Lexus rounded the first

corner—and out of sight—the veteran FBI agent began to panic.

"Let's move!" he yelled.

The group of agents piled into the SUVs and chased after them. A few seconds later, they could see the Lexus, racing through the streets of D.C.

Flynn rode shotgun. "There! They just took a turn."

"I got 'em, I got 'em."

He flipped on the blue light and siren and called it in to the D.C. police and US Secret Service, since they were driving right near the White House.

"Suspect is a white male, about six feet tall, medium build. Driving a maroon Lexus sedan...now turning onto..."

"Constitution," the other agent said.

"Constitution Avenue. Request immediate backup and pursuit."

The D.C. dispatcher relayed the message, and the Washington streets came alive with police and federal agencies. Two minutes later, a Maryland State Police helicopter was en route.

Flynn smiled.

What a piece of work. Who the hell thinks he can run from the FBI in the middle of Washington, D.C.?

* * *

Max was pressed back into his seat at the unexpected acceleration.

The lawyer glanced in his rearview mirror as he drove.

"Who are you?"

"That's not important. This is: don't let yourself be taken into custody again, understand? They might not have enough to arrest you with right now, but they will. That's what I'm being told."

"Told by whom?"

He didn't answer.

The Lexus's engine roared as the driver swerved through the busy D.C. traffic. Max held on to the door handle and his seat, tensing his legs against the floor for stability. He could see blue flashing lights both in front of and behind them.

His body jerked to the right as the driver took a hard left turn on Fourteenth Street.

"Why is someone trying to set me up?"

"We don't know yet."

The driver reached in the backseat and threw a small backpack on Max's lap. "Here. Put this jacket on. Make sure you leave your phone and any electronic devices in this vehicle. You know the drill." The man smiled.

With the smile was an unspoken acknowledgment that he knew about Max's background.

"Got it," Max said, a twinge of apprehension in his voice.

He unzipped the backpack. Two phones. A gun, with several magazines taped together. A Ziploc bag filled with cash, prepaid debit cards, and false IDs. All with Max's face. He examined one of them. It was quality work. Must have taken a while. How long had they been planning this?

The driver took a hard right on Constitution Ave. The Washington Monument was out the left side of the window now. The speedometer read over eighty miles per hour, the slow-moving traffic whipping by as the sedan zigged and zagged in between lanes.

He was a good driver. But also a little lucky. They barely missed hitting a woman crossing the street. She had been looking down at her cell phone.

"Put this on."

The man handed Max a large black motorcycle helmet. Tinted visor. Max did as he instructed.

By the time they took the circle around the Lincoln Memorial, the police cars were pretty far behind them. But Max wasn't worried about the ones behind them. He could see blue flashing lights and halted traffic on the bridge crossing the Potomac.

Max said, "Tell me you aren't going for one of the bridges."

"Not yet."

The Lexus swerved around the circle and jerked to the right, going off the road at over fifty miles per hour.

"Wait," Max said, realizing where they were going.

The ground in front of them dropped off into a steep incline. Max couldn't see what was beyond.

"*Hey...wait...*"

It looked like they were about to go off a steep drop-off in the road, heading towards the Potomac.

"*Hold on,*" said the driver.

The Lexus launched over the long concrete set of stairs that led down to Ohio Drive, twenty feet below. The sedan crunched into the bottom of the stone steps and skidded into the ground as the driver turned left and braked.

It wasn't enough to stop the collision. They hit a Mercedes sedan first. Sideswiped it while going about thirty-five miles per hour. Max jolted around in his seat. He clenched his teeth so that he wouldn't bite his tongue in the crash. Another car bumped them from behind, its driver pumping her fist.

Drivers slammed on their horns as the Lexus momentarily came to a halt. The man in the Mercedes started to get out of his car, furious and swearing. But Max's driver just put his car in reverse and backed up a few feet, shoveling the car to the rear. It cleared enough space for them to break free. He drove forward, leaving the angry drivers behind.

They raced to a spot only fifty yards away, under the bridge.

"Alright, listen up. You have a heads-up display on the inside of your helmet. Do you understand what that is?"

Max couldn't believe what he was hearing. "Yes."

"It's going to project turn-by-turn navigation onto your visor. That will tell you where you're supposed to go. The other bikes are going to leave you and rejoin you at various spots. That will ensure that you can't be followed."

"Other bikes?"

"Yeah. Now get out."

Max opened his door and stepped out under the over-pass formed by the Arlington Memorial Bridge. The Lincoln Memorial was just behind them. Cars' tires thumping overhead on the bridge.

He now wore the black leather jacket and a black motor-cycle helmet, visor down. The sedan driver was dressed the same. So were two others, already waiting in the shadows of the bridge. They straddled identical black Ducati motorcycles.

Max's heart beat faster as he saw the two empty bikes.

One of the bikers yelled, "Bloody hurry up. We've only got a few seconds before the police arrive. Whatever you do, make sure you keep up."

* * *

The Maryland State Police helicopter flew over the Potomac just as the Lexus barreled into traffic.

The pilot looked down through his chin bubble—the glass window by his feet. "That's them, right?"

The copilot said, "Looks like it. Idiot just wrecked his car, and he's still not stopping."

"Can't see him anymore. He just drove under the bridge tunnel. Hold on, I'm coming around left."

"Roger, coming left."

As they maneuvered, four black motorcycles shot out from underneath the bridge and began speeding down the road that paralleled the Potomac River.

"You *see* that?" said the pilot. He stayed over the river, turning the aircraft to follow the motorcycles.

"Yeah. Those guys are really moving," said the copilot.

The pilot said into his radio, "Dispatch, Maryland State Helicopter 223 is just west of the Lincoln Memorial. We have four black motorcycles heading north at over seventy miles per hour and are pursuing them. Recommend—"

"Hey, they just took the exit..."

The pilot watched as three of the bikes took the bridge. But one of the motorcycles continued heading west.

"Shit. Now what do we do?"

"I'm following the three. We'll stick with the group and see if we can get a squad car to follow the other." Dozens of blue lights were converging on the scene. The pilot veered left to stay over the group of three racing bikes.

"Dispatch, Maryland Helicopter 223...one of the motorcycles is now headed west on Ohio Road, but three of them have taken the Roosevelt Bridge and are now on...uh...stand by..."

"Another one broke off."

"Yeah, thanks man. I can see that."

"Dispatch, make that *two* bikes are on the George Washington Parkway. One has continued south on...stand by..."

"Now they're all going in different directions."

"Well, shit," said the pilot. "What the hell...?"

"Which one are we supposed to follow?"

"I don't know. I'm coming up. There are too many tall buildings over here."

"We're gonna lose them."

The motorcycle he was following turned into a side street and then took another turn out of view behind a tall building.

The pilot looked at his copilot. He shook his head.

"Bud, I think we already did lose them."

* * *

It had been a while since Max had ridden one of these, but it came back fast enough. His trouble wasn't riding the Ducati. It was keeping up with the other three riders. They were lightning on wheels. The engines blazed into a fierce, high-pitched whine, the traffic zooming by so fast it felt like Max was traveling in a fighter jet.

Each rider had a set path. It took a moment for Max to get used to the turn-by-turn navigation being painted up onto his visor by a set of lasers. Max had to train his eyes to continuously flip between the transparent map and the actual outside world as they raced down Ohio Drive, only feet away from the Potomac River.

Max had done some riding in France. He'd even spent time at a racetrack in Italy once. He wondered if they knew that. They must have. This kind of riding would have been a death sentence to the uninitiated. None of this was a coincidence, Max realized.

He followed the pack of other bikes, weaving in and around traffic. But as three of them took an exit—which was what his turn-by-turn navigation told him to do—one of the motorcycles peeled left and kept traveling along the road next to the Potomac. They were separating.

He took a chance and glanced up at the helicopter overhead. It all made sense now. This was the only way they were going to escape so many police, and an aerial pursuit.

Each route must have been preplanned for this exact situation. They hit speeds over one twenty on the straightaways, the engines making a deep guttural sound. His chest rattling, heart pounding. The high-speed turns forced Max to remember how to hold his body. He leaned forward, his legs straddling the seat, knees bent at a sharp angle, only inches away from the ground.

The three motorcycles raced over the Theodore Roosevelt Bridge, weaving in and out of traffic. They bolted around a lone police cruiser, its lights flashing. If he hadn't been holding on for dear life, he might have laughed at the blurred expression of shock on the police officer's face as they whizzed by. Max felt sorry for him. He was only trying to do his job.

But so was Max. And him getting thrown in jail wouldn't help anyone.

They sped down Wilson Boulevard, and Max could feel the air pounding against his black leather jacket. His stomach fluttered as he accelerated even faster, the engine screaming. People stared at them as they raced past. But only for a split second. After that, they were gone.

They were moving so fast that there were no police cars in the area now. Another of the bikes turned and it was just two of them. They raced through Clarendon and then slowed to a mere forty miles per hour as they turned a corner.

Minutes later, the two other bikes had re-joined them for

their entrance into the lower parking garage of Ballston Mall.

They drove at a normal speed up through the garage, turning and climbing higher and higher, up through the levels of parked cars. The lead bike stopped in the corner of the top level. Very few cars up this high in the garage, and no people around.

Everyone began taking off their helmets and outerwear. Removing their gloves. Moving fast. No one would look the same when they left. The bikes were parked in a row, lined up neatly next to each other in the corner. No fingerprints or other biometric evidence. Just four black racing bikes in one of the few blind spots in the garage.

Each of the other three riders left in a different direction. None of them so much as spoke to Max. One of the riders, now wearing a sweater vest and khakis, left via the parking garage stairway. Another rider—a woman in sunglasses and a bland dress—took the elevator. The last rider was the man who had pretended to be the lawyer. He looked completely different now, as he walked through the double glass doors into the Ballston Mall. Hands in the pockets of his denim jacket. A Nationals baseball cap on his head.

Max stood waiting, watching the only other vehicle nearby. An Audi Q7 SUV that was parked next to the bikes. Tinted windows. Engine running. When the three others were gone, the door opened, and a man got out.

"She's all yours, mate," he said, with a British accent.

"Thanks."

"Do me a favor. Try not to blow this, eh? As I'm not sure you'll get another chance."

Max knew his face. He'd worked with him on an operation in France once. What was his name?

Max spoke quietly, his voice a whisper. "You're MI-6, right?"

The man smiled. "I wouldn't know what you're talking about."

"That was an interesting exit strategy."

"One of my personal favorites, now that you mention it."

"Who asked you to do it?"

"Mum's the word, chap."

"So you're not going to tell me what this is all about?"

The man took out a piece of paper and handed it to Max. "Call this phone number tomorrow. Six p.m. Eastern. Repeat that back."

"Six p.m. Eastern. Tomorrow. Who am I calling?"

"She's one of ours. She'll help you from here on out. And do us a favor and don't go asking her what you just asked me. You know better."

The man patted him on the shoulder and walked through the double doors of the Ballston Mall.

Max got in the Audi and drove.

5

"How did this *happen?*"

Special Agent Jake Flynn had never been in the office of the deputy director of the FBI before. Honestly, he'd expected it to be nicer. But it was just as cramped as all the other shithole office space in the J. Edgar Hoover building. Every year they talked about how they were going to start construction on a new FBI headquarters in Maryland or Virginia. But that would require the government to agree on something.

And the only thing that anyone in the government could agree on right now was that Flynn had screwed up *royally*.

"Sir, I apologize. I take full responsibility. We had no reason to believe that Max Fend would flee. A man pretending to be his father's lawyer came to the safe house where we were questioning him, and—"

"Why were you questioning him there? Why were you questioning him at all? My understanding was that the NSA and DNI feedback was that the evidence wasn't strong enough."

"Sir, after speaking with the Cyber Division and our

counterparts in the French government, we were confident that the updated evidence they were about to provide us would be enough to grant a warrant for Max Fend's arrest. We were already in the process of moving on Fend. I thought there was a chance we might end up charging him with something, so I decided to ask him to voluntarily answer questions at our safe house in D.C...."

"Wait. Hold up. You're saying this man claiming to be a lawyer arrived at one of our D.C. safe houses?"

"Yes, sir."

"As you were questioning this Fend kid?"

"Yes, sir."

"That didn't strike you as odd? That he *knew* your exact address?"

"In hindsight, sir, it is a bit strange..."

The deputy director dug his tongue around his lips, breathing out his nose. Flynn figured that he was probably trying to sort out whether to kill him quickly, or slowly.

"Mr. Flynn, you have made a mess of this. Some guy that you brought in for questioning runs away from you? Fine. Go get 'im. Bring him back in and charge him. But this...this is out of control."

He held out his hand, gesturing towards the TV screen in the corner of his office.

The cable news channels had run nonstop coverage of the footage. Everyone loved a good car chase. A car chase in D.C.? Even better. Throw in four black motorcycles? Now *that* was viral video gold.

Since D.C. had countless cameras and tourists with smartphones taking pictures, there was ample video for the networks to use. They kept showing footage of the Lexus sedan getting air as it jumped the concrete stairs next to the Lincoln Memorial. Then the driver and passenger jumped onto four identical black motorcycles that were waiting under the tunnel overpass. The Fox News banner still read, "Car Chase of the Century." The subheadline read, "Criminal masterminds make their motorbike escape from the FBI."

It was humiliating. And nothing pissed off the front office of the FBI like humiliating headlines.

The deputy director said, "So the lawyer shows up to an FBI safe house. An *unlisted* FBI safe house. Then what happened?"

"The lawyer says that the only way he'll allow further questioning is if we conduct it at his office the next day. He says he needs to confer with his client. As we're all getting into our vehicles, I get the call from the judge that the updated evidence is in and we have his approval for an arrest."

"You didn't follow proper procedure there. DNI's going to be pissed that you went around them because you didn't like their answer the first time. This is a mess."

"Sir, respectfully, what the hell was the DNI's office thinking?"

"They get input from other intelligence communities, Flynn. You figure it out. Keep going. Tell me what happened next."

"So I tried to get Fend out of the car. I was about to place him under arrest, when the lawyer peels out and speeds away. At first I thought it was some type of joke. Him showing us up. That kind of thing."

The deputy director just shook his head in disapproval.

"So then the sedan drove off and my men began to pursue."

"Back up. Tell me about the original evidence that made you decide to arrest him."

"We have a team from the Cyber Division that's been down in Jacksonville. They've been working with CIRFU."

CIRFU was the FBI's Cyber Initiative Resource Fusion Unit. The group was a combination of FBI and private sector cyberexperts, as well as Carnegie Mellon's Computer Emergency Response Team, and the FBI's Internet Crime Complaint Center.

"What did they find?"

"They were able to piece together electronic data that links Fend to the hackers. It's highly probable that this Max Fend kid granted access to a foreign entity. And he had a business associate—a Russian. Sergei Sokolov. We think the Russian had been working with a criminal hacker group. We believe that the hackers broke into the Fend network and tried to download a bunch of their data. Fend also does defense contracting. Usually these hacker groups try to sell the technology or hold it for ransom."

The deputy director said, "So you're telling me that the owner of Fend Aerospace—Charles Fend—his own son is the bad guy here? Why would he do that?"

"I don't know. We're looking into it. He's been working as a consultant in Europe for the past few years. The reports we got on him say that he's been associated with some questionable people over there. It's possible he's been compromised."

"Compromised by whom?"

"The data that we got from the Cyber Division says that the hackers were located in Syria—but that they were probably working with Russian or Eastern European cyberexperts."

"Jake, listen to me. You need to be careful. Charles Fend has been around for a long time and has a lot of friends in this town. His lawyers have been calling us nonstop. You can't just go arresting his son without stone-cold evidence."

"I understand, sir. I'm sorry this happened this way. I was afraid we were going to lose our chance."

Flynn expected to be removed from the case. But it didn't appear to be going that way...yet. Maybe they wanted to save that card for when they really needed a scapegoat for the press.

The deputy director said, "Okay. Here's how it's going to go. You'll stay on the case for now. I'll brief the director on what you told me. In the meantime, keep this quiet. The press still hasn't said his name. Let's keep it that way. Don't let anything out about Max Fend beyond our own agency. Is that understood?"

That was odd. Charles Fend's son would be a high-profile fugitive. Flynn was surprised that Max Fend's name wasn't already in the news. He figured it was only a matter of time until one of the networks picked it up. That would help massively with the search. Tips to local law enforcement could locate him within twenty-four hours. Why on earth would the FBI not want Max Fend's face on a billboard everywhere they could get it?

"Sir, it would really help our search if..."

The deputy director shook his head. "No. Did you just hear me? Absolutely not. Let me be clear. Do not speak the name Max Fend to anyone in the press."

Flynn shifted his weight from one foot to the other. "Sir, excuse me, but why is that?"

"The director has had enough embarrassment. It was suggested to him from above that we should keep the Fend family name out of this until we are one hundred percent sure that the facts support our case against him."

"But he evaded us—"

"Did he? A few moments ago, you told me that he was going to voluntarily answer questions."

"Yes, but—"

"And you never officially placed him under arrest."

"I was about to."

"Flynn…maybe you aren't getting this. Read between the lines. We're being asked to keep the Fend name out of the press for now."

Flynn stared at him, visibly frustrated.

Seeing this, the deputy director said, "And there may be other factors that you aren't yet privy to."

Flynn didn't know what to say. "Sir, you want me to find Max Fend, but not tell any member of the public that we're looking for him? And you think that the press isn't going to pick up that it was him escaping on one of those motorcycles?"

"That's what we're being asked to do, yes. Listen, Flynn. Sometimes it's better just to put your head down and follow orders. Okay? Now I've got to go brief the director."

The deputy director walked through the side door of his office that connected to the FBI director's own office.

Jake Flynn walked out of the room, glad at least to be done with the ass-chewing. He wasn't sure what had just happened. *Something doesn't add up.* Yeah, sure, Charles Fend was wealthy and had friends in high places. But why was the FBI willing to give him cover after running away like that? Max Fend's occupation was listed as consultant. Last time Flynn checked, consultants didn't run away on motorbikes like they were in some damned James Bond movie.

Just who the hell *was* Max Fend?

* * *

For now, Special Agent Jake Flynn was still the senior agent assigned to the Fend Aerospace case.

In the past few weeks, he had learned more about the type of aircraft and how automated flight worked than he had ever wanted to.

Agent Flynn looked over his notes again, at the profiles of the main team members.

There was the senior engineer for the project, Bradley Karpinsky. Flynn had learned that Karpinsky had been passed over for the project lead position. One theory was that he harbored a grudge, and maybe he had offered to sell secrets to a foreign group. But nothing Flynn had seen led him to believe that Karpinsky would have purposefully tried to sabotage the aircraft.

Another theory suggested that a competitor had hacked into the system. Their aim may have been to expose safety flaws, in order to reopen the government bidding for the lucrative automated flight network contract in the FAA's NextGen program. But careful investigations by the FBI on all major competitors had turned up very little.

Foreign governments and organizations conducted cyberhacking attacks on US companies and government websites every day. It was a low-risk, high-reward crime. Most hackers were petty criminals. Low-level scum that tried to use phishing techniques to try and gain access to email or network passwords. From there, they could try to discover more and more information, until they found something truly valuable and either sold it or put it to use.

But this hacker group was very professional. Flynn knew that because of the facial expressions on the FBI Cyber Division's chief investigator.

"I've only seen this level of sophistication a few times,"

the man had told Flynn. "And both times, it turned out to be Russian state-sponsored activity."

Flynn decided to take another look at Max Fend's personnel file.

Princeton University, class of '02. A football player. Wide receiver. Graduated in the bottom half of his class. Then he went to work for the Department of Defense in D.C. right after college—some entry-level job. He then quit that role and moved to Europe to become a consultant.

Flynn figured that after realizing what real work was, Max Fend must have gone whining to his dad to get him some cushy job on the French Riviera.

But now Agent Flynn had new facts to inform him. What had he seen? How had he behaved in the interview? Calm. Polite. Confident, but not overly cocky. He seemed to resent any suggestion that his father's money got him a job. He was respectful and his answers seemed honest. None of this fit with the personality sketch of a spoiled rich kid turned international white-collar criminal. Max Fend had carried himself with the same swagger Flynn had seen in many of the FBI agents that he worked with.

Something wasn't right. Had Flynn made a mistake?

Flynn looked at the TV screen. The news was playing the car chase over and over again. The screen cut to the motorcycles, crossing the bridge, one of them peeling off by itself down Ohio Street.

He did a Google search on Max Fend. There was a smattering of articles. Mostly low-end "most eligible bachelor" type stuff from years ago, when he was at Princeton. Heir to one of the largest private companies in the United States. There wasn't much on him after he graduated college.

Flynn decided to double-check his FBI file. It took him a few moments, but he found what he was looking for.

Max Fend had gone to work for the Department of Defense right out of college and worked there for nearly two years. That meant that he had a Single Scope Background Investigation on file. The investigation was required for anyone trying to get a government security clearance in the United States.

After leaving the DoD, he had lived in Europe, working for a US-based consulting firm there.

Flynn used his FBI computer to gain access to Max's latest Standard Form 86. It had last been updated in 2003. Nothing interesting.

He decided to contact the Department of Defense and see if anyone there who had worked with him could provide any extra information.

Flynn found the reference on Max's security clearance form. He dialed the number, wondering if the man still worked at DoD, or if he used a different phone number now.

"Hello?"

"Hello, my name is Special Agent Jake Flynn, with the FBI. I was hoping to speak with you about one of your former employees. A man by the name of Max Fend. Are you familiar with him?"

Silence. "Uh, yes, sir. I remember him. He's the son of the airplane billionaire, right? How can I help?"

"Yes, that's him. Were you his supervisor from 2002 to 2004?"

"That's right."

"Listen, I'm going to be down near your office this afternoon. Would you have time to speak with me? Say around one p.m.?"

"I have a meeting. Can we make it two?"

"No problem."

At two p.m. sharp, Jake Flynn was sitting in a private meeting room at the DoD manager's office.

"What type of work was Max Fend involved in when he worked with you?"

"Standard stuff. Accounting, mostly. Some procurement for defense programs. He was a new guy, so it was entry-level stuff."

"And are you familiar with where he went to work after that?"

"I've got my suspicions, yes."

Flynn sat up straighter in his seat.

"What do you mean by that?"

The DoD manager squirmed. "You are FBI, right? So I guess it's fine to talk to you about this. We see a few Max Fend types every year. Not billionaires' sons, mind you. I mean guys like him. I think someone in Langley's human resources department must have my section flagged. I've been here nearly thirty years, and it seems like we're always seeing them."

"Langley's human resources?"

"Yeah. You know, Langley. Like the CIA."

"I'm familiar. What's Max Fend got to do with the CIA?"

The man cleared his throat. "Well, every couple of years, we get a few of their new guys. We're asked to find something for them to do for a year or two. They tend to stash them here before they ship off."

"What do you mean, ship off? You mean like go to a new DoD job?"

"I don't think it's with the DoD. But who knows? I could be wrong. Look, man, I just hear things, okay? I don't want to get in trouble."

"What kind of things?"

"Well...one of my employees, she has family down near

Williamsburg. So she goes there a lot. She says that she's seen a couple of these guys down there over the years. Almost always right after they leave their job with me."

"In Williamsburg?" He scribbled on his notepad: *Max Fend—CIA???*

"Yeah. There's a bar there that they all hang out at, I think. But this girl who works for me, she goes there, and she's run into a few of them. I probably shouldn't be saying this."

Flynn fought the urge to roll his eyes. "Sir, you are helping an investigation. Please speak freely."

"I heard that they go to Williamsburg and start their training. The Langley guys probably use the time working for me to do their in-depth background checks or wait for new classes to start."

Flynn frowned. "And this is in Williamsburg?"

"Yeah, you know. The Farm."

* * *

Flynn found that in times of uncertainty, it was best to speak with trusted friends. He decided to give his buddy Steve Brava a call. Steve had started off in the FBI with him but had transferred to the DNI's office when that organization had been created. The man would shoot straight with him. He could get access to information that others couldn't. And most importantly, he could be trusted.

"Jake, good to hear from you."

"Steve, you too."

They exchanged pleasantries for a few moments.

Steve said, "You see all this car chase stuff on the news?"

"Yeah...actually, that's part of the reason I'm calling," Flynn said.

"Really?"

"Yeah. Listen, this has got to stay quiet."

"Say no more. What can I do for you?"

"Hey, I'm looking...unofficially...at a man by the name of Max Fend."

"As in Fend Aerospace?"

"Yes."

"Okay."

"I got a tip from someone recently that the CIA sometimes stashes guys within the Department of Defense before they go off to start their training at the Farm in Williamsburg. Does that sound right to you?"

"Yeah, sure. That's possible. Probably gives them time to do a full background check. And places like the Farm have to schedule classes just like any other big government school. So it might take guys a few months before they're ready to class up. So what?"

"Is there any way you could check out Max Fend, and see if he was one of those guys?"

"Sure, I could do that. But, Jake, why don't you just go ask the CIA?"

"I will. I just like to check multiple sources."

"Alright, I'll see what I can dig up for you."

6

Max Fend's first stop was at a storage center in Leesburg, Virginia. He drove in at night, wearing baggy clothes and a golf visor pulled down low over his forehead. He typed in the code and heard the beep, the chain fence sliding over to one side. He drove along the rows of storage units and parked in front of his rental.

He fidgeted with the lock until the right combination was entered. It snapped open, and Max lifted up the sliding garage door. It stopped with a bang. Max then flipped the light switch, illuminating two trunks in the center of the otherwise empty storage space. A stale smell hung in the air.

The rented-out garage had been his own personal decision. After operating as a field agent for over ten years, he didn't trust anyone. He had his own plan to disappear, if need be. A "break glass in case of emergency" plan that no one else knew about but him.

Max closed the garage door behind him and found himself alone with his stash. He moved quick, his hands and eyes racing from item to item. He knelt on the floor as he worked.

Max emptied the contents of the first trunk and then closed it to serve as a surface to work from. He placed a laptop on the closed trunk, plugged it in to a large portable battery, and powered it up.

He took the phones, IDs, and prepaid debit cards that the MI6 agents had given him and threw them all into the empty trunk. Max would use his own items.

He took out his own prepurchased phone and entered the number he was supposed to dial tomorrow night at exactly six p.m. He named the contact SECRET AGENT. No reason he couldn't have a sense of humor about it.

Max connected the computer to his phone and used it to access the Internet. He accessed a secure cloud drive and opened a spreadsheet file. The file was his little black book. People whom he had known and worked with over the years. Max paid a virtual assistant—a very capable and trustworthy one—quite a good sum of money to keep this list up to date. Should he ever find himself in a certain place, in need of someone who had a particular skill, he could rely upon this list.

There were several hundred names on the spreadsheet. He could sort by column: name, country, state (if in the US), and skill set.

He needed someone close. He didn't have the time or the inclination to travel far right now. He set the filter for the eastern half of the United States. All within range. And all had rural areas that he could fly into easily.

Next he sorted for skill sets. He had decided on just five skill categories. Procurement. Tactical. Tradecraft. Transportation. And cyber. Each person had multiple columns. Some people on his list had multiple skill sets.

He filtered for cyber. A half dozen names came up. While they were each listed as living in the stated locations, he knew from looking at several of the names that most would be out of the country. On assignment.

One name stuck out. Renee LeFrancois.

Max hadn't seen her in years. He clicked on her name and looked more closely at her updated file. His virtual assistant was expected to keep each personnel file current. It was costly, but Max had the means.

He read over her file. One thing surprised him. She had been married. He hadn't known. Then again, it wasn't like she would have invited him to the wedding. Her file said she'd gotten divorced two years earlier. She now lived alone and did contract IT security work. No obvious red flags.

Max still didn't like the idea of going to her. She didn't have experience in this type of thing. Her computer skills were off the charts, but who knew how she would react when she found out that he was a wanted man?

Not to mention their personal history. Things hadn't ended badly for them, but they hadn't exactly ended well, either. He tried to think of the last time he'd seen her. It must have been at least eight years ago. Princeton reunions, he thought. Drinking together on the dance floor under a massive tent. Screaming into each other's ears, trying to have a meaningful conversation over deafening music. That meeting had been bittersweet.

Max pushed out any personal feelings he might still harbor. He needed to be clinical about this decision.

He once again looked over the list of personnel who were located on the East Coast of the US. Most were "Tactical" experts. Those were the types of men who specialized in weaponry and warfare. They weren't on the list for their knowledge, but for their skill. They were the black bag job boys.

Max didn't need people like that. He had already

prepared for something like this. For running and hiding. He had supplies, transportation, and money all lined up. Some people prepped for a future Armageddon; Max prepped for the day when someone might come after him.

What Max really needed was someone who could help him investigate who had done this to him, and what he was up against. Someone who could understand the world of cyberespionage. That field was a mystery to Max.

That left two names.

One was actively employed by the National Security Agency. Max didn't want to go to him. There was too much risk. Max was being pursued by the US government. Most of the people on his list got their paychecks, in some way or other, from Uncle Sam.

He sighed, frustrated by the painful realization. That might cross off ninety percent of his contacts.

He would have to try Renee. She was trustworthy, and in relatively close proximity. She wasn't, nor had she ever been, employed by the US government. And when she was able to access a computer, she was magic.

Max closed up his laptop and slid it into the backpack that contained his prepared items. His own false IDs, weapons, and cash.

There was a good chance that everything the MI6 team had passed on to him was perfectly usable. But he hadn't procured it himself. What if the IDs were flagged? What if the phones were being tracked? Even friendly operatives made a habit of doing that. No, the best way to stay alive was to assume that everyone and everything else might be compromised.

Five minutes after he'd entered, Max walked out of the garage and locked it behind him, got into his car, and drove to the Leesburg Executive Airport.

* * *

Max left the Audi in the parking lot across the street from the airport. He pulled the backpack tight on his back and then hopped the fence, landing in the grass.

Leesburg Executive Airport was small by most standards. It was mostly used by general aviation and private aircraft. One of those planes was his.

Washington, D.C. airspace restrictions were notoriously onerous—there were precise rules that general aviation aircraft had to follow in order to get in and out of the area. But Leesburg Executive had a special triangular cutout in the Air Defense Identification Zone around D.C. That would help make things a bit easier.

Max doubted the FBI knew about his plane. Max's virtual assistant had used a shell company to make the purchase and pay for the maintenance and hangar fees.

It was a single-engine piston. A Cirrus SR-22T. He had hired a local operator to take care of it and lease it out every so often to one of the local flight instruction companies, just to make sure that it was working. Until today, he had never flown it personally. He would always rent the same type of aircraft from other locations.

He climbed in and threw his bag in the passenger seat, sliding the seat belt through one of the straps and clicking it in place. He loved this aircraft. The Cirrus interior was similar to that of the finest luxury automobile. And it flew like a dream. The plane would travel at over 200 knots without breaking a sweat.

Max filed his flight plan under an alias and flew west out of the D.C. airspace, using visual flight rules. He then canceled his flight plan while he was airborne over Front Royal, and turned off his transponder. If and when investi-

gators looked up his flight path, they would expect him to
have landed there.

It wasn't much of a diversion, but it might throw them
off the scent for a bit. More likely, they wouldn't expect him
to be traveling this way at all.

He then turned south and flew to Charlottesville. The
Blue Ridge mountain air made the flight a little bumpy, but
it wasn't too bad.

An hour later he made a night landing on the cool
blacktop of the Charlottesville Albemarle Regional Airport.
The tower was already shut down for the night.

Max tied down the aircraft and placed the chocks in
front of the wheels. No one else was out this time of night.
The only sound was of summer crickets. Lightning bugs
glimmered in the sky.

He walked toward the Signature Flight Support building
and checked his watch. It was getting late. Almost eleven
p.m. The automatic doors opened up, and a rush of cool air
came over him. The air conditioning felt good. A girl stood
behind the front desk. She looked as if she was about to
close up shop for the night.

"You need fuel, honey?"

"Yes, please. Top it off if you would."

"Will do. May I have your card?"

"Actually, I'll use cash if you don't mind."

"Um...okay, sure."

Probably didn't hear that too much. Fuel cost for planes
could be in the thousands of dollars. Much higher, even, for
the jets. But Max wanted to leave the smallest trail possible.

"You need a cab?"

"That would be great, thanks."

"Where you going?"

"Local area."

She smiled at him. "You know, I'm about to get off. If you don't mind, I'd be happy to give you a lift." She was cute. And interested, by the look in her eye.

"Sure. That would be great." She called the fuel truck. Max could hear its engine grumbling outside and its brakes squeaking as it came to a stop next to his plane.

She took him to her car, apologizing as she cleared off trash from the cramped passenger seat. He had her take him to the Double Tree Inn. She parked in the parking lot.

"So...you want to have a drink or something?" She twirled her hair, chewing her gum.

Max had two voices in his head. The voice of reason told him that he had been stupid to have her drop him off. That he needed to keep a low profile, and even right now his face might be on the news. The other voice sized up her measurables and provided him a firm thumbs-up.

"As much as I would love that, my girlfriend is supposed to come by later..."

"Oh. Sorry." She giggled.

"Appreciate the ride." He ducked under the door and swung it shut. Max waited for her car to leave before whipping out his phone and dialing the number.

"Hello?"

"Renee," Max said.

"Who is this?"

"Renee, it's Max...*Fend*. I need your help."

Silence on the other end. Shock, perhaps. He had expected that. This would be a lot to ask of her. To drop everything, and risk her career—not to mention legal troubles—to assist him. But he needed someone he could trust.

* * *

Princeton, 2000

They had met at Princeton. Max was a minor celebrity there. The sons and daughters of some of the most famous people in the world walked the campuses of elite Ivy League institutions such as Harvard, Yale and Princeton. Indeed, some of the students at those schools were already celebrities themselves. Actors and actresses. Olympians. Budding stars in the tech industry.

Max was well known because of who his father was, and barely a day went by that he wasn't asked about being the son of Charles Fend.

Cap and Gown was one of Princeton's eating clubs—sort of a cross between dining halls and coed fraternities. Prospect Avenue was lined with large mansions, each one home to one of the eating clubs. On nights like this, warm Saturday nights during football season, they erupted into massive parties. Celebrations of life.

Max loved the parties. But it also meant that he had to answer the same question over and over again. *Are you really Charles Fend's son?* Yes. *Oh my God, that's so amazing.* Yup. Sigh.

The deck had a nice wide view of the backyard. He had walked out onto that second-floor wooden deck, hoping to take a break from it all. A Dave Matthews cover band played on the stone patio below. At least three hundred people were at the house. The girls on the field hockey team were already dancing in front of the band.

He stopped when he saw her sitting alone on the unlit wooden balcony. Crutches at her side. A cast on her leg. Leaning back and looking up at the clear night sky. Stars twinkling. She looked peaceful, but lonely.

She heard his footsteps on the wooden planks and glanced up at him. A guarded look.

"Good evening," said Max.

"Hi."

"How'd you hurt yourself?"

"A field hockey accident."

"Ouch. Sorry. Anything I can get you?" He was just being polite. He had expected her to say no.

"God, yes. A beer would be great. Be a dear and bring two, if you wouldn't mind."

Max laughed. "Sure."

She was his kind of girl. The right priorities. And a proper planner. He hobbled down the creaky wooden stairs of the mansion and made his way through the crowded basement. The sophomores were manning the beer kegs. He waited about five minutes and was then handed several full plastic cups of cold beer. It sloshed and spilled a bit on his way back up the stairs. But she was grateful when he arrived with them.

A big smile, which he suspected was a rare thing for her. Dark hair. Strong cheekbones.

"You're a lifesaver." And an accent.

"Where are you from?"

"Montreal, originally."

"What's your name?"

"Renee."

"I'm Max, Renee," he said, sticking out his hand.

"I know." She shook it.

"Mind if I join you?"

"Be my guest."

"Those your teammates out there dancing?"

"They are. Normally they would try to get me out there. I despise dance floors, so the crutches are a nice excuse. But

I'd give anything to be playing still. I'm afraid I'm done for the season."

"Sorry to hear that. But happy for my luck."

She flashed a wry smile and raised her plastic cup in a toast.

They spent the rest of the evening talking on the balcony. It would be the first of many evenings that they spent together. While Max had dated many women, Renee would be the only one he really would characterize as a serious girlfriend. Their on-again, off-again relationship was all at once passionate, comfortable, and painful. They made a "clean break" upon graduation. In all, they dated for nine months. She was a year younger, and—given the field he was entering—it didn't make sense to continue on. He had never explained to her why he had broken it off. That only made it harder.

* * *

Present Day

Renee and Max agreed to meet the next morning. He used one of his prepaid cards to pay for the room at the hotel and then spent an hour scanning the news.

The lead story was about the G-7 conference that was being held at Camp David in a few days. It would include Russian attendance for the first time in a few years. The Russian president was attempting to mend relations in the West. The bloc of nations would become the G-8 again in a special ceremony.

The rest of the coverage was about the motorcycle chase.

The talking heads were going crazy about the car chase

in D.C. But surprisingly, Max wasn't mentioned. Now why was that?

He could think of only one reason. Someone in the government didn't want Max Fend's name put out there.

That was a good thing for Max. If he just had to avoid law enforcement, he could do it. But if he had to avoid going out in public...that was another thing entirely.

Max wondered how long this gift of anonymity would last. With the right spin on it, this could really be a big news story. Rich playboy son escapes from FBI in high-speed motorcycle chase through the streets of D.C. That was the way he would write it up, if he were trying to make headlines. The news would plaster his face on every TV and electronic device in America.

Max was already known to a lot of people who read the gossip columns, thanks to his father—and maybe his own extravagant lifestyle. That had been a necessary evil. But being involved in this motorcycle chase would skyrocket his reputation into the stratosphere.

He sighed as he thought about his father. What must he be thinking? What was the FBI telling him? Max doubted his father would believe that he would sabotage Fend Aerospace. But the fact that he had run away from law enforcement—that would likely plant a seed of doubt in his mind. And the nature of the escape would raise even more questions.

There was nothing Max could do about it now. He did a quick calisthenic workout, took a shower, and went to sleep.

* * *

The night had been a disaster for Renee. She had gone out

to dinner with a client. He was older. Late forties, but not bad looking.

They were barely halfway through dinner when he had crossed the line. Suggesting that he could come back to her place for drinks. Maybe Renee was smiling too much? Maybe she had dressed too provocatively? She hated herself for thinking like that. And the worst part was that Renee had actually considered it. He wasn't anything special, but it wouldn't have been that bad to have male companionship once in a while. It had been too long.

But there was something about him that didn't sit well with her. He was too pushy. She excused herself and went into the bathroom, taking out her phone. One thing a married cheater should never do is try to date a hacker.

Renee found out everything about the man within a few minutes. The disgusting pig had been lying to her about his personal life. He must have taken the ring off before they had dinner.

Renee should have known. Clients didn't normally come to see her. But he'd said he was going to be in the area for business. And her contract was up for renewal soon.

When Renee had gone back to the table, she said, "May I see your hand?"

"Excuse me?"

"Your hand. Please let me see it."

The man frowned. He started to, and then thought better of it.

"What's wrong, Renee? Did I say something? Look, if you don't want to have drinks, that's fine—"

"You've been married for fourteen years. And you have four kids."

His face went white...and then red. Eyes narrowing. "You checked up on me while you were in the bathroom? Who the hell do you think you are? Look, I don't think we can do business. I can't work with someone I don't trust."

"Neither can I."

She stood, glaring at him. Then she walked away, not bothering to let him say any more.

For a moment, she had thought of threatening him. She could demand that he switch her account to a different buyer, or she would...what? Ruin his marriage? Hurt his children? Better to walk away. Hopefully, he wouldn't spread nasty rumors about her to other potential clients. She sighed. She didn't need the money that bad.

What was it about that type of man? It was like they were drawn to her.

She kept telling herself she didn't need anyone else in her life. But it was hard doing everything alone. And she worried about growing old and not finding anyone. And she wanted to have kids, before it was too late.

After college she'd had one serious relationship that lasted for six years. He had been in pharmaceutical sales. She had moved to follow him to Charlottesville for his work. They'd married after a year of dating.

When she thought about it now, she didn't know why she had said yes. She didn't really love him. It had just seemed like the thing everyone was doing at the time. All of her girlfriends were getting married. It was like musical chairs, and no one wanted to get left out.

She had wanted to travel. To compete in road races. To meet new and interesting people. To get drunk at concerts. To hike the Appalachian Trail. She wanted to live life. To have the adventure.

All her ex wanted to do when he was home was sleep and watch TV. He had wanted her to be his housewife. To stay at home and make meals, and to take care of the kids they were going to have.

Thank God she hadn't gotten pregnant with him. If she had, she probably would have stuck with him, even after she'd found out he was cheating on her. Bored out of her mind and faking it for the sake of the kids.

Kids. The word made her want to cry. She was almost forty. And while she would admit it to no one, she desperately wanted to have children.

But he had taken her for granted. It wasn't just the cheating. She could forgive that, if it were an honest mistake. It was the lack of passion in him. She was a romantic, and he was...a mistake. She'd felt guilty for feeling that, until he'd cheated on her. Then, truth be told, she'd felt relief. She had an excuse. It had been time to fish or cut bait, as the expression went.

He wanted to keep fishing. She cut bait.

The sad part now was that her life hadn't gotten much more adventurous. She ran road races, and had done a few mini-triathlons. She tried to schedule one big vacation to somewhere fun every year. But her love life had been pretty nonexistent. She usually worked from home. The only places she really went were the gym, church, and the grocery store. None presented her with great opportunities for meeting people.

Work was at once an escape and a worry. It took her mind off the worry that her life wasn't progressing as planned. But the work itself wasn't exactly curing cancer. Still, the job paid well, and it gave her freedom and control. Renee's clients didn't care when the work got done. Most of the time, they didn't even understand what it was that she was doing. Corporate IT security. She was an anti-hacker. She liked to joke with her niece, who adored Harry Potter books, that she was like a witch who specialized in the Defense Against the Dark Arts.

Renee had started off after college in one of the big multimillion-dollar corporations. Now they were her competition. *They* didn't see it that way. They didn't know she existed. But she had a book of business. About six figures a year. Nothing to scoff at, but it could dry up in a heartbeat. And she always felt the pressure.

And loneliness. And guilt. She was thinking about seeing a psychologist or a psychiatrist—whichever one didn't give you medicine. She didn't want medicine. Just someone to tell her how to get her life back on track. Maybe a life coach? No. She had read that many of them were people who'd been laid off.

Renee kept telling herself that in another year or so, things would finally change for the better. She would get a new big contract and would have more time to get things done. It would be easier then. She would then read more, work out more, and travel more. She would call up her best friends from college and demand that they go hike the Appalachian Trail with her. She had so many adventures that she wanted to have, before she grew too old, and before her life began to fade away into memories.

Memories.

It was funny how strong some of them could be, when they came back and slapped you in the face. Renee hadn't thought of Max in quite some time.

"Who was that on the phone?"

"No one, Mom."

"It didn't sound like no one." Renee's mother came to visit every six months or so. And whenever she did, she always gave Renee advice that she didn't want.

"Just an old friend, Mom."

"A boy?" Nosey.

"The friend was male, yes."

"Does your old friend have a name? Tell him to take my daughter out. She needs a man in her life."

Renee walked into the living room, where her mother was knitting and watching a home-buying show with the volume down low.

"Enough, please," Renee said.

"You're much too young and pretty to give up on men now."

"*Mother.*"

"Well, I'm only saying. What happened with the nice man who took you out tonight? You came home early."

"He's a client. I won't be seeing him again."

Her mother looked up from her knitting. "Well, that's a shame."

"I'm going to my room, Mother. I need to get a little work done. What are your plans tomorrow morning—do you need the car? I have something in the morning."

"No, dear. I'll be fine. Goodnight."

"Goodnight."

Renee went into her bedroom and sat on her bed, bringing her computer onto her lap. Time to find out what Max Fend had been up to over the past few years, and what kind of trouble he was in.

7

Four Days Before the Fend 100 Flight

The next morning, Renee was there waiting for him in the lobby of the hotel, a laptop resting on her knees, and a cup of steaming coffee lying on the hotel rug next to her chair. She put the computer down next to the coffee and stood, extending her hand.

"Hello, Max."

A quiet, steady voice. That same lovely French Canadian accent. She'd changed her hair up a bit. It was shorter. And he saw that she'd added a long flower tattoo that wound down her milky-white leg.

"Renee. It's good to see you again." A quick embrace.

"Why don't we go somewhere we can talk, Max?"

He took her back to his room.

Max and Renee sat on two opposite ends of the room's ugly couch.

She began. "You're in trouble."

"How much do you know?"

"As much as I could find out, before speaking in person.

I looked at everything I could get my hands on last night after you called."

Renee held dual Canadian and US citizenship. She had always been very good with computers in college, but while there, she had mostly been concerned with playing field hockey. The tech companies had come at her hard her senior year. She had gone to work for a cybersecurity firm after graduating.

When they'd last seen each other at a reunion party in 2008, Max had asked her about her job. She had been coy, saying only that she worked for a small Canadian firm. Max knew how to spot a lie. The answer had piqued his interest, and he'd used his resources to look into Renee's work the following week.

Max was surprised to discover that Renee had gone to work for Canada's Communications Security Establishment in Ottawa for a few years. The CSE was Canada's version of the National Security Agency. From what he could decipher, she was one of their cyberwarriors. Then she'd left and had gone to work for herself...probably about the same time she'd met her ex-husband.

Max had thrown her name into his little black book spreadsheet.

"Are you guilty?" she asked.

"Of what, exactly?"

"The FBI thinks that you gave some foreign cybercriminals access to your father's company network. This allowed them to steal information"— she looked down at her notes —"something about an autonomous test flight. I haven't read up on that yet. But I'm sure you are more than familiar."

"Well, to answer your question, then, no." He shook his head. "I'm not guilty of that."

She raised an eyebrow. "What are you guilty of?"

"Good looks. A voracious appetite for life."

She tried not to smile. "I've missed you. But you don't need to put on your little show for me. Remember, I know who you really are."

"And who's that?"

She shrugged. "Not this act that I've read about."

They stared at each other for a moment. Each trying to unmask the other.

Max shrugged. "I hate it when my reputation gets ruined."

"If you were the little brat the gossip columnists make you out to be, I wouldn't be talking to you. But I knew you before you went away to Europe and got put in the magazines with your shirt off."

"You saw those?"

"Oh, yes. Quite the heartthrob to the tweens and moms who read that sort of thing."

"Moms and their daughters have always loved me. What can I say?"

Renee didn't respond.

"I checked you out. Your work in Europe seemed..."

"Interesting?"

"Controversial."

"What do you want to know?"

"How did you get involved with all those people?"

"Which ones?"

"Max, the things I read about...the FBI file says that you've been mixed up with several groups...well, they aren't the types of people I would expect you to know."

Max leaned forward, his elbows resting on his knees. "Let's get this out of the way now, because you'll need to know. Renee, when I was in Europe, I wasn't just a consultant. That was a cover. A nonofficial cover."

"What do you mean, a nonofficial cover?"

"Intelligence agencies have two types of operatives. Ones who are official government employees...and ones who aren't. The official cover agents are the ones who work in the State Department or some other section of government. But really, they serve multiple masters. You might have seen news stories about how Russia will send home several of our diplomats, claiming that they're spies. And then we send home several of their diplomats, claiming the same thing. Those people are under official covers. They get diplomatic immunity. Protection."

"Wait, are you saying that you worked for the intelligence community?"

"Yes."

"As in...like...you were a spy?"

"Yes, Renee. I was an illegal. I had no diplomatic immunity. And my posting was unrelated to any government agency."

"You were a spy, Max. I'm still trying to wrap my head around this."

"I understand."

She blurted out, "I worked for the CSE. In Canada."

He laughed at her expression. As if she'd been holding it in for years and had finally found someone she could admit it to.

"I mean, the work was pretty boring. Nothing like being a spy. I was trapped in a windowless room all day for a few years. But it was all super hush-hush." The words flew out of her mouth, like she was trying to match confessions.

Max smiled. "Actually, I know."

"You *know*?"

"I'm familiar with your professional background. That's part of the reason I've reached out to you."

"Hmm. And I thought you missed me."

"I do."

Her voice was excited. "So who did you work for? The CIA?"

"DIA. The Defense Intelligence Agency."

"Since when?"

"Pretty soon after I left college."

"That long?"

Max nodded.

"So is that why you were running around with all those bimbos in France? It was a cover."

"Some of those bimbos meant a lot to me..."

Renee rolled her eyes. "Fine. Maybe we should just get down to business, shall we?"

Max said, "Very well. I want you to come work for me. I want to hire you. I need help. Someone with your talent. Someone I can trust. And someone who won't turn me in, because they believe me when I say that I'm innocent."

Renee pursed her lips, not speaking.

"I understand if you have to say no. But you saw what the FBI thinks. Someone's after me."

She cocked her head. "How long would the contract be for?"

"Until this mess is cleared up." Max smiled, his wide, charming smile.

"Yes, well. If you want me to drop everything and come work for you, you'll need to make it worth my while."

"Nothing is off the table."

"What's the pay?"

"I'm not sure if you're aware of this, but I'm painfully wealthy."

"I am aware. Although last time I checked, those who are running from the law face problems when accessing their bank accounts."

"I've got my own stash under the mattress. Turns out Grandpa was right after all. Besides, if you do your job well, I won't be running from the law for long, right? How much do you make now, annually?"

She told him.

"Consider it tripled. Next?"

She tried not to look too pleased, which was difficult. She said, "I will need job security. You're on the run. If I help you, and we're caught, I'll be considered an accomplice."

"Doubtful."

"That they wouldn't consider me an accomplice?"

"No. That we would be caught." He winked.

"You're almost famous. Your father is famous. What happens when people start finding out that it was you racing out of Washington on a Ducati racing bike yesterday?"

"It wasn't a racing bike, it was the model—"

"*Max.*"

"We won't be caught. We'll just need to move fast. And send what we find to the Feds. There seems to have been a dreadful misunderstanding, is all."

"I know, but still. You can't very well expect me to leave my other contracts on a whim like this without knowing that I'll be taken care of. I've got a life, after all."

"I'll do whatever it takes to give you peace of mind. But we can't stay here. If you decide to help me, it will require travel. I don't yet know who or what I'm up against. So I think that it would be best if we...if we were able to disappear for a few days. Is that possible for you?"

Renee thought for a moment. "My mother is in town.

She won't be happy, but I can tell her that I have a work trip. Yes, Max, it's possible."

Max nodded. "So, are we good? You'll agree to help me?"

She pretended to think about it. Truth be told, she wanted nothing more than to get away for a few days. This sounded like interesting work. And a good friend was in need. Beneath Max's wild act, she knew that there was a decent man there. She had to help him.

"Alright. Let's get started."

"Let's."

"Tell me your story, Max Fend. And let's try to figure out who might be after you."

Max recounted the last twenty-four hours. He had given her hints on the phone last night, but this was more in depth. It took him about fifteen minutes to catch her up. Most of it she was already aware of, having made the connection that he was the one who had escaped law enforcement the previous day. But she did stop him several times with questions.

"Wait. You said you were going to go to work for your father? At his company?"

"Yes."

"So you don't work for the DIA anymore?"

"Correct."

She looked at him in disbelief. "So when did you stop working for them?"

"Last year."

"So if you're no longer in, how were you able to escape law enforcement in D.C. like you did?"

He smiled. "That's the other part of the mystery. I don't know who set me up, and I don't know who helped me escape. But I have my suspicions."

Her jaw dropped open. "So you're saying that you didn't

know the people that rode the motorcycles with you out of D.C. before you took part in all that?"

"They obviously planned it, but I didn't know it would happen. I recognized one of them. He was MI-6, I believe."

"British intelligence? Like James Bond?"

"Yes. I met him in Europe several years ago. An operation I took part in there. But I don't know the man's name. Just the face."

"So you *think* MI-6 broke you out of the FBI's custody? That's insane."

"Technically, I wasn't in custody at the time."

She gave him a questioning look.

"They hadn't placed me under arrest. I voluntarily went in to answer questions. Although, I'm pretty sure that they were about to arrest me. The guy outside my window was yelling and reaching for his gun. Never a good sign."

"If they didn't think that you were guilty then, they certainly must think you are guilty now."

"Because of the car chase?"

"Yes."

"Well, OJ was still presumed innocent after his car chase."

"I don't think that should be your standard of excellence, Max."

"You're probably right. See, I was smart to hire you."

"So why did you run?"

"MI-6—if that's indeed who they were—leads me to believe that there was more to come in terms of evidence against me. The man who helped me to escape warned me not to let myself get taken into custody. He informed me that someone was trying to set me up. Knowing that I was innocent, his advice seemed of high quality. Plus, I tend to believe folks like that."

"Folks like what?"

"Spies with elaborate motorcycle escape plans."

"Ah. Them."

"Someone's set me up to take the fall in this Fend Aerospace hacking thing. I wasn't even aware of a problem. Some sort of network intrusion involving Russian hackers. My father must have known, though."

"And he didn't tell you?"

"No, actually. It's very unlike him to keep things from me, but perhaps he didn't think I needed to know. But the people who helped me get away implied that there was more incriminating evidence to come. So—I would like you to help me find out who did it, and why they did it. Can you do that?"

"I can certainly try," Renee said.

Max held up his phone. "The MI-6 team gave me a phone number. I'm supposed to call it at six p.m. tonight."

"And who will you be speaking with?"

"A woman. A member of their team, I presume. They said it was someone who would be able to help me out."

"Let me be there when you make the call," Renee said. "I'll set some analytics software up. Perhaps we can learn more about who's on the other end."

"Excellent. Thanks." He stood up. "Renee, there's something else that I'll need help with."

"What?"

"Do you know a good bakery around here? I'm famished."

8

Fend Corporate Jet
30,000 feet over Atlanta, Georgia

"Mr. Fend, we'll be landing in another forty minutes," the stewardess said.

"Thank you."

The stewardess disappeared back towards the front of the aircraft.

Charles sat across from Maria Blount. Her red hair was pulled back. She had been discussing the hacking incident. He hadn't told her anything about Max. Charles thought that it was best to keep that to himself for now.

"Should we work with the FAA to postpone the Fend 100 flight?" Maria said.

Charles shook his head. "No."

"But if..."

"This is only going to increase the pressure on us, I'm afraid. If we don't put on a good show next week, the different stakeholders might get spooked."

"But the cybersecurity investigators said that they weren't able to penetrate all of our firewalls."

Charles looked out the window of the jet as he spoke. "You went over the data they stole. What do you think?"

Maria looked glum. "They have the Fend 100 aircraft blueprints. Those alone are worth a lot to us. But they weren't able to access the servers that held the AI program."

"So? What's your prognosis, doctor?"

"If our aircraft design gets into competitors' hands, that would be bad. And Wall Street will punish us if we don't secure the FAA's NextGen contract. That's the most important thing to us now. We need that government contract finalized."

Charles tapped his fingers against his armrest. "Our corporate cybersecurity experts tell me that these hackers are like Somali pirates. They'll seize our precious information and hold it hostage for an indefinite period. Or like you suggested, sell it to the highest bidder. We can't postpone the Fend 100 flight. If we delay that flight, we give the hackers and our competition more opportunity to hurt us. Delaying the Fend 100 flight would delay the finalization of the NextGen contract with the FAA—or worse, put it in jeopardy."

"That would be awful for the company."

"Yes, it would."

"So what do you want to do, Charles?"

"We need to ensure that we improve our cybersecurity efforts. The FBI tells us that the hackers attempted to steal our AI technology, but they were unsuccessful. Fine. But they also warned us that they would keep trying. I want you to make sure that we are improving all of our security. Under no circumstances will we allow someone to steal the Fend 100's AI program."

"I understand. Who would do this sort of thing?" Maria asked.

Charles continued to look out the window. "The leeches of the earth. The Fend 100 flight must go off without a hitch. The sooner that happens, the less vulnerable we will be."

The stewardess walked back down the aisle. "Mr. Fend, you have a phone call, sir."

He thanked her and walked to the front of the jet, where the corded satellite phone was plugged in.

"Hello?"

The voice on the other end was one that he hadn't heard in quite some time. "Hello, Charles."

Charles closed his eyes, tightening his grip on the phone. "I had hoped that we were finished."

Charles could see Maria trying not to be too obvious in her attempt to eavesdrop on the conversation.

The voice on the other end said, "We *were* finished, Charles. We were. But it seems that our old friend has renewed his interest in you and your company. And now there is another consideration, I'm afraid."

"And what is that?"

"Your son."

9

Camp Peary
Near Williamsburg, Virginia

The fact that Max Fend had been working for the CIA wasn't a problem, per se. But the fact that Max had lied about it to the FBI during their investigation—well, to Jake Flynn, that *was* a problem. Maybe that was standard procedure for them. Flynn didn't know. But he needed to find out.

Flynn drove down early in the morning. He could have gone to Langley. But if Langley was anything like the FBI headquarters, Flynn preferred to stay as far away from there as possible. The farther away you get from government headquarters, the more people smile, and the looser their lips become. Although he wasn't quite sure if that would apply in this case.

The Farm, as it was known, was the CIA's training ground near Williamsburg, Virginia. Officially, the place was known as the Armed Forces Experimental Training Activity, or Camp Peary. The land was owned and run by the

US military. But much of the base was used to train officers in the CIA's Directorate of Operations. He'd had to get special permission from both the FBI and CIA to gain access to the base. His interview was set up with someone the CIA thought would best be able to help him out.

The CIA man's name was Caleb Wilkes. By the looks of it, he was in his late forties. Maybe early fifties. Thinning gray hair. Suit jacket with no tie. Top button undone.

"You comfortable? Can I get you anything?"

"No, I'm fine, thanks," replied Flynn.

Wilkes closed the door and sat down across from Flynn. "We were surprised that you called us asking about Max. Mind if I ask what led you to believe that he worked for us?"

"Sure. I'm looking at Max Fend as part of an ongoing investigation into Fend Aerospace. When I was looking at Max Fend's background, I came across his Defense Department security clearance form. He worked for the DoD for a few years after college. So I talked to his contact that he had listed on his security clearance for when he worked at the DoD."

The CIA man listened but didn't speak.

Flynn went on. "So the guy gets talking, and he tells me that he thinks that they get a few people a year stashed there by CIA's personnel department, awaiting further assignment. He said he thought Max was one of them, but couldn't be sure. The more I thought about it, the more his job overseas seemed like a good cover for CIA employment. I think the fact that we're both sitting here tells me that I'm warm."

Wilkes nodded. "Is that it? Anything else I need to be aware of? You understand the sensitivity here. If there's a way that we can improve our process, I'd like to get that feedback."

The CIA man's voice was impassive. Flynn wondered if

he already knew about Max Fend fleeing in a car chase yesterday.

Flynn said, "That's it."

"And the reason you're investigating Max Fend? What's his connection, if you don't mind my asking?"

"We're just looking into a recent Fend Aerospace incident, involving their automated flight system."

Caleb Wilkes stayed still. "I see."

Flynn flipped open a small notepad and clicked his pen. "Mind if I take notes?"

"Actually, I'd rather you didn't. This is a courtesy discussion. And I'm afraid it will be a short one. Normally we never discuss former employees, but we'll make an exception to help aid your investigation. You see, Max Fend actually didn't work here for very long. Your friend at the DoD was probably right. I'm afraid that we do stash people there —and in various other jobs within the government—while we're running background checks. We can't be too careful."

"So you're confirming that Max *did* work for the CIA?"

He held up a finger. "Yes, but not for long. He washed out of the program."

"Why?"

"Performance. He just wasn't up to our standards, I'm afraid. But I implore you—keep this to yourself. We don't normally provide information on *anyone* who has been to this school, and that includes washouts."

Flynn lowered his voice a little. "You mind if I ask you a question? Is this place really what everyone says it is? It's really a spy school?"

Caleb smiled. "It's not exactly a well-kept secret. They have many books and TV shows about it. But most of them aren't very accurate." Flynn noticed that he didn't really answer the question.

Flynn nodded. "But you *are* sure that Max Fend never worked for the Agency beyond being here?"

"Correct."

"And how long was he at this...*school*?"

"I would have to check the record again. Sorry. I only glanced at it just before you arrived. I think it was a matter of weeks. Maybe a month, tops. It's quite rigorous training."

The FBI agent tapped his pen against his blank notepad.

"And to be clear, Fend is no longer employed by the CIA?"

Caleb Wilkes's smile looked fake now. Annoyance in his eyes. "Again, that's correct. He's no longer with the Agency."

"Why did you guys recruit him, if he wasn't up to your standards?"

"We recruit a lot of people. Sometimes you don't know who can handle the pressure until you put them in the cooker. A lot of them don't make it through. But we funnel most of those to other CIA roles, if they're fit for those types of assignments. It would be a waste not to. Security clearances are expensive, and take a long time."

"But you didn't do that with Fend?"

"What? Send him to another CIA role?"

"Yes."

"No. Not with him."

"Why not?"

"He wasn't suited for other roles."

"Why not?"

"He just wasn't." Wilkes's eyes narrowed.

"When's the last time you spoke to Max?"

"Years ago. Just before he left our employment."

"And what exactly is *your* position here?"

"I can't say."

"How is it that you remember Max Fend so well if he was only here for a month, over a decade ago?"

Caleb tapped his temple. "Memory like a steel trap. It's a gift."

Flynn wasn't getting anywhere. He decided to take a chance. "Can I ask you a question? Did you happen to see that motorcycle chase—the one in D.C. yesterday?"

"Of course," Wilkes said. "It's been all over the news."

"What did you think of it? Like, as in, what is your *professional* opinion?"

Wilkes stared at Flynn for a moment and then said, "It was a competent group. Professionals. They were able to evade law enforcement in one of the most highly secured areas in the world. Then they disappeared. I couldn't have planned it better myself."

Flynn stared into Wilkes's eyes. His investigative instincts were colliding with his sense of interagency propriety. The FBI agent in him won out.

"*Did* you plan it?" He watched Wilkes's face carefully during the response.

Wilkes laughed. "No. I definitely did *not*. While I said that I couldn't have planned it better, and that might be true, I would like to think that I'd have planned it *differently*."

"How so?"

"I wouldn't have made the escape so...*public*. That's against everything we teach here. If we make the news, we're doing something wrong."

"So you think the people who did that wanted Max to make the news?"

"Perhaps." He shrugged.

"Do you know if Max Fend ever worked for any foreign governments? Foreign companies? Or acted as a foreign agent in any capacity?"

"No, I told you. He was only here for a month."

"What about after the CIA?"

"You are asking about what Max Fend went on to do after his time here? That, I wouldn't know."

While this CIA guy may have been a well-trained liar, Flynn had been a federal investigator for over twenty years. He had a great built-in lie detector, and he was pretty sure that Wilkes's last answer was a whopper.

"Look, Wilkes, I'm just trying to make sure he wasn't involved in anything that I need to investigate further. We had an incident at Fend Aerospace that involves billions of dollars in technology. And there's evidence of foreign interference—as in industrial espionage. It might even have national security implications. There are foreign nationals who'd *love* to get their hands on that technology."

"And you think Max Fend was helping them? The son of the owner of the company?"

"You'd be surprised how often family is involved in crimes against each other."

Wilkes said. "No, I wouldn't, actually. But look, I'm sorry. I just don't have anything for you. I've told you all I know. Max Fend did *not* work for the CIA."

Flynn rubbed his chin. "Alright. Between me and you, I thought it was a long shot anyway. I see no reason to keep digging. Thanks for your time."

"Of course."

They stood, and Wilkes walked him out to his car.

"I appreciate your help today."

"No problem. Always glad to help the FBI."

* * *

Special Agent Jake Flynn drove west along I-64, towards

Richmond. From there he would take I-95 north and head towards the FBI's Manassas office. Flynn planned to make a quick stop there before catching a flight to Jacksonville in the afternoon.

He went over the interview in his mind, getting more and more frustrated as he replayed it. Flynn had met guys like Wilkes before. Spooks. Some of them really thought they were better and smarter than everyone else. Like they were the only *real* cowboys, and everyone else in law enforcement was just pretending.

Guys like Wilkes thought they had license to manufacture a false reality when it suited their needs. It became hard to tell what was real and what wasn't. They were good at it. After all, it was what a professional spy did for a living.

If the CIA had Wilkes teaching at the Farm, he probably had decades of field experience. Every lie he told was likely mixed in with just enough truth to convince Flynn to believe him.

But Flynn *couldn't* believe everything he had just heard. He didn't believe that BS line about having the memory of a steel trap. What kind of asshole says something like that? Wilkes had a certain level of familiarity and interest in Max Fend that was *way* more than he should have had. There's no way a guy like Wilkes would have wasted his time talking to the FBI about some washout. Max Fend was more than Wilkes was letting on. Flynn could feel it.

His phone rang. He looked down at the caller ID. Steve at the DNI's office. Perfect timing.

"Jake, it's Steve." His voice sounded funny, like he didn't want to talk too loud.

"Hold on, let me pull over." Flynn pulled off at an exit and parked in a gas station. "What's up?"

"I looked into what we had been discussing yesterday."

"Yup. And?"

"Something isn't right."

"Really? Can you go into it?" He didn't want to say the name if it was that sensitive.

"In person."

Flynn looked at the clock. He would have to forego his planned stop at the FBI's DC field office in Manassas.

"I've got to catch a flight this afternoon, but I've got a little bit of time. Can you meet me for coffee? I can be up there in a few hours."

"Text me when you get here."

The drive took two hours. I-95 was backed up around Dumfries, but no more than usual. They ended up meeting at a little coffee shop in Springfield, Virginia.

Steve said, "So I checked the personnel file for Max Fend —or I started to, anyway."

"And?"

"The system that the DNI network uses will trigger alerts if I look at things I'm not supposed to. But I know this much: he worked for one of the intel agencies. If Max Fend had never worked in the intel world, I wouldn't have found anything on him. But there's definitely a DNI personnel file on Max Fend."

"What was in it?"

"I don't know. But I could see the classification level of the file. And in this case, it was above what I'm allowed to access. *Way above*."

"What does that mean?"

"I'm not sure. I'm afraid if I dig any further it'll trigger an audit on me. We don't want that. I'll get in trouble...or get both of us in trouble."

"Let me ask you this—would you have seen that file if

he'd worked for the CIA for a month and then washed out of their training program?"

Steve thought about it and then shook his head. "Nah. I don't think so. The file would have looked different, or there may not have even been one for him."

"Okay. Listen, Steve, I just came from Camp Peary. I met with a guy down there who represented the CIA. He just completely denied that Max Fend ever worked for them. He said he was in training for a month, and then washed out."

"That's what they told you?"

"Yeah."

"That seems strange, considering the classification of his personnel file."

"Yeah, I'm not buying it either."

Steve said, "Well, maybe he just works for another agency."

"What do you mean, like who?"

"A lot of the agencies have spies, Jake. It's not just the CIA out there in the field, you know."

"But the guy down at the Farm said—"

"Jake, I gotta tell ya, in my experience—a lot of these CIA field agents are like politicians, but with different motivations. You can tell when they're lying by whether their mouth is moving or not."

"You think he would lie to an FBI agent conducting an investigation on one of his men?"

Steve shot him a skeptical look. "Come on, man. You know how it is."

Flynn sighed. "Well, what can I do?"

"Let me talk to someone else at my work. It's okay, I'll be careful what I say. And he's trustworthy. If I find anything else out, I'll call you. It might be a few days."

"Call me whether you find anything out or not. I want to know."

"Got it."

"Thanks, Steve."

"You bet."

Flynn looked at his watch. He needed to be on a plane to Jacksonville soon.

10

Max and Renee stopped off at her home so she could speak to her mother and grab her things. Max waited in the car for ten minutes until she was done.

They ate their breakfast in the MarieBette Cafe and Bakery in Charlottesville, Virginia. The place was crowded with a mix of locals and University of Virginia students. Max had a penchant for good French pastries, and MarieBette made some of the best ones he'd tasted in the States.

"I have a house in Georgia. I'll fly us there this morning. It's out of the way. No one will see us. We'll make our call at six tonight and see what we can find out. And you'll have time to do your thing."

"Sounds good."

Max wiped his mouth with a napkin and stood. "Okay— I'll wait in the car. If you don't mind paying? I'd prefer as little interaction as possible."

"Sure." Renee closed her laptop and placed it in her bag. She ordered two cups of coffee to go and a few more crois- sants, and paid for their food.

A few minutes later, they walked through the Signature

Flight Support building at Charlottesville Albemarle Airport. Max wore his aviator sunglasses and kept his head facing away from the man behind the counter, who was paying much more attention to the cling of Renee's shirt than to Max. That was fine. If the FBI questioned him later, he would be that much worse of an eyewitness.

Max untied the plane and threw the chocks back inside the storage compartment, along with their travel bags. He got into the cockpit and helped Renee strap her seat belt on and plug in her headset. Then he went through his checklist.

He held open the aircraft door, yelled, "Clear prop!" and started up the 315-horsepower engine.

Max checked the weather one last time on his phone. Severe clear all the way down to Brunswick. He called ground control and began to taxi, holding short of the runway. He then told the tower that he was departing to the south using visual flight rules, and they cleared him for takeoff. Max smiled to himself as he saw Renee tense up out of the corner of his eye, her thighs flexing and her hands grabbing the seat as the aircraft vaulted forward down the runway.

Then he pulled back on the stick ever so slightly, and the Cirrus was airborne. It was a smooth climb out. A little left stick and they were headed toward the south horizon.

* * *

"Can you hear me okay?" Max asked Renee over their pilot headsets.

They were flying southeast now, sitting side by side in the cockpit, green pastures and farmland beneath them.

Renee was on her laptop, using her satellite connection to get work done while they traveled.

"I can hear you fine. I'm reading an article on you. On your father, actually. But it mentions you. It's a write-up about the Fend 100, and a profile on him."

Max looked over at her and then back out the windscreen of the aircraft.

She quoted, "While Charles Fend is known as a pioneer in the aviation world, his son Max has yet to make his mark. Max Fend has lived in the lap of luxury in the South of France for the past decade. He is best known for throwing decadent parties at his villa in Saint-Jean-Cap-Ferrat, located in a region of France known as an exclusive vacation spot for the ultra-rich. He often hosted celebrities and the wealthy elite from around the globe. Controversy erupted last year when two men were found dead on the premises. While rumors swirled regarding Max Fend's connection to the crimes, he was never charged, and was reportedly out of the country when the deaths occurred."

Renee looked at Max again. "I've been meaning to ask you about that."

"I've promised you honesty. Ask me anything."

"Did you kill those two men?"

The drone of the plane engine was the only sound for a few seconds.

"Yes, I did."

"Why?"

"We had a disagreement."

"Over what?"

"How to treat a lady." Max glanced at her. "Have you flown in a small plane like this before?"

Renee frowned at the obvious change of subject. "Actually, yes. In Canada. When I was younger, my family spent a lot of time on the West Coast. North of Vancouver. Have you been there?"

"Yes, actually. It's quite beautiful. Lots of great hiking and fishing."

"Yeah. My father has a cabin there. It's pretty remote, so sometimes we would get there by float plane. That was a lot of fun."

"A float plane, huh?"

"Yup."

"Always wanted to try that. This one can't land on water, but it does have its own parachute."

Renee made a face. "Are you messing with me?"

"No, I swear." Max pointed up at the ceiling. A black oval covering with a bright red and white warning label was above them.

"What is that?" Renee was reading it now. "Oh my. You *are* serious. This plane actually has a parachute?"

"I figured with all of the trouble I get into on the ground, it's best that I take the proper precautions when I'm in the air."

She smiled at that. "Have you ever used it?"

"The parachute? No. You would only use it in a dire emergency. But I must admit, I've always wanted to try it. It has an exceptional safety record."

"If it's all the same to you, let's just land normally."

Max laughed. "Not a problem, my dear."

* * *

The aircraft touched down on a tiny runway near the shores of southern Georgia. Jekyll Island. The airport was nothing more than a long strip of black pavement, with a few Cessnas parked next to a small shack.

The island was part marshland, part golf course. On a secluded strip of beach were a scattering of vacation homes, one of which Max owned.

A rental agent was waiting for them with a car. Max had had Renee order it while they were flying. They'd provided false information and paid using one of Max's prepaid cards. The rental agent tried to make small talk in the airport parking lot, but they kept it to a minimum.

They stopped at a small grocery store and picked up some essentials, then drove to Max's property. The house didn't look like much, but it was quaint. A dated two-bedroom ranch underneath a low-hanging weeping willow. More sand than grass in the yard. A few leaning palm trees.

Max said, "The view in back gets better."

It certainly did. While the house was old and beat up out front, the backyard was a narrow sandy passage right down to the beach. Rows of perfect tube waves rolled into the shore. It was mid-afternoon, and the sky was a deep blue. After throwing their bags in separate bedrooms, they went outside and sat on two wooden beach chairs, facing the water.

Max cracked open two beers and handed one to Renee. He stared off towards the Georgia shore, a few hundred yards away, a cool sea breeze rustling the trees in the yard.

"I got this place a few years ago," Max said. "I was home for a month, visiting my father, and I wanted somewhere I could go to get away from it all."

"Do you buy a lot of property on a whim?"

"It's relaxing here. The neighbors are far enough away that we don't see each other. The beach is relatively undiscovered. And most of the year, the weather is warm."

"It's very nice." Renee opened her laptop and began

typing. Without looking up, she said, "Why did you start down that path?"

"What do you mean?"

"Your father being who he was, you could have had any life you wanted. But you chose to be in the intelligence world. Why?"

"Honestly? Probably because it sounded exciting. Like an adventure."

"And was it?"

"I think the hope of an adventure is what attracts a lot of us at first. But you find out pretty quick that it's not like they portray it in the movies."

"What is it like?"

"You have to pretend a lot. Some might call it acting. And you have to document and pass on everything. In a world where so much is accessible by computer, the intelligence agencies are more reliant on human sources than ever."

"That seems counterintuitive. Why?"

"Because cyber data is too easily tracked. A lot of the best spies and terrorists stay off phones and Internet. So the best way to track them ends up being old-fashioned tradecraft."

"Did you like the work?"

"Sometimes. Sometimes not."

"So why did you stay on?"

"Because people need protecting. It's a noble cause. You did work for the CSE. And you work in cybersecurity now. You must know as well as I do that there are evil men in this world. I don't know how they got that way, and I've given up trying to find out. But I saw it enough to want to fight them."

"So you joined for an adventure, and stayed on to protect us from bad guys?" She was smiling.

"And probably 9/11, if I think about it. September eleventh changed everyone, I think. I was in New York City when it happened. I had actually skipped class to go visit my father. I never did anything like that—skip class, I mean. But I hadn't seen him in a while, and it was early in the semester. I planned to make it back for football practice. My father and I ended up watching the smoke from the first building when the second airplane hit. That was the moment—when the second aircraft struck. People were still trying to figure out what was going on when it was just one smoking tower. But the second aircraft hitting—that was when the world changed."

Renee looked up from her computer as Max spoke.

"I remember seeing the people who jumped off the burning towers. Their bodies falling through the air. Their choice was to stay and burn to death, or jump off. Maybe it wasn't a choice. That was the most terrifying thing I've ever witnessed. When you see something like that, and you know that there are these men out there who intended for it to occur—men who celebrated when it happened—it makes you realize that there is good and evil in this world. And I guess I just wanted to fight for good."

"Sometimes I think it takes a truly shocking event to wake us all up out of our slumber." Renee paused. "So, you see yourself as...what exactly? A knight?"

He smiled. "I guess. Something like that."

"So why the act? Why do you pretend to be the spoiled rich boy, if that's not who you really are? Does the DIA tell you to pretend to be that character?"

Max shrugged.

"Come on, Max, give me an answer."

"Are you psychoanalyzing me now? Should I lie down?"

"If it would help." The wind blew a few strands of her

dark hair across her face. She stroked it out of the way with her fingers.

"Because if people think I'm the cliché of a rich billionaire's son, they're expecting to see certain things," Max said. "I give them what they expect. It's a convenient mask. And then they don't see anything else I might do."

"It allows you to be anonymous?"

"It allows me to be sneaky."

"And the act didn't get too distasteful for you?"

"No. I'm good at pretending. I feel like all my life, I've pretended. When you get good at it, the act requires less effort. And if they think you wake up at dawn, you can sleep till noon. Or in my case...if they think you're sleeping till noon, no one knows that you might be sending intelligence to your handler at dawn."

She touched his arm. "So if you were satisfied being a spy, then why did you decide to get out?"

"I didn't decide to get out. They *forced* me out." He started to say something else and then bit his lip. "We can talk more about that later. Right now I need you to find out as much as you can before our call with the MI-6 agent."

"Sure. That's fine." Renee began typing. She shot him a curious glance as he got up and walked away.

11

Jacksonville, Florida

The Fend Aerospace business center was a tall metal-and-glass structure that rose up just west of the St. John's River. It housed a sizable chunk of the managers in the company - those involved in finance, purchasing, marketing, and sales. Charles Fend and the c-suite executives had their offices there, along with a select group of project managers and R&D scientists.

The view was excellent. From the eighteenth floor, one could see the St. John's River winding through the city. The football stadium stood to the north, and Naval Air Station Jacksonville was to the south. Multiple bridges cut across the shimmering river.

Special Agent Flynn sat across the glossy conference table from the senior Fend 100 program manager. She looked nervous, which was understandable considering that she was talking to the FBI. Most people Flynn spoke with were nervous.

Flynn looked at his notes. Maria Blount.

Charles Fend had personally hired her away from a London-based competitor. Maria had gotten to know Max Fend informally in the two years that she'd been with his father's company. Red hair. A nice smile. And very smart. Aerospace engineering smart. Not that Flynn was a dummy, but these people were all brainiacs. She'd graduated near the top of her class at Cambridge and had turned down a job at NASA to work on this project, for God's sake. Flynn would have to bring his A game.

"I appreciate you guys blocking off your afternoon for me."

"Of course."

"Tell me about Max Fend," he began.

Maria blinked. "Max? Well, I've known him for a number of years through his father. He's a good soul, Max. A little bit of a comedian, I think, but sharp, and eager to learn. He'll fit right in."

"Do you have any reason to believe that Max Fend would be angry with his father?"

She was taken aback. "No. No, of course not. Why do you ask?"

"Have you seen any suspicious behavior? Talking to anyone that you didn't know? Or perhaps asking questions that were unlike him?"

Maria thought about it. "He was asking a lot of questions about the automated airliner. The Fend 100. But *everyone* has been asking questions about that. And it's completely appropriate for Max to ask those sorts of questions. He'll be coming to work for Fend Aerospace, as you know."

"Yes, I'm aware. What kinds of things was he asking?"

"I don't know," Maria said. "The basic questions. How it worked. Who controlled the aircraft at different phases of the flight. That kind of thing."

"Did you see him using the Fend computer network the day of the network breach? Or at any time leading up to that incident?"

"What do you mean, the Fend computer network?"

"Did you see him use any company computers on the fifteenth of last month?"

"Yes, I think so. But again, that's completely appropriate and normal behavior."

"I'll decide that, thank you."

"Very well. I apologize."

"It's no problem. Confirm for me this—you had a computer network breach, right?"

"Yes."

"And the day after, you had a test flight for one of your Fend 100 prototypes, right?"

"Again, that is correct."

"Was there a risk there? Was the Fend 100 aircraft affected by the hacking incident?"

"No."

"You sound very sure of yourself."

Maria frowned. "Look, I understand that it's your job to investigate this computer security incident. But in my opinion, it's silly to think that someone logging in to the Fend network's email system could gain access to the datalink that controls the Fend 100 remotely."

"Why do you say that?"

She rolled her eyes and sighed, exasperated. "Do you mind if I bring in Bradley? He's better at explaining this type of stuff."

"He's the chief engineer on the project?"

"Yes."

"Sure. Please bring him in. I'll wait."

Bradley Karpinsky entered a moment later. Flynn said,

"Mr. Karpinsky, I was just talking to Miss Blount here about the external computer breach that occurred on the Fend network."

"Okay." Karpinsky shrugged.

He was going to make Flynn do all the work. Flynn hated guys like this.

"Miss Blount was telling me how she thinks it's implausible that anyone could have gained access to the Fend 100 aircraft through the company's computer network."

"I would have to agree with her on that," Karpinsky said.

"Would you mind elaborating? Using laymen's terms?"

"Well, for one thing, the system that remotely controls the Fend 100 is a closed system. There is no connection to the company's main computer network."

"But our Cyber Investigation division has identified that your company's computer network was penetrated by foreign entities."

"So we heard," Karpinsky said. "So what?"

"I'm just trying to cover all my bases. I want to figure out what the hackers were after. Some of my cyber experts raised the question that the aircraft itself could have been tapped into. I would like to hear your opinions on that theory."

Maria whispered, "They think it was Max."

Flynn frowned. "Excuse me. I never said that."

"Well, you were asking all those questions about him. It doesn't take a rocket scientist to see where you're going."

Flynn realized that she actually *was* a rocket scientist.

Karpinsky let out a snort. "Max Fend? Look, don't repeat this, but that kid is more interested in buying a new boat or whatever it is rich folks do. And I doubt he would have the skills needed to gain entry into our computer network."

Agent Flynn said, "I take it you don't have a very high

opinion of Max Fend?"

"Not really, no."

"Why is that?"

"His father's setting him up with a comfortable job here when he's done with school. But the kid's done nothing to earn it," Karpinsky said. "Meanwhile we're all busting our asses so that his dad can make history."

"*Bradley.* Come on," Maria said.

"Well, it's true. You know it is."

Flynn watched the exchange. What Flynn didn't bother to mention was that Max Fend himself didn't need much skill to open up the Fend network to criminal hackers. He just needed *access* to the Fend Aerospace computer network. Inserting a preprogrammed thumb drive, or clicking on the right external link, would create a hole in the firewall—the hackers would do the rest.

Karpinsky's comments raised two questions in his mind. First, was it really implausible that the Fend 100 had been accessed through the company's separate network breach? Flynn made a note to ask his cyber team about that. He had taken their word for it. He would have to dig there.

The second question in Flynn's mind was whether Karpinsky held a grudge against Charles Fend, because he felt that Max was getting favorable treatment.

Flynn decided to change up the questions. "Mr. Karpinsky..."

"Please, call me Bradley."

"Bradley, if you were going to seize control of the Fend 100, how would you do it?"

"I wouldn't."

"But if you *had* to—do you see any possible way for a criminal organization to do so?"

Karpinsky rubbed his chin. "I mean—hypothetically—

and I mean this is *way* out there—but if someone was able to access the actual aircraft...maybe then they could mess around in there and—"

Maria shook her head. "I doubt that's possible. We have so many security measures."

"Yeah. She's right. I mean, we have teams of engineers crawling all over the aircraft every day. We treat it like a NASA rocket launch. We check everything eight different ways to make sure there are no defects. That's why I told your FBI investigator that I don't think this computer network breach is a safety concern—more like a corporate security issue. Hackers trying to steal the design and software code. That is my worry."

Flynn said, "You're saying that the hacking incident isn't a safety concern because no defects showed up on your tests?"

"Right."

"Look, this might sound crazy, but I've gotta ask this," Flynn said. "I've heard reports about people on commercial flights hacking into the aircraft's controls through the onboard Wi-Fi network. Does the Fend 100 have any security flaws like that? Something that hackers could have taken control of?"

Maria looked at Karpinsky and they both shook their heads.

Maria said, "No. That's not possible. I think I read an article in *Wired* magazine about that. Some engineer claimed to have changed the aircraft's trajectory. But that's just not realistic."

"Why not?"

"Oh, I remember this one. We looked into that," Karpinsky said. "We think the engineer in the article was able to access that aircraft through the IFE system."

"IFE?"

Karpinsky sighed the way IT people did when talking to "non-computer" people. "The in-flight entertainment system. He probably used the port in his seat to get into the IFE system. Then, on his computer, he saw some data that he thought was the avionics system data, and he tried to manipulate it."

"The article I read said that he *did* manipulate it."

Karpinsky rolled his eyes. "That's not possible. The data is routed through a different bus."

"So then how—"

"Okay, let me put it this way. My daughter has a pretend steering wheel on her car seat. When we go to the grocery store, she turns the wheel and she thinks she's moving our car, but she isn't. That's what happened with this guy. The data bus we use on commercial airliners is a secured, closed system. It is not possible for a passenger to hack into it."

"And the security breach didn't affect the Fend 100 that was flying that day?"

"Correct," Karpinsky said. "We analyzed the electronic data stats for hydraulics, avionics, electrical and mechanical controls, along with their built-in redundant systems and fail-safes. Any interference with the normal signal would be detected and flagged to us. We're clear to proceed with our test flight."

"And when is that flight?"

"Four days from now."

* * *

They took a break around five-thirty p.m. Sandwiches and drinks were brought in from a local place down in San Marco.

Flynn asked to speak to one of the test pilots who worked on the program. They brought in a guy named Tim Hutson. Karpinsky stepped out for a meeting.

"So are you going to be flying the Fend 100 during the big test flight in four days?"

"That's right."

"And you used to fly for the Air Force?"

"That's right. C-141s, among others. I was a test pilot before I retired and started working here."

"Excellent. I saw a bunch of Air Force jets at an air show once. What do they call them? The white ones that fly together?"

"The Thunderbirds?"

"Yeah. That's it. They were incredible. Wow. Hey, thank you for your service."

"Thanks."

Flynn looked at Tim. "Can I ask you something? As a pilot, what do you think of all this automated flight stuff?"

Tim said, "I think it's going to put guys like me out of business."

"Really?"

"Sure. I mean, autopilot functions have been around for decades. And they're getting better and better. Hell, now any kid can buy their own quadcopter drone and control it with a smartphone."

"So you're saying that the technology is already there."

"Yeah, has been for years."

"So then what gives? Why is everyone making such a big deal out of automating commercial airliners?"

"This is more than just a few safety measures. Your car has cruise control, right?"

"Sure."

"Okay, well, think of today's autopilot in planes as being

the equivalent of cruise control in cars. The Fend 100 autonomous flight is like those driverless cars you hear about all the tech companies testing out. We're actually using some of the same technology. There are very sophisticated computers on board that will—potentially—be able to completely replace the pilots."

"From the tone of your voice, I'm picking up that you're a bit skeptical?"

Tim said, "Most people want to know that there's a human being up front, making sure everything goes smoothly. An expert, ready to take charge if anything goes wrong."

"Do you think pilots are still needed?"

"Right now I do, yeah. I think with any new technology, you're gonna have bumps. And flying is an unforgiving business. Small mistakes have big consequences. I would want a pilot on board."

Flynn ate a potato chip. He looked at Maria, who was shaking her head in disagreement. "Maria, what are the arguments for automated commercial airliners?"

"I mean...aside from the massive profits, and it being part of our company's main growth strategy?"

"Yes. Aside from all of that."

"Safety. Cost efficiencies. Do you know how many car accidents there are in the United States every year?"

"A lot, right?"

"Yes. Over thirty thousand people die in road crashes every year. Thirty thousand. Think about that number. Not only that, but another two million are injured. *Two million people*. That's almost one percent of the entire population. Every stinking year. Compare that to aircraft accidents. The fatalities are in the hundreds."

"What has this got to do with robot pilots?"

"Her point is going to be that robots make fewer mistakes than people," Tim said. "She's saying that bringing autonomous driving and flying to market will save lives."

Maria nodded. "It *will* save lives. Lots of them."

Flynn looked at Tim. "You seem skeptical. You still don't trust a robot to do your pilot job."

"That's because he's a dinosaur." The gruff voice of Bradley Karpinsky, who stood in the doorway, wearing his light blue lab coat.

Maria looked at her watch. "Your meeting go okay?"

He plopped down at the head of the conference table. "Yes, thanks. Maria's right. Computers are smarter than people. It's not even close. Tim here"—he pointed at the pilot—"is going to get tired. He's going to drink alcohol. He's going to forget things. He's going to have to pee. He's going to get sick. Distracted. Sometimes, he'll underperform."

"Never," said Tim. "Except maybe the part about getting drunk. But not while flying."

"A computer—or a robot, if you will—will never get tired, sick, hungry, or have to go to the bathroom," Bradley said. "It will be ruthlessly efficient. Do you know that even today, if you're flying on a commercial airliner, the hardest landings are given to the computers? Did you know that?"

"That's not entirely true," Tim said.

"What does he mean?" Flynn asked.

"He's referring to the fact that—depending on the airline and the type of aircraft—if weather minimums get bad enough, the pilots are required to have autopilot fly the landing," Tim answered.

Flynn stopped chewing. "Are you serious? What do you mean weather minimums—like if it gets too windy?"

Tim gave him a funny look. "No, sorry. I mean ceiling and visibility. If the clouds get too low...the best way to think of it is when it's really foggy out. That gets the visibility way down. So in that scenario, when the cloud layer is basically zero, and the visibility is zero, then a lot of airlines require that their pilots use an automated approach. In essence, the computers will fly the landing."

"No shit. Wow. I had no idea."

"Most people don't."

Flynn said, "What if the computers mess it up?"

"The pilots are right there, ready to take the controls. But in reality, with the improved navigational equipment on board and the reliability of the automated flight software, the computers never make a mistake."

Flynn said, "So is your Fend 100 as simple as that? You guys just hit the autopilot button and the pilot leaves the plane?"

"There are three modes of operation in the Fend automated flight software," Bradley said. "Type one—normal, pilot-controlled flight. Nothing out of the ordinary. Type two —remote-controlled flight. A pilot from the ground controls the airplane. This is the way the military controls its drones. Finally, we have type three—this is the really innovative stuff. This is where machine learning and artificial intelligence come into play. And it's where Fend actually adds to the value chain."

"Bradley's never had trouble talking up his own program," Maria said.

Karpinsky frowned. "Fend's type three automated flight means that the computers inside the aircraft are doing everything. They handle all the communications to and from ground controllers, tower controllers, and all other air traffic controllers throughout the flight. Much of this is through data exchanges. But there's an actual voice action-response mechanism that'll supplement the pilot. And the machines are *learning*. Getting better every day with the sum learning of the entire system."

"So how does a computer know what to say like a pilot would?"

"That part is pretty easy. It's just a bunch of code. A bunch of if-then statements, so that it knows what to do in every scenario. For instance, before it goes into class bravo airspace, it knows that it has to establish two-way communications with the class bravo air traffic controller. So it won't enter that airspace until it does."

"What if the radio failed, and it could never establish communication in the first place?"

"Then it would keep going through the if-then statements until it got to the correct course of action. Tim, as a pilot, what would you do?"

Tim said, "It depends—but if all else failed, I could set the transponder to 7600 and keep making my radio calls in the blind. Then basically keep flying the approach and land on the runway and hope they can hear you."

"And that is what the computers would have the aircraft do," Bradley said. "It would automatically know who to talk to, what to say, where and how to fly. No humans required. And it would be taking in data from a variety of sources, *including* the radios. If the air traffic controller called up the aircraft and told it to turn, our computers would follow orders—as long as there wasn't a more pressing need, like a fuel emergency. And this is just how a human pilot would behave. Right, Tim?"

"That's the theory."

Bradley frowned. "Tim's a purist. He believes that all planes should have people in them."

Tim said, "Bradley, let me ask you something. Have you ever used the voice-to-text feature on your phone?"

"Yes."

"And did it transcribe everything perfectly? I doubt it. I once told my mom I was going to get her a birthday cake, but instead my phone told her that I got her birthday crack."

"I understand your point."

Tim said, "Same example—but with typed text messages—if the autocomplete feature on your phone messes up and changes what you meant to type, it might give your text message a completely different meaning. Those are two separate technologies. Voice transcription, and text autocomplete. Billions of people around the world use those technologies. Yet everyone knows of stories where they have failed, leading to unintended consequences."

"This is true," Bradley said. "Voice recognition is challenging. But it's constantly improving. And your phone needs to be able to interpret anything. We're able to cut down a lot of errors because of the standardized terminology in aviation. Pilots and controllers are expected to use precise terms and phrases."

"My point isn't that voice-to-text is a weak link here," Tim said. "It's that when you replace a complex human worker with a robot, you're probably going to have a lot of errors that the human would never make. Because humans are critical thinkers, and we can use all our senses and experiences to help make decisions."

Jake Flynn listened as the pilot and engineer went on arguing their points to each other. He wondered how it must feel to know that computers were about to make your job obsolete.

* * *

After a brief break, they came together again so Flynn could finish up his questions to the Fend 100 project team. It was well after business hours now, and Flynn could see that he was wearing out his welcome. "Okay, talk to me about your upcoming test flight."

"We're calling it a final approval flight," Bradley said. "The type certification has already been granted by the FAA, but this is more about the contract. The FAA wants to make sure our first passenger flight goes well, and they're going to evaluate us while it happens."

"So if it goes well, what happens?"

"We get the NextGen contract for autonomous flight. You're familiar with NextGen?"

Flynn shook his hand back and forth. "I've read about it. But refresh me."

Bradley looked at Maria, who smiled politely. She said, "The Next Generation Air Transportation System. NextGen. It's the new national airspace system that the United States will adopt over the next ten years. The plans will transform the way planes and air traffic controllers navigate and communicate, and the way the industry manages flights in the United States."

"What are the major changes?" Flynn asked.

Maria looked at her watch. "How much time do you have? How about I give you the high-level version? Today the US air traffic control system primarily uses radar and radio communications. NextGen will change that to use more GPS and data transfers. It allows planes to shorten their routes by going directly to the airports, instead of using inefficient navigational beacons. The data exchanges will reduce how much time it takes to get information back and forth between the planes and the controllers. Think of it as using text messaging instead of voice communication. Texting saves time, right?"

"Right."

"Before, controllers had to read out long chains of instructions. The pilots would then read it back. That took up a lot of valuable time. Mistakes were sometimes made. The data exchange method is quicker and more precise."

"So that's it? That's NextGen?"

"There's a lot more to it than just that," Bradley said. "But those changes *are* major changes. It might sound simple, but making it happen is a massive amount of work."

"So how does Fend Aerospace fit into the NextGen plans?"

"Many companies are part of it. I mean, it's transforming the entire commercial aviation industry," Bradley said. "The commercial *airline* industry alone is almost ten percent of the US GDP. And it's growing fast."

"Wow. I didn't realize it was that big."

"Prior to NextGen, automated flight wasn't permitted," Maria said. "There are still a lot of regulatory hurdles, but we're lobbying hard, and things are looking up. As long as everything goes well during our FAA final approval flight in a few days, we think there's a very good chance that Fend Aerospace will be the main contractor for automated flight when that part of NextGen comes online."

"Won't other aircraft manufacturers just make their own technology?"

"Well, that's why this is so important to us as a company," Maria said. "Fend Aerospace isn't building technology just to be used in its own planes. We're creating the hardware and software that allows aircraft to be preprogramed, and—if need be—controlled remotely. *All* aircraft in the NextGen Automated Flight Program would use this technology."

Karpinsky said, "Our strategy is to own the entire

autonomous flight software *platform*. All the major aircraft manufacturers and airline companies will become our customers. Think of the Fend 100 as our iPod. But we're also creating iTunes. So if the FAA decides to use the Fend 100 platform, everyone will buy from us."

Maria said, "It would be the standardized brain for every aircraft that wants to fly using automated flight in the NextGen aviation system—so all commercial flights, as well as logistics flights. Like FedEx. There are a lot of those, too."

"So what's the problem?" Flynn asked.

"Competition. Right now Fend has a leg up. We earned the bid for the US program. But European and Asian markets are modernizing their airways as well. Ideally, we would form the global solution. But that's probably not going to happen. We would probably create a licensing agreement with the leading European and Asian companies to share the tech. But first, we have to prove that it can work in the US. Everything culminates in our FAA final approval flight in a few days."

"I didn't realize this flight was so important."

"Oh, yes. If this flight goes well, we'll advance to the next tranche of funding. And our fifteen-year contract with the government will go into effect. That's everything for Fend Aerospace."

"Let me ask you a question. What would happen if all your technologies were given to your competition? Say, through a cyberattack?"

"That would be catastrophic for the company," Maria said. "But we've made sure that can't happen. After the cyberattack last month, we've really upped our IT security standards. The data for the Fend 100 is in the Fort Knox of IT security. And it isn't accessible through the Internet."

Flynn nodded. "Good to know."

12

Max and Renee spent the afternoon doing research and waiting for their phone call with MI-6. After two hours of Max watching Renee type, she sent him out to get some food.

Max returned and cooked her the best frittata she had ever eaten.

"My God, you're a good cook. Where did you learn that?"

"Europe. But the secret to this was the ingredients. Roast tomatoes and onions from the local farmers' market. I have to admit this is one of the better ones I've made."

She smacked her lips, finishing every bit of the dish.

Max and Renee sat in the living room of the beach house talking and working until six p.m. He had just gotten off the phone with the local fuel truck owner. The man was filling up his Cirrus now.

"It's time." Time to call the female MI-6 contact.

She nodded, sliding over on the couch. "Here. Sit."

Renee had connected her computer to Max's phone. It would run a series of programs designed to gather more information about who they were talking to.

At precisely six o'clock, Max dialed the number. Renee sat close enough that she heard everything.

The person on the other end answered, "Hello?" A woman's voice. So far so good.

"I was given this number to call." Said Max.

"Did that person give you a car?"

"Yes."

"What type?"

"An Audi." A minor identity check.

"I'm glad to see that you are out on your own."

Max said, "Can you tell me why you assisted me with my problem?

"Our organization attempted to find a mutually agreeable solution with our counterparts in US government. But they weren't interested. Due to the nature of the emergency, we took matters into our own hands."

Max pressed the mute button and looked at Renee. "So what does that mean? Counterparts in US government? As in the CIA?"

"That's what it sounds like, yes."

"So she's saying that MI-6 contacted the CIA regarding me, and the CIA wasn't interested in helping me out?"

"I think that's what she's saying."

Max unmuted the phone and said, "What do you mean by 'the nature of the emergency'? What emergency?"

"I can't go into it in too much detail in this format. I'll need you to come meet me."

"Where and when?"

"Key West. Tomorrow evening. Can you make it?"

Max looked at Renee, who shrugged. He said, "I can make it. What are you doing in Key West?"

"Look up Sailing Vessel Bravo. You'll see."

Renee typed a few keystrokes into her web browser. Max could see that *Sailing Vessel Bravo* was the name of a massive sailing yacht owned by a Russian billionaire, Pavel Morozov. Last spotted off Key West, Florida, a few days ago.

Max hit the mute button again as he looked at her screen.

"Morozov," Max whispered.

"You know him?" said Renee.

"I know of him."

"And?"

"Not a nice guy."

He could hear the woman on the phone say, "I need to go."

He unmuted the phone, "Where will I find you?"

"The Southernmost point. Sunset."

Max heard a beep and saw that the call had ended. He looked at Renee.

"Were you able to get anything useful?"

"A little. The transmission definitely came from the Florida Keys—that's where the cellular data was routed through. Other than that, not much."

"Okay. At least we have a lead. Let's find out everything we can about Morozov, and how he might be related to me or my father's company."

* * *

They were both on their computers for the next few hours, researching Pavel Morozov and his crew. While they had found out a lot about him, it had yet to reveal an obvious connection to Max or his father.

Max let out a sigh of frustration. "Anything?"

"Be patient. Your conversation with the MI-6 contact

helped me identify potential computers and IP addresses to dig into. I have programs running right now that should give us more information, but it'll take time. When shall we go to Key West?"

"I figured we'd fly there first thing in the morning."

She looked at her watch. "It's getting late."

"I'm going to take a walk on the beach. I need to clear my head."

"Okay. I have my phone if you need anything," said Renee.

Max took his phone and placed it in the pocket of his cargo shorts. He walked barefoot past the small grove of palm trees in his backyard and out along the hard-packed sand beach. He fought the urge to contact his father. Nothing would be stupider, he thought. But he hoped that the old man wasn't taking this too hard.

He walked for a good twenty minutes, the cool saltwater lapping the fine white sand off his feet. A nice breeze blew against his face, a sliver of moon rising over the horizon. He loved coming here. A shame it had to be under these circumstances.

* * *

While Max was gone, several of Renee's sources in the hacker community began to return her messages. They were contractors, mostly. While Renee worked almost solely for nongovernmental organizations these days, she knew people who were plugged in to the state-sponsored cybersecurity world. Unlike the way pop culture portrayed the intelligence agencies, the community was not a tight-lipped vault of top-secret information. Private contractors had permeated just about every crevice of the modern intelligence apparatus. One of the results of that trend was that, for a price, Renee's contacts would be able to provide her information on just about anyone or anything.

Her first order of business was to confirm that it was actually MI-6 they were dealing with. Renee's paranoia worried that it could be some elaborate trick, designed to look that way to Max.

So far so good.

Word on the street was that it was indeed an MI-6 team that had been responsible for Max's motorcycle escape out of D.C. No one knew *why* they'd done it, but it was very likely members of that specific British intelligence agency. The team who had executed the operation had gone underground. No one had seen or heard from any of them in the past forty-eight hours. A dead end.

Renee's second order of business was to reach out to someone she knew on the FBI's Cyber Forensics and Training Alliance. She wanted to find out more about what had prompted them to investigate Max in the first place.

Her source was able to provide her with what the FBI knew about the Fend Aerospace network intrusion, and the evidence that linked it to Max.

The hackers had stolen some data on the new Fend 100 aircraft, but they were unable to access the most secure information on the Fend 100's AI program.

The FAA had agreed with Fend Aerospace that there was no safety concern with the aircraft test scheduled for the next week.

Then why so much interest in Max Fend?

Renee's source told her that the FBI had received information from Interpol about Max's ties to Eastern European and Middle Eastern criminal enterprises. While Max's shady dealings might have piqued the FBI's interest, it was his association with a Russian mobster that put Max at the top of the suspect list.

The Russian mafioso was a man by the name of Sergei. Sergei had taken a leap off a building only a few weeks ago. The French government had provided the FBI with Sergei's communications records. They showed that Sergei had been working with a cybercriminal group that was operating out of Syria.

Furthermore, Sergei's communications implicated Max as being complicit in the Fend Aerospace cybertheft. The communications had been sent only hours before Sergei's death in Gibraltar.

But this information had been delivered electronically. Easily faked, Renee thought. The FBI thought that Sergei's death had been ordered by the Syrian hacking group he'd been working with—tying up loose ends and increasing their share of profits.

Renee's work in the cybersecurity world had exposed her to many of these criminal hacker organizations. They were white-collar criminals. Murder usually wasn't part of their skill set. Sergei's death smelled of something different, Renee thought—a ploy.

The FBI's working theory was that Max intended to sell access to Fend technology to the highest bidder. The technology could be worth billions.

Renee wanted to point out the flaws in this theory—namely that Max was the son of Charles Fend, and already filthy rich—but she decided to stop asking questions. While her contact wasn't an agent, and she trusted that he would keep her inquiry confidential, one never knew. Dig too deep, and she might trigger the FBI to look into her.

Lastly, Renee wanted to check up on Max's departure from the DIA. His story didn't quite add up. He seemed happy with his work there. His explanation of how his cover had been blown didn't seem like a fully adequate explanation for why he would have to leave. She would ask him more. But first, she wanted to try and find out what she could on her own.

After a few moments, Renee was conducting an encrypted chat with one of her former counterparts in the Canadian cyberintelligence organization, the CSE. There was a small video window so that she could see her friend as he typed, and her friend could see her. It was a security measure, to make sure that the conversation was actually with the intended person. The CSE folks were just as paranoid as she was. That was where she had learned it. She was surprised at what she read.

Renee: What do you mean?

Anon: It says that Max's cover was blown.

Renee: How?

Anon: Something involving a Russian arms deal. He was supposed to help facilitate the sale of weaponry from a Russian supplier to a buyer in northern Africa. But something went wrong.

Renee: What happened?

Friend: Max ended up killing the Russian arms dealers. The DIA and CIA decided that his cover was blown. There are phone records that indicate the Russians knew he was an American operative.

Renee: How would his cover be blown if both of the Russians were killed?

Anon: Don't know.

Renee: And so the DIA just let him walk away? They don't use him at all anymore?

Anon: Apparently.

Renee: Seems unusual.

Anon: Agreed.

Renee: So who does the intelligence world think is after him? Were you able to find that out?

Anon: There are two theories. One is that it is related to the people that he killed. The Russian group settling old debts.

Renee: And the other?

Anon: The other theory is that Max is dirty. That he might have been turned while in Europe. That would also explain why the DIA wanted him out of their organization, if they suspected that.

Renee: They wouldn't just ask him to leave. They would investigate him, right?

Anon: Maybe they couldn't prove anything, but didn't want to take a chance keeping him.

Renee: So what, then? People think he really gave someone access to his father's company? Why? Money? He's as rich as a Saudi prince.

Anon: No idea. Don't shoot the messenger.

Renee: Okay, thanks.

Anon: Renee, be careful. I don't know what's going on, but if this Max Fend guy is wanted by this Russian mercenary group, he probably isn't a good person to be around.

Renee: Understood. Send me what you can on the Russians.

Anon: Will do. And I don't have to tell you that if theory #2 is true—you better watch your back.

Renee: Thanks, goodnight.

Renee closed the chat window and made sure to delete the

conversation history. She leaned back on the couch. The lights were off in the living room of the beach house. The dim computer screen illuminated her face. She looked out at the dark beach. She could hear the waves. Max was walking out there somewhere. Was it really just to clear his head? Or was he calling someone else?

She shook her head. She had known him for a long time. Before he had gotten involved in the espionage world. He was a good man. Right?

* * *

Max came back in, wiping the dry sand off his feet. The screen door shut with a snap behind him. "Anything new?"

"I just reached out to a few people. That MI-6 team has gone underground."

"Okay. Well, we don't need them anymore anyway. We know we have to go to Key West."

"I also looked into the evidence the FBI has on you."

"And?"

"A lot of it's circumstantial. But there's an Interpol report that ties you to several organized crime syndicates in Europe and the Middle East." She filled him in on what she knew.

"Sergei? That little Russian bastard? He was nothing. Just a regional...and he's dead?"

Renee nodded. "Any idea what information he might have had that led to you?"

Max's eyes darted from side to side as he thought. "He was plugged in to the type of people who make money off ransomware. But it was petty stuff. They would lock up a thousand people's computers and make them each pay like three hundred bucks to get back their files. It was a volume game. You must know more about that stuff than I do."

Renee nodded. "That's what most of the small-time groups do. High-volume, low-dollar ransoms. The bigger fish go for corporations and can ask for millions of dollars. But those targets are harder to hit. And the penalties are worse if you're caught."

"You think Sergei thought I might be a good target?"

"Either he or someone he was connected with. It makes sense."

"Looks like my past is coming back to haunt me. Nothing I can do about that now, I guess."

"Were those connections related to the work you did for the DIA?"

"Of course." Max frowned. "Why else would I have associated with those types?" He walked into the kitchen. "I'm going to make something to eat. You hungry?"

"A little."

Max dug around the freezer. A few minutes later, he walked back into the living room with paper plates of steaming microwaved pizza.

"Anything else?"

"Are you really going to keep asking me that every few minutes?"

He put a plate of pizza in front of her. "Sorry. Just anxious."

She blew on it and took a small bite. "It's okay. Here's what I'm doing right now. Some of the software programs I've been running have returned information that I can use. They've identified computers that were in close geographic proximity to the device the MI-6 agent was using to communicate with you. So now I'm sending back pings to those computers, to see if any more information turns up. I have to be honest—I don't think we'll learn anything. But it's worth a shot."

"Yes, it is."

"So how did you start off in the intelligence world? Like...how did they hire you?"

Max chewed his pizza and took a swig of sweet tea. "It started when we were at Princeton. My senior year. That's when they first approached me. I was at a career fair. Looking at sales jobs. I wanted to make money on my own. I've always had an aggressive streak. Not sure if you've noticed."

"Maybe a little."

"So we had quick little interviews at this career fair. You probably went to some of them, at those big conference hotels near town. They conducted separate interviews in each of the hotel rooms, all going on at the same time. At least a hundred other students came. I thought I was interviewing for a financial sales job. I'd been through two of those interviews already that day. But my interviewer wasn't part of a financial sales firm. He was a DIA recruiter. It took me a while to figure that out, though."

She nodded.

"So he asks me a series of questions. Everything's normal. They were all behavioral questions. Tell me about how you would respond in this situation. Tell me about a time you led a team. That sort of thing."

"Then what?"

"Then he asks me about my mother's death. She died in a car accident when I was just a child. But I hadn't told him that."

"He asked about that?"

"Yeah. I mean, you know I was very young when it happened. I didn't really know her. But still, it was unexpected."

"So because the interviewer brought up your mother— you knew that they knew more about you than normal."

"Yes. At first, I assumed they must know about it because they knew about my father. I wasn't famous at the time." He winked. "That came later."

Renee rolled her eyes. "I think you have a complex."

"Yes, I'm quite complex."

"You misunderstand."

"You're French Canadian," Max said, "it's probably getting lost in translation."

"I speak better English than you."

"That's up for debate."

She pouted.

He grew more serious. "Anyway, my father was famous then. Still, it wasn't common knowledge—my mother's death. So when the interviewer asked about her, it caught me off guard. But more than that, it was the question itself that was strange."

"What did he ask you?"

"He asked me—hypothetically, if I found out that a criminal had been responsible for my mother's death, would I be comfortable killing that person, if I knew that I wouldn't be caught?"

"What did you say?"

"I didn't hesitate," Max said. "I said yes."

"Interesting interview."

"Then he said, what if there was a job where you could save people's lives by fighting the worst types of people in the world—would I be interested?"

"And you said yes."

"I did. Then he asked if I would be able to keep secrets, and lie, and commit acts of espionage, and things like that. Obviously, I kept giving him the answers he wanted."

"The interviewer asked you if you would be able to commit acts of espionage?"

"What? Oh. Hmm. Yes, that is a little too obvious for a first interview, isn't it? My memory fails me. Somewhere in the series of interviews they threw that one in. I had to go through several interviews. But really, once I figured out it was them, I was in. They had just released a Jason Bourne movie in the theaters. And I didn't want to go into the real world."

"Peter Pan syndrome?"

"Maybe."

"That was around the time that we broke up."

Max looked back at her, a flash of guilt on his face. "Renee..."

A beeping sound emanated from her computer. Renee sat up, looking at the screen. A frightened look crossed her face. "Shit."

She began typing.

"What is it?" Max asked.

She hit a series of keys and then powered down her computer. "Dammit. Shit. Shit. Shit." She punched a pillow on the couch.

"What?"

Renee looked at him. "Give me your phone."

Max narrowed his eyes. "What is wrong?"

Renee was looking around the room. "I think we should leave."

"What? Don't be silly."

"I mean it, Max. I think we should go. First give me your phone."

Max sat up straight. He handed his phone to her. "Renee, how worried should I be right now?"

Renee hooked his phone up to her computer. "I have a

program on my computer that alerts me when someone is—well, the best way to describe it is when someone is 'looking' at me. And someone was definitely checking me out. They know where I am. They know where *we* are."

"How?"

She was typing. "Shit. They accessed your phone. When we made the call, they were able to use its GPS signal somehow. Max, I'm sorry. I was careful. I don't understand how they were able to do this..."

"*Who* knows where we are?"

"I'm not sure, but I think..."

"Renee, *who*?"

"I'm assuming the people who wanted to set you up. Someone used your call to the MI-6 agent to track us down."

"How is that possible?"

"The techniques they used were very sophisticated. I'm sorry. I wasn't expecting it."

Max said, "Okay. Well, we're in the middle of nowhere. Your alert just went off, right? It would take a long time for anyone to get here—"

She was shaking her head, frowning. "No."

"What do you mean, no?"

She let out a stream of French profanity. "That was so stupid of me."

"Renee. Calm down. We've got time."

"No. *We don't.* The timestamp was for two hours ago."

"Two hours ago? That's when they first had our location?" Max looked a bit more concerned. "Maybe you're right. Maybe we should leave."

As he spoke, the power in the house went out.

* * *

The four Russians were all former Spetsnaz. Mikhail was the most senior. He wasn't in the same shape he used to be in, but he was still deadly. The others were all younger. Fit, athletic, and capable, these three had been part of the Forty-Fifth Guards Detached Spetsnaz Brigade. Air assault troops.

For the past few years, they had each been working for Morozov. He paid well and always had interesting work.

They'd gotten the call while waiting in their hotel room in Jacksonville. They had located the Fend boy. Morozov expected Fend to show up near his father. He was only an hour or so away from Jacksonville, where Mikhail's team had been waiting.

It took them ten minutes to get to Craig Airport. Morozov's pilot was already in his helicopter, rotors turning.

Once the aircraft took off, the team began putting on their night vision goggles and checking their weapons. Mikhail spoke to the pilot on his headset.

"How long?"

"About thirty-five minutes. I'll put you down on the beach. Send me a message when you are finished and I will pick you up from the same spot."

Mikhail texted Morozov's computer men on the yacht. They were the ones who'd alerted him of the opportunity.

Mikhail texted: *Kill or capture?*

The response was immediate.

Will shut off power when you arrive. Kill any personnel in the house.

* * *

The only lights that had been on were the kitchen overhead and the bathroom light in the master suite. Both lights went out simultaneously. Someone had intentionally cut the power.

Now Max had two choices: hunker down and fight, or try to make it to the vehicle and run. He didn't know where his adversary was coming from. Helicopter noise was coming from the beach. But what if some were arriving by car? What if some were circling around the property? If they were out in front of the house, they might just be waiting for him to walk outside towards his car so they could pick him off.

"How are you with firearms?"

Renee shook her head. "No. Max, I don't want—"

"Follow me." It was dark, but the light from the moon shone in through the windows.

Max took Renee into one of the bedrooms and threw the mattress up. There was a storage chamber underneath, which he opened. It held weapons and tactical gear.

"Oh my God. What, are you prepping for doomsday?"

"I like to be ready. Just in case. Quick, put these in." He took some earplugs and handed them to her.

"Why?"

"Trust me. And take this."

He handed her an MP-5.

"No. Max, I don't like guns."

"Renee, I'm sorry, but we don't have time. Take the gun. There. Now the safety's off. It's in single-shot mode. You just point and shoot. And make sure you aren't pointing it at me."

* * *

The Eurocopter hovered just above the beach, and all four

Russian mercenaries hopped off. The helicopter took back off and circled overhead.

The Russians had been told that there was likely only one target. He would be well trained. And the fact that the helicopter had just dropped them off meant that he would be expecting them. They sprinted down the beach.

"Here!" Mikhail shouted when his GPS told them that they had reached the right location. He gave a command and they fanned out into a line, about five yards between them. They scanned the backyard of the house and looked for movement in the windows.

"There," one of the Russians said. The man depressed a button attached to his AEK-919K Kashtan submachine gun, emitting a green laser that was visible to all of them through their night vision goggles. It pointed to a room on the northern side of the house.

Two of them approached the back door. Another crept around the side of the house, keeping his Saiga 12-gauge semiautomatic shotgun pointed at the window in question. Mikhail stayed back, on a mound of sand in the backyard, keeping his weapon trained on the house and searching for any sign of the man inside.

There was no movement. No flashlights. No voices. Doubt crept into Mikhail's mind. He didn't like how still it was.

* * *

Max watched the attackers approach from the living room window. He hunched over behind the couch. Renee was on the other side. There were four of them. He could see their silhouettes making their way over the small sandy mound in his backyard, their weapons trained on the house. A laser pointer shot out from one of them, pointing at Max's bedroom.

Max risked a whisper. "Can you take the one on the left?"

"I don't know, Max." Her voice was quivering.

"Relax, Renee," he whispered. "It's going to be okay. Just point and shoot—when I say three, shoot. After that, we go to my car and head for the airport. Understood? Whether we get them all or not, we'll make a run for it. Okay?"

"Understood."

"One...two...three."

He fired two three-round bursts. The rattle of the MP-5s rang out in the night air. Empty shells fell onto the hardwood floor. Bullets holes appeared in the walls. Splinters of wood and chunks of plaster flew through the dark room.

Max watched his two targets drop to the ground. Then he turned towards Renee's side. She was frozen, her finger off the trigger. Damn.

Max took aim at a section of the wall where he thought Renee's target might have been, then he fired at the remaining silhouette that had stayed back near the beach.

He saw the dark figure fall down in the sand, and more bullet holes began to appear on the eastern wall of Max's home—the attacker in the backyard was firing at them.

Max flattened himself on the floor and dragged Renee down with him.

"We need to get out of here."

"I'm sorry," she said, her voice muffled by his earplugs. In the moonlight, he could see her eyes, wide with fear and anguish. Household items exploded around them as an attacker fired into the home.

"Let's go." Max quickly looked back up and fired several more bursts from the MP-5, until his magazine was empty.

"Come on!"

He grabbed Renee's arm and they both ran out to the Toyota in the driveway. Max emptied his magazine and reloaded another. They were both treading backwards, aiming their weapons around the house in case anyone jumped out.

They got in and Max started the vehicle and slammed on the accelerator. They sped off down the road, the sound of a helicopter looming overhead.

* * *

"Who were they?" Renee asked, her voice near hysterical. She was in the passenger seat, looking behind them.

"I don't know. But I heard one of them say something in Russian."

Max turned right and floored it, speeding through the closed gate of the Jekyll Island airport.

"Who would be able to come after us this quickly?"

Max slammed the brakes and the car came to a halt. "I have some ideas. Were you able to bring your laptop?"

"Yes, I got it," Renee said, patting her messenger bag.

They both exited the vehicle and hopped the airport fence. Max looked back in the direction of his house. It was about a mile away now. He could still hear the sound of the helicopter. He couldn't be sure, but he thought it was a little louder now.

"This is our plane. Get in." Max threw the bags and weapons into the back cargo hold and then thought better of it.

"Here." He handed Renee one of the MP-5s and an extra magazine.

She took it with both hands, not asking questions.

Starting up the aircraft went quick, but taxiing seemed painfully slow. When the helicopter buzzed them for the first time, Renee let out a yelp.

This was what Max had been afraid of.

If he got airborne, there was no way a helicopter could keep up with his fixed-wing aircraft. The helicopter would max out around 150 knots. His aircraft would leave it in the dust. But that was only after he took off and climbed out. Right now, he was vulnerable.

It was dark, and they could barely make out the helicopter as it looped around and headed back in their direction. They were still on the taxiway, but there was a lot of flat pavement in front of them.

"Hold on," Max said. "I'm going to try and take off here."

"Are we on the runway yet?" Renee said, looking at him with incredulity.

"No, we're on a taxiway. But I think I can make it. If I take off now, the helicopter might get one more pass in before we take off. Then we'll lose him. If I take the time to taxi all the way down to the runway, he'll be able to keep shooting at us the whole way."

"But?"

"But we might not have enough runway to take off..."

"What did you just say?"

"Never mind. I'll tell you later."

Max pushed the throttle forward and the engine let out a fierce whine. They were both pressed back into their seats as they moved faster along the pavement.

"Here they come again."

Max could see the nose of the helicopter dipping down as it raced towards them from the left side.

He looked at his airspeed indicator. Forty knots. Fifty

knots. *Come on...* He could see little yellow bursts of gunfire coming from the helicopter's rear cabin.

A bullet burst a hole in the Plexiglas window on his left-hand side.

"What should I do?" asked Renee.

"Fire back."

Renee took a deep breath. She reached over him and aimed her MP-5 out his window, firing three shots towards the hovering helicopter. The gunfire was very close to Max's face, and he reflexively turned away. He could smell the odor of the spent rounds and felt the shells dropping on his lap.

"*Careful*," Max yelled, his ears ringing. "That's enough. Just have a seat." Perhaps Renee might be better as an observer.

Renee sat back in her seat as the helicopter sped overhead.

There. Takeoff speed.

Max pulled back on the yoke with his left hand. The airflow through the broken window was intense, but otherwise, there was no sign of damage.

They quickly gained altitude and Max turned south, along the beach. The moonlight illuminated the surf. Renee was still looking behind them. The helicopter lights grew more distant.

"Relax. They won't be able to catch us."

Renee's chest was heaving. "Where to now?"

"Key West."

13

Three Days Before the Fend 100 Flight

Special Agent Jake Flynn arrived at Jekyll Island, Georgia, the next afternoon. The local news reported it as a burglary gone wrong, thanks to the local police. The FBI had a great relationship with local law enforcement around the country.

Many local police had attended the FBI's National Academy in Quantico, Virginia. The National Academy allowed local police to improve their law enforcement standards, knowledge, and training. It also forged strong bonds between the FBI and local police for when cooperation in the field was needed.

And it was needed today.

Flynn had first seen the report of the Jekyll Island incident in a bulletin when he'd logged on to the FBI email system from his hotel in Jacksonville that morning. He hadn't thought much of it at first. Three men, dead. The location was strange, but he figured it was probably drug-related. Some meth deal gone bad.

Then his phone rang.

"Hi, I'm looking for Special Agent Jake Flynn. This is Special Agent Mike Gagliardi. I'm the SAC with ATF down in Brunswick, Georgia."

"Mike, this is Jake Flynn. What can I do for you?"

"You the one looking for this Max Fend guy?"

Flynn sat up in his chair. He wondered how the ATF knew he was looking for Max Fend. But hell, he would take all the help he could get. Any further pretense was pointless.

"Yeah. Why?"

"Well, we're working with local police on this Jekyll Island thing. Have you heard about it yet?"

"I was just reading up on it, actually. It says three dead. That right?"

"Yeah. Forensics is looking at it now, but they were 9mm rounds. They think they were all fired from MP-5s. And the dead guys at the scene were carrying Russian-made weapons. The type that Russian special forces use. We've been running their prints but haven't found anything yet. We're working with Interpol now to see what they have. Looks like a professional hit went wrong."

Flynn was intrigued. "*Really?*"

"Yeah. First time they've ever seen anything like this down around here."

"So what's it got to do with Max Fend?"

"Fend's fingerprints are all over the house. The owner is an LLC. Still tracking down someone to speak with there. Looks like it might have been some sort of safe house. If I had to guess, Max Fend was the one being attacked, and he and at least one other person killed these three guys."

Flynn looked at his watch. "Alright. Let me figure out transportation. I'll be there as soon as I can. Mike, thanks for the heads-up."

"No sweat."

Flynn checked the directions and called his office to let them know where he was headed. A few hours later, he was pulling up to the crime scene.

The Jekyll Island Police Department was more than happy to help them keep the news media and local gawkers at bay. The ATF forensics team had finished their initial evaluation by the time he got there. The Russian hit team had been using AEK-919K Kashtan submachine guns and some type of semiautomatic shotguns. Both weapons were types favored by Spetsnaz commandos and Russian mercenary groups.

"Jake, you'll want to see this."

One of the local FBI agents took him into one of the bedrooms. The mattress had been flipped up. Underneath were opened trunks. One of them was filled with cash. Stacks and stacks of twenties. Most were in US dollars, but there were tens of thousands of dollars' worth of foreign currency as well.

The other trunks were filled with equipment. Guns, mostly. And silencers, ammunition, eavesdropping equipment. Passports, IDs, night vision goggles. Knives, medical equipment, and phones.

"This guy looks like he was ready for something. Either he's dirty, or he's..."

"James Bond?" one of the men offered.

Flynn nodded. "Right. So which is it?"

He decided that he needed to pay another visit to the CIA.

* * *

"Special Agent Flynn, this is Maria Blount, the program manager for the Fend 100 aircraft."

"Yes, of course, Maria. How are you?"

"You asked me to call and update you on the upcoming test flight."

Flynn sat in his hotel room in Georgia. He was going over his notes from the crime scene on Jekyll Island. Not something she needed to hear about. He needed to switch gears.

"One moment, please. Just trying to find my notes."

Jake Flynn kept meticulous notes on his laptop. He usually brought a notepad to interviews and when investigating crime scenes. He would then transcribe it all into a Word file later. That way he could search for keywords and have a more durable record of everything he found.

"Okay. Go ahead."

"We're still on schedule for the Fend 100 flight to proceed in three days' time," Maria said. "We've gone over everything with the FAA approver who's been working with us, and they've signed off. The FAA has no safety concerns about the computer network intrusion that was detected."

Flynn didn't think the FAA was the best one to make that judgment, but he didn't say that to her. He was getting the distinct feeling that there was a lot of push from Washington for this flight to occur.

"Maria, let me ask you a question. What would happen if they were to postpone this flight?"

"Oh my. That would not be good. We've been working on this product launch for some time. Billions of dollars have gone into it. And not just our company. Many of the airlines—our potential customers—are waiting for the Fend 100 system to get approved by the government so they can start making their orders. Like we talked about when you were here, this is a major building block in the future of commercial aviation. A lot of people, and a lot of money, are depending on it."

Flynn frowned. "Okay. But you are feeling good? No safety concerns?"

"If you're asking if I feel pressure to have this flight go on as planned, yes, of course I do. But we would never approve it on our end if we thought it was unsafe."

"That's good to know."

"Will you be coming down for the big day?"

"We'll see. I kind of doubt it. But I wish you the best of luck."

"Thank you, Special Agent Flynn."

They hung up.

The gears in his head were turning.

14

They landed in Key West just after dawn. Both of them were exhausted. He kept his sunglasses and a hat on and tried to keep his face pointed away from anyone who might be watching.

The fuel truck pulled up to their plane. "You guys want fuel?"

Max had Renee do the talking. "Yes, please," she said, "fill it up."

"Okay." The man looked the plane over. "Say, it looks like you guys got a broken window. How'd that happen?"

"Bird strike," Max said.

"Must have been a big bird."

"It was."

Max walked through the FBO lobby and hailed a cab. Renee paid for the aircraft parking fees and asked to see if they had someone who might be able to fix the window while they were in Key West. More funny looks when everything was paid for in cash. But no hassle.

Renee then walked outside and got into the waiting cab.

Max stood next to her, his baseball cap pulled down low over his head.

"Where to?" the cabbie asked.

"Know anywhere we can find a rental on short notice?"

"I know a guy, sure."

The "guy" was mopping up the inside of a bar on Duval Street. It was early morning, and the only people outside were the walkers and joggers. Renee negotiated a price, and they were able to rent out a two-bedroom cottage a few blocks away from the center of town.

Max collapsed on the couch shortly after they got in the door. Renee went into one of the bedrooms and did the same. They hadn't slept all night, and the adrenaline had long since worn off. They both slept for several hours.

Max awoke in the late afternoon. He walked through the home and out onto the tiny back deck. The small area was surrounded by green tropical plants. A quaint blue swimming pool. Three wicker deck chairs.

He changed into a pair of running shorts—the most appropriate thing he could find in his bag—and walked out to the private pool area. He placed his phone on the outdoor table and slid into the cool water. He dunked himself, got out, and lay down on one of the deck chairs. He grabbed one of the colorful folded towels that had been laid out by the property manager and used it as a pillow. Max took his phone and started catching up on the day's news.

The incident in Georgia wasn't being reported accurately. The local papers were calling it a burglary. The *Atlanta Journal-Constitution* mentioned something about a possible meth gang. While the news stories didn't give him much information, the pictures did.

Special Agent Flynn, the man who had questioned him

in D.C. two days before, was photographed on the scene, wearing a navy-blue FBI raid jacket.

Renee walked out onto the pool deck. "Enjoying the vacation?"

"I hate to waste a chance to relax." He gripped her shoulder. "Are you alright? After last night, I mean?"

She stood close to him. Nodding ever so slightly, she whispered. "Yes. I think so. I've never seen or done anything like that before." He could see how upset she was.

"Like I said, you did well. Thank you. Look, if any of this gets to be too much...I'll understand if you need to stop."

Her expression changed, determination flashing in her eyes. "You need my help."

He nodded.

She sat on the chair next to him and opened up her laptop. Max watched her type for a few moments. He admired her bravery. It couldn't have been easy for her.

After some typing, Renee said, "I just started looking at the tracking data I was able to collect last night. The hackers who located us—when they did that, it allowed me to collect some of their electronic identification info. I know more about them now."

"And who are *they*?"

"I think they're connected to an outfit called Maljab Tactical."

"I know that name." He searched his memory. "How do I know that name?"

"Tell me about the Russians that ended up dead at your home in France," Renee said.

Max looked up at her. "They were part of an arms deal."

"Were they connected to the Russian mobster that got killed in Gibraltar? Sergei?"

"Sergei set up the introduction, but they weren't Russian mafia."

"How were you involved with Sergei?"

"I ran him. He was an informant and an asset. Because of his mafia affiliation, he was well plugged in."

"Did you trust him?"

"I never trust any informant as far as I can throw them. Informants get to where they are by being either too dumb or too morally corrupt to know better."

"So Sergei introduced you to the two Russian arms dealers, and then you killed them? He must have been pissed off at that," said Renee.

"He didn't give a shit. Sergei was paid off. Cash cures all kinds of heartache in that line of work."

"You paid him as a way to say sorry?"

"That's the way things are done. The Russian arms dealers I killed weren't part of his organization, so he didn't care as long as it didn't get him in any trouble. We made sure it didn't point to either of us. Officially, I was out of town."

"When did you kill those two men?"

"The incident happened about a year ago."

"And you were pulled out of France when?"

"Shortly after."

"A year ago."

"Yes."

"So that was the last time you were in touch with Sergei?"

"Yes."

"So then he gets in touch with a hacker group and what...remembers his old rich friend Max?"

"Maybe he saw an article about the Fend 100 and thought of me?"

"Okay, so let's play that out. So they come up with a plan to hack into the Fend Aerospace Company and steal all their data. They might sell it to the competition. They might hold it for ransom and have the company pay them off. That's the way those things normally work. But when you go after big fish like that, a company like Fend Aerospace...they usually can afford to bankroll their own white hat or black hat hackers. People like me. People who can track down and upend the ransomware."

Max rubbed his temples. "So what are you saying?"

"None of this makes sense yet. It doesn't make sense that Sergei would find a hacker group all by himself and come up with this plan. And it also doesn't make sense that they would frame you."

Max said, "Well, we know it isn't Sergei's family mafia business that's after me anyway. They wouldn't have killed him."

"What about the two arms dealers?"

"You think that's what this is about?" Max asked.

"The men who attacked us in Georgia and the arms dealers are both Russian, for starters."

"Yeah, but those two were low-level nothings. The people who just attacked us in Georgia were professionals, Renee."

"Tell me more about how it happened in France," she said again.

Max sat up, eyeing her. "The DIA had me facilitate a meeting between the Russian suppliers and one of our assets in northern Africa. Libya, I believe. I was essentially just a matchmaker. A middleman. I would help connect people who were looking for certain hard-to-get items with the type of people who could procure them."

"And?"

"As you're aware, the rule of law is not quite as strict in different parts of the world. So while most of the match-making I did was legit, much of it was not."

"How did you not get in trouble with French authorities?"

"The DIA took care of that. The French government knew enough not to get in my way."

"And these small-time Russian arms suppliers—these were men that the DIA instructed you to set up a deal with?"

Max nodded. "The agent was embedded with a terrorist group in Libya. He needed to prove to his group that he could get them access to arms. We were trying to help him set up that deal."

"Why didn't you go through another channel? Why use this Russian group?"

"Part of my job was to continuously make new contacts. In this case, I was trying to establish a connection with the Russian group. It was two birds with one stone. I figured they'd supply the arms, and the DIA agent in Libya would get what he needed."

"But it didn't work out that way."

"No, it didn't."

"I think I'm starting to see a connection. The hackers that found us in Georgia were part of Maljab Tactical. Maljab Tactical worked all over the Middle East, including Syria. And they specialized in cyber operations, among other things."

Max raised his head. "Very good, Renee."

"Maljab Tactical is the subsidiary of a larger Russian mercenary organization—Bear Security Group. I'm curious if those 'small-time' arms dealers you were with might have been connected to Bear Security Group as well."

"I know Bear Security Group. They're huge. They're the primary Russian mercenary group in Syria and Crimea."

"Right," said Renee.

"So what is Maljab Tactical? Remind me."

"Maljab Tactical is a small subsidiary of Bear Security Group. Do you know who they sell to?"

"Who?"

"To Muslim extremist militias. One of their biggest clients is the Islamic State. Maljab is basically a Russian-owned mercenary group that trains jihadist fighters. It's made up of mostly Uzbek fighters—along with other mercenaries from Muslim-majority Russian Caucasus republics."

"So they're Russian private security consultants who work specifically for jihadists?"

"Pretty much. There's a lot of money flowing into these groups from wealthy radicals in the Middle East. Hiring companies like Maljab Tactical is seen as a great return on investment, rather than just giving the money to the groups directly."

Max said, "Because a professional defense contractor like Maljab makes these groups much more effective."

"Exactly."

Max nodded. "Yes. Now I remember them. Maljab Tactical was in Syria and Iraq. They improved Islamic State's recruiting numbers by managing their social network outreach—they made ads similar to what you would see from a Fortune 500 company. And they improved their combat effectiveness by giving them top-notch weapons training."

Renee said, "And Maljab Tactical is part of Bear Security Group. Bear Security Group is owned by a wealthy Russian named Pavel Morozov. You said you know of him. What do you know?"

Max said, "My work over the past few years has primarily been in Europe and the Middle East. As CEO of Bear Security Group, Morozov is head of one of the largest private armies in the world, and the largest mercenary group in Russia. They do all the Russians' dirty work in places like Syria and Ukraine. I encountered Morozov only once, but it was enough. It was in Syria."

"What happened in Syria?"

"I did some work with a US military task force there. Special Forces types. Whenever we did work in Syria, we had to be careful. We didn't want to get into a shootout with the Russians who were operating there. They were well trained and well armed. And starting a gunfight with them could have led to bigger and worse fighting between Russian and US forces. Oftentimes Bear Security Group was working alongside the Russian military. We had to treat them the same."

"What were you doing there?" Renee said.

"A meeting. Making an introduction between a rebel group and an arms dealer. The US wasn't willing to *officially* sell arms to this group, but we still *wanted* them armed. My man was seen as the workaround. But this Syrian rebel group was unstable. A junior varsity team." Max sighed. "When it happened, we could see a lot of it from the windows."

"When what happened?"

Max nodded. "So one day when I was there, a few local fighters who were in this rebel group—they were nothing more than teenagers—made the mistake of going head to head with the Russians."

Renee raised an eyebrow. "I can't imagine that ended well."

"It didn't. Bear Security Group was there—embedded

with the local Russian military unit. They took turns going out with the Syrian military when they did security patrols. Morozov himself was in the country, visiting his operational commanders.

"The teenage fighters from the rebel group took one of the Syrian security patrols hostage. Only three hostages, but they were *soldiers*. Shortly after, a few more of the rebels came in to reinforce the two idiots who started it all. I don't think they really wanted to be there, but it was too late at that point. Two of the hostages were Syrian Army. But *one* of the hostages was one of the Russian mercenaries. *Big mistake*."

"What did the Russians do?"

"Morozov moved dozens of his men into the area, clearing out all the civilians for blocks around. The Syrian Army showed up and tried to take control, but Morozov told them to piss off. He didn't want anyone to see or interfere with what he was about to do."

"Even the Syrian Army?"

Max took a sip of his water. "Even them. When the rebels saw they were surrounded by well-armed men, they sent out a list of demands. They thought they could negotiate. I don't think they thought they would be dealing with the Russians. They expected Syrian Army or government representatives to come."

"So what happened?"

"Morozov had his men sweep the local area. He got the names of the rebels—the men who'd taken the hostages. Then he had his men find their *families*."

Renee shook her head.

"Morozov instructed his men to begin cutting off limbs of family members and sending them inside to the Syrians."

Renee gasped and placed her hand over her mouth.

"The Syrian rebels started *pleading* to negotiate. Never a good sign. They sent one of the hostages out for nothing in return, hoping it would be a sign of good faith. They told the Russians they would lay down their weapons and release everyone else. They were begging the Russians to let them surrender."

"What did Morozov do?"

"He accepted. Then he waited until they came outside and laid down their arms. I remember seeing the Syrian rebels standing there, unarmed and dumbfounded. Waiting. Morozov stood twenty feet away, flanked by his commandos. Then he walked up to the group of *hostages*—the two Syrians and the one Russian—and executed them. The Syrian rebels just stared at him in disbelief. Morozov shot the *hostages. Including his own man.*"

"What? *Why?*"

"He said it was a message to anyone else who worked for him, never to put themselves in that position of weakness. He then killed all but one remaining family member of each of the Syrian rebels. The rebels were forced to watch. When Morozov was finished, he let the rebels leave, unharmed. He told them that if they ever did anything like this again, he would finish the job and kill the remaining relative. I heard from someone else once that leaving a single family member alive was a sort of calling card. He believed it was the great deterrent. Anyone thinking of seeking revenge on him would just have to look at their one living family member, and they would stand down."

"He is...*evil.*"

"Yes, Renee. He is."

* * *

Max got up and sat at the edge of the pool, dipping his feet in. "Okay. Thinking out loud here. Walk me through this. So far, you've linked the cyber group that located us in Georgia to Maljab Tactical."

"I believe so, yes."

"And Maljab Tactical is a subdivision of Bear Security Group."

"Right."

"Bear Security Group is the big one. Pavel Morozov's outfit. The largest Russian mercenary organization, filled with Russian ex-military special forces types."

"That's correct."

"And we just got attacked by guys who fit that description. Russian ex-military."

"Yes."

"And you think these people are related to that small-time outfit that tried to kill me in France? The two men."

"All I have to go on is that they're Russian, they're dirty, and they tried to kill you—but I'm picking up a definite theme here. Are you?"

"Bear with me," Max said. "Sometimes I need to be hit on the head by a hammer to see it. This is all helpful, Renee, but it doesn't answer a key question—*why*?"

"Why are there Russians trying to kill you, or why did they try to set you up for sabotaging your father's company?" Renee asked. "Because assuming that we are talking about the same entity, they seem to have changed strategies. They don't seem to want you alive anymore."

"I guess I need both questions answered, really."

"Let's start with you telling me why two Russian men tried to kill you in France."

Max looked up, remembering. "There were a group of people over that night. Lots of booze. Several dozen of my clients. The Russians were invited. It was my second meeting with them, and I wasn't sure what to expect. And... well, let's just say we had a disagreement about how to treat a lady."

"What do you mean?" Renee said.

"There was a young French woman there at my place that night. Early twenties. Blond hair. Beautiful figure."

Renee raised an eyebrow. "Was that description necessary?"

"What? She *was* beautiful. Great birthing hips. You know how I love those. There's nothing wrong with me pointing that out."

"I see your sense of humor still has poor timing."

"Don't ruin the story, Renee. Anyway, the two Russians were there and the girl brought a few friends. But the Russians were just getting way too drunk and obnoxious. Major buzzkill. So the girl's friends decided to leave. She stayed because she was interested in me, I believe."

"Of course."

"What? I can't help it. My good looks are both a gift and a curse."

"Please just continue."

"So I was hoping to get what I needed from the Russians and send them on their way. I went into another room to make a phone call—working on another deal. The girl was pretty drunk. She was alone with the Russians only for a moment. They were trying to get her into one of the bedrooms. She said no. I heard the commotion and got off my call. I told them to leave. They didn't. One of them grabbed the girl and started dragging her into the bedroom screaming, and the other Russian just stood there smiling, typing on his phone."

"Typing on his phone?"

"Yes. In the after-action report, the DIA showed me an intercept from their phone records. The guy had sent a message to someone. We never found out who, but I assume it was his boss."

"What did it say?"

"It said something about me being an American agent."

"And then you killed them?" Renee said.

"Well, I tried to work it out peacefully, but they left me no choice."

"And so that's how your cover was blown? You stood up to them when they attacked the French girl? And from that, they knew you were an agent?"

"It seemed like they were testing me. I think they wanted to see what kind of things I would let slide. Hell of a litmus test."

Renee shook her head. "You think Morozov sent those two?"

"Why? That was a year ago. Why send them to blow my cover back then, and then kill Sergei only a few weeks ago?"

"I'm not sure. There's still something missing here."

Max stood. "Well, you keep digging. That's what I'm paying you for. In the meantime, I've got a hot date with an MI-6 agent. Maybe she'll be able to help."

* * *

Max threw on a navy-blue polo shirt and khaki shorts and began walking down Duval Street. He stayed on the side streets mostly, trying to keep as low a profile as possible.

The sun was low in the sky, and the Key West shops were lit up with bright lights. The surface of the road was wet from a recent rain. Lush green trees overhung many of the stores and restaurants. Happy tourists, many of them liquored up from their rum-based drinks, walked along the street. Live music blared out of many of the bars.

Max walked down the full length of Duval Street and finally arrived at a waterfront bar and restaurant with outdoor seating. Orange barstools. A mix of patrons wearing bathing suits and floral shirts. Street entertainers in the courtyard, one playing guitar quite well. Two others walked along on stilts, juggling. Max found himself thinking this would be a fun place to retire to.

He sat down at a table in the corner, out of view of most people. He had a few minutes to kill before the meeting time.

"What'll you have?"

Max looked up to see a skinny waitress holding a pen and paper.

"Hmm." He searched the table for a drink menu. "To be honest, I haven't had a chance to look at—"

"He'll have a mojito. So will I."

A tanned woman stood over him. She wore Ray-Ban sunglasses and a tube top covered with tropical flowers.

"I guess I will," Max told the waitress, who went off to fetch their drinks. He stuck out his hand. "My name's Max."

She shook his hand. "Don't be silly, dear. We know each other." Wide smile as she leaned in and kissed him on the cheek.

She sat down, crossing her legs. Max noticed that her tight black skirt revealed quite a lot of skin. He decided he didn't mind that one bit.

"Of course we do. Remind me of your name?"

"Charlotte Capri." She had an accent. British, he thought. So far so good.

"It's a pleasure to see you again, Miss Capri."

She didn't reply. Just kept giving him that bright smile.

He disliked not being able to see her eyes behind the sunglasses. Max found her rather striking. Full lips. Smooth and tanned skin.

The drinks came quick. Tall glasses. Crushed ice and mint. Limes, rum and sugar. Hard to beat. Max took a sip and found it deliciously refreshing.

Max held up his glass and toasted with his guest. "So I take it I don't need to meet you at our location anymore? Where was it again?" He wanted to hear her say it.

She said, "The southernmost point? No. This will be fine."

"So what can I do for you?"

"Actually, I think it is I who might be able to do something for you."

"And what might that be?"

She leaned forward in her seat, pulling down the sunglasses, and Max saw that her eyes were not playful and flirtatious the way her voice sounded.

She leaned in and whispered in his ear. "I know about the cyber intrusion on your father's company—the one that the FBI has been investigating. Someone hacked into the Fend 100 program. *And they're going to do it again.*"

Max put his drink down.

"What do you mean, they're going to do it again?"

"We need to go somewhere more private. Somewhere we can talk. We're too out in the open here."

Max fought the urge to look around. Tourists were everywhere, enjoying the ocean view. The pink-and-orange sky—the perfect sunset of Key West—mesmerized most of the crowd.

"Alright. Let's go." Max stood, took another sip of his mojito and then signaled the waitress to come get the check.

She took his hand. "Come on, follow me."

They walked through the crowded street and then stepped into a dive bar. A man onstage wearing a cowboy hat played guitar and sang into a silver microphone. The woman kept gripping Max's hand as they weaved through the throngs of dancers.

They stopped in the corner of the bar. It was so loud he could barely hear her. But she pressed in close to him, speaking into his ear. "We'll just stay here and pretend we're dancing. The noise will make it impossible for any listening devices to work. I can't be completely sure that one of us wasn't followed. So we need to take precautions."

The crowd around them screamed as the guitar player switched to his next 1980s rock ballad.

Charlotte Capri swayed to the music, playing the part. "I know who you are, Max Fend," she said. "And I know who you've worked for in the past." She brought her head back a bit, locking eyes with him.

"Alright," he said. "So who are you really? And how do you know about the cyberattack on my father's company?"

"You can call me Charlotte, just like I told you. I suspect you already know who I work for." She gazed into his eyes.

"For queen and country?"

"Indeed."

"They have me working for a Russian businessman right now. His name is Pavel Morozov. Have you heard of him?"

"I have. So what are you doing for Morozov? What's your cover?"

"I'm an executive assistant." She smiled.

"Like a secretary?"

"Sort of, yes. He's on a working vacation. Morozov sent his yacht so he could stay on board while he was here. He's going to do a month-long tour of Florida and the Caribbean, meeting with investors and business partners along the way. I'm helping to manage things for him."

"What does he have to do with my father's company?"

"A few months ago, a member of the Russian mafia named Sergei began fishing for a buyer. He was selling access to Fend Aerospace's corporate data center. Word on the street is that you knew Sergei."

"We were professional acquaintances."

"Morozov got word of this plan. But he knew that Sergei had worked with the Americans before, and he didn't trust him as a partner."

"Morozov was right. Sergei would have sold him out if it suited him. So Morozov stole Sergei's idea?"

"More or less. Morozov went and commissioned his own hackers. Their objective was to steal the most valuable technology your father's company owns—the artificial intelligence software for the Fend 100 aircraft."

"I'm told that they failed."

"That's right. They were able to steal some of the aircraft blueprints but couldn't get into the hardened servers located in the Fend 100 control center—the ones that housed the AI program."

"You said that they were going to try again. What's changed? Why would it work the second time around?"

She looked worried. "There's a vulnerability window. When the Fend 100 is flying, it uses an encrypted datalink that sends information back and forth between it and the Fend 100 control center. This sort of opens up the firewalls for the Fend 100. We think that the first cyberattack planted a virus that will allow Morozov's hackers to take advantage of this vulnerability window."

"How?"

"I don't know. We're still trying to find out. But the point is that there will likely be another attempt to steal the Fend 100 AI data—during the big demonstration flight they're having in a few days."

"Why is MI-6 so interested in this?"

She shrugged. "Morozov is wrapped up in a lot of bad things. This is just one of them. It's possible that he intends to do the same thing as Sergei—sell the information or hold it for ransom. That's standard operating procedure for these cybercriminals. But there is a darker scenario—there are many people who are very concerned about what one would be able to do with the technology."

"What does that mean? What could he use it for?"

"Your father's company has big defense contracts for drones. The AI software he's developed doesn't just have commercial implications. Imagine how AI learning machines could improve the effectiveness of combat drones. The AI software could turn them into a robot air force, thinking and learning on their own—dominating the battlespace."

Now Max understood why someone like Morozov might be interested. His expertise in the defense sector, and his connections at the highest levels of the Russian government, would make this a valuable steal.

"You said Morozov was going to hack into my father's plane again. When?"

"In a few days. Fend Aerospace has their final approval test flight with the FAA. It will have people on board this time. Mostly reporters and company executives. The FAA has already declared it safe. Now they want to observe it with passengers aboard. We think he'll try to hack into the network during that flight—during the vulnerability window."

"None of this explains why I was set up. What's all this got to do with me?"

"We think Morozov knows about your background in Europe—you had a lot of connections there to unsavory characters. And he needs someone to divert the FBI's attention—an inside man at Fend Aerospace. If they're off worrying about you, then that's taking eyeballs away from him."

Max had an idea about that. Renee's theory was holding water. "So he just wants to hang this on me because he thinks I make a good scapegoat? That still doesn't explain it."

"There is one more thing. I'm not a hundred percent sure, but I think that Pavel Morozov really does have someone working on the inside at Fend Aerospace."

Max couldn't stop his jaw from momentarily dropping. "Who?"

"I don't know."

"What do you know? Why would you say that?"

"That's what MI-6 thinks. The cyber experts there think it seems logical. They think that someone with inside knowledge and access to the Fend Aerospace network would be needed to pull it all off. That's how they were able to frame you. And that's how they know so much about the Fend network."

"Has Morozov or his team mentioned anything about someone on the inside of Fend Aerospace?"

She shook her head. "No. It's an MI-6 theory that they want me to look into. Morozov runs a very tight unit. They're some of the best-trained operatives in the world. Many of them are former FSB. His security team is all former Spetsnaz."

"I met some of them recently," Max said. "Nice guys."

She swayed to the music like she was just a regular tourist, here to dance. "That was quite an escape," she whispered into his ear. "He was very upset about that." A smile. She really was attractive.

Max could feel her body pressing up against him. He smelled her perfume, too. It smelled good.

"So one minute he's trying to set me up to take the fall for my father's company sabotage. Then he's trying to kill me. Why? Why not just kill me in the first place?"

"We think that at first, he needed you to take the fall. But now that the FBI has taken the bait, he doesn't need you alive anymore."

"Isn't he worried about this all leading back to him?"

"It won't." She seemed very sure of herself.

Max thought about telling her that Renee had already traced it back to one of his subsidiaries, but he didn't want to give her more information than he needed to. Not yet.

"In a few days, he'll be taking his yacht to Jacksonville," Charlotte said.

"Jacksonville? Where Fend Aerospace headquarters is located?"

"Yes."

"Why in God's name would he do that?"

"I think he wants to be there when it happens."

Max shook his head. "I need to warn my father. He needs to cancel the Fend 100 flight."

"Absolutely not."

"What? Why?"

"We went out on a limb and freed you, Max. We gave you a second chance for a reason. We have a plan. Now hear me out."

He folded his arms. "What do you want me to do?"

"They've planted a computer virus in the Fend network.

One that will allow them to steal the Fend 100's AI data during the flight next week. But you can stop it, Max."

"How?"

"MI-6 is working on a fix. It would be another software program—one that would serve as a sort of antidote to the virus they put in there. This would make sure that they couldn't hack into the aircraft."

"So why do you need me?" Max said. "Why not just contact the CIA?"

"We've tried working with the CIA on this, but they aren't seeing things our way. They preferred to wait. We wanted to move. They weren't sure what to do about you. We decided that the best option was to break you out of custody in D.C. and get you to help us out."

"Why?"

"You hold your father's confidence, Max. He'll listen to you. You can't let him cancel the flight—this cyber antidote is the best way."

"What will it do?"

"It will allow British intelligence—and the US, when they get on board—to turn the tables on Morozov's hackers. It will make sure that they can't steal the AI data. And it will give us the incriminating evidence we need to bag Morozov."

Max was taken aback. Was she saying that the CIA and MI-6 wanted to let Morozov conduct another cyberattack on his father's company?

"Who are you working with at the CIA?"

"Caleb Wilkes."

"Wilkes?" Max knew the name. Not well, but well enough. Wilkes was CIA counterintelligence. He was a very shadowy figure—even for Langley.

"He's the one who's going after Morozov," Charlotte said.

"He intends to take him down or turn him. He's fishing. And trying to let out enough reel that Morozov doesn't break the hook."

"Is Wilkes on board with this plan?"

"We're working on it."

"What's the problem?"

"I don't know why Wilkes doesn't see it our way. So far we haven't been able to convince him to take an alternate path. But now we have you involved. I'll give you a thumb drive with the cyber antidote to plug into the Fend 100 control center. Can you do that?"

Max thought about it. "Yes. I think so. Do you have the thumb drive now?"

"I won't be able to give it to you until the night before. They're still working on the software program. You'll have to meet me in Jacksonville."

"Okay."

"I need to go."

"How will I hear from you?"

She reached up and gripped the back of his neck, leaning in like she was going to kiss him on the cheek. Her lips hovered over his ear. "The night before the test flight— I'll call you and tell you where to meet me. Give me your number."

She held out her phone and he typed a number in.

She looked into his eyes. "It will be alright, Max." Then she softly kissed him on the cheek, turned, and disappeared into the crowd.

* * *

Pavel Morozov watched the speedboat approach from the

second deck of his yacht, which was anchored several miles north of Key West.

His security man looked at Pavel, and then at the girl. Pavel gripped her ponytail with his strong right hand, pulling back so that her head was arched over the rail of the vessel. The drop was a good forty feet to the warm water below.

The girl had been pretty, before his knuckles and ring had gone to work on her face. Her eye was swollen. Blood dripped down from her nose and lip.

The security man nodded toward her. "Would you like me to finish her?"

Pavel shook his head slowly. "No. Please just send up our new arrival."

The woman who had just arrived on the speedboat came up a minute later. Pavel looked her up and down. "Ah, hello, Miss Capri."

Charlotte regarded him, her eyes glancing at the scared and bloodied woman that Morozov was holding by the ponytail.

"Good evening, Mr. Morozov."

"Did you have a good time tonight?"

"I did."

Pavel looked back at the girl by his side. The position of her body looked painful, but she didn't cry. She didn't beg. Her eyes were afraid, but her voice was silent.

Morozov stared at her. "I intend to drop you into the sea. But before I do that, is there anything else you care to tell us? If it is helpful to me, perhaps I will change my mind about your fate."

Still the woman didn't say a word. She just sniffled quietly.

With his left hand, Morozov removed a small black

object from his pocket. He kept holding the girl back with his right hand. With his teeth, he carefully pulled open the folding blade of the knife.

The girl he was holding began struggling to free herself from his grasp, her eyes widening at the sight of the blade.

"Do you want to do it?" Pavel asked Charlotte.

She let out a sound of disgust and walked away.

Morozov smiled. He turned back to the girl and shoved the knife into her back several times, careful that he punctured her lungs. He then flipped her over the rail and off the yacht. Her legs had been tied together, with weights attached to them. That would send her down to the bottom.

Her body made a big splash, but it was dark. Morozov couldn't see her after she sank below the surface. But he felt good, wiping his bloody hands on a towel. It was always satisfying to remove a bad employee from his organization.

15

When Max returned to the cottage, Renee was still out back, sitting by the pool, her computer in her lap. She looked relieved when she saw it was him.

"Worried?" Max said.

"A little."

"Good. That's healthy. You were right about Bear Security Group. Pavel Morozov is involved." Max filled Renee in on who he'd met and what he had learned.

"Do you trust this woman? The MI-6 agent?"

"They freed me from the clutches of the FBI."

"You don't think a good lawyer could have done that?"

"Depends what the FBI has on me."

"But you're innocent."

Max waved off the comment. "If what Charlotte said is right, the CIA is intentionally allowing Morozov's cronies to hack into my father's network. Someone in our government has an agenda."

Renee looked up from her computer. "Do you believe that?"

"I don't know. It sounds reckless. There must be another side to the story."

"I wonder if there's a way we could find out who at Fend Aerospace might be working for Morozov."

Max looked up. "That would be a big help. Do you think you could do that?"

Renee was looking at her computer again. She whistled.

"What is it?"

"I'm taking another look at Morozov's boat. It's really something." She turned the computer so he could see.

"That's Morozov's?"

It wasn't a normal yacht. The ship was a massive gray vessel that looked like a futuristic version of a sailboat. Giant metal masts rose up two hundred feet above the deck. Narrow tinted portholes lined the sleek hull. There was a helipad. Multiple spots for small motorboats to pull up. Wooden sundecks. Indoor and outdoor pools.

"It's incredible."

"It says here that it's one of the most expensive ever built."

"How much?"

"Nearly half a billion dollars."

Max looked up at the sky. "Hmm. I'll think about it."

"About what?"

"Getting one. I'm sure that would help with my playboy reputation."

"Right," Renee said. "It arrived in Key West just two days ago." She looked up. "So they were here at the same time that hackers from this region located us in Georgia."

"You think that they did it from the yacht?"

"I don't know. This yachting website says Morozov is taking it around the Caribbean and Florida for the next month."

"Why?"

Renee typed some more. "Because when you're rich," she said, "you can do whatever the hell you want. You know that." She smiled at him.

"Easy, now."

"It appears as though he's throwing a party on the yacht tomorrow night."

"Oh, really?" Max was interested. "I wonder why I wasn't invited."

"A lot of big investors are showing up. You know, Max, if I can access the computer network on that yacht, that might be an opportunity to—"

"No," Max interrupted, a stern look on his face. "That would be a terrible idea."

"You wouldn't have to go, of course. They would recognize you. But they don't know me."

"That's an even worse idea."

Renee looked hurt. "I may not be an expert at fieldwork like you, but I was a trained member of the CSE."

"What did they train you in, how to avoid paper cuts before you sat down in front of your computer terminal?"

She frowned. "We didn't use paper. Security protocol."

"Renee, dear, now I haven't been to a good yacht party for the ungodly rich in months—and that is a long time for me—but if I walk onto that yacht, I would get shot in about ten seconds. And you..."

She crossed her arms.

"Renee, the truth is, I feel guilty for dragging you into this in the first place. You could have been killed in Georgia. I won't place you in harm's way like that again."

She saw the look on his face and knew she wasn't going to convince him right now. "Well, I'd at least like to get a better look at this thing. Maybe we can just go check out the yacht from a distance?"

"That's a more reasonable idea." Max took off his sandals and placed his bare feet in the cool pool water. "You know, Renee, I think it's time I treated you to a nice trip on the water."

* * *

Two Days Before the Fend 100 Flight

Max and Renee snapped the buckles of their life vests. The sound of seagulls overhead mixed with the clangs of the sailboats floating in their slips. Deep-sea fishing boats motoring out into the Caribbean. The smell of salt in the air. Max loved the sea.

"You guys want to rent one or two?" said the freckle-faced kid working the counter of the Jet Ski rental shop.

"One should be fine," Max said.

Renee said, "Two."

The kid looked back and forth between them.

Renee whispered, "I'm not going to be one of your pretty girls, hugging you and hanging on."

"Don't say that. You look great in your bikini."

She frowned.

Max turned to the boy behind the counter. "Two Jet Skis will be fine, my friend."

A few minutes later, they were headed out of the small harbor, their engines barely above idle. Renee was the first to pass the buoy, which signaled the end of the no-wake zone. She immediately gunned the throttle, and a spray of white seawater shot up from behind her. She looked back at

Max, smiling as she left him behind. A second later, he accelerated and felt his body sliding back as he neared fifty miles per hour.

The wind and seas were calm. Uninhibited by a rough ocean, the Jet Skis skimmed above the water at a very high speed. Riding them was pure fun.

Max reminded himself to do this again soon. They zoomed in between Sunset Key and Wisteria Island, turning right, towards Fleming Key. From there, they headed towards a group of tiny islands about two miles to the north, a large sandbar interwoven between them.

They arrived at Cayo Agua. The small island was barely more than a few hundred yards around, carved apart by multiple turquoise seawater streams. Both Renee and Max slowed their Jet Skis and headed into one of the inlets. The water below was crystal clear, and Max saw flashes of color darting underneath him. Tropical fish, not used to being disturbed here. As they slowly motored along the stream, they were surrounded closely on either side by tropical plants and trees. Banana trees. Mahogany trees. Coconut palms. A scattering of bright pink orchids. It was at once quiet and beautiful.

Renee turned her Jet Ski towards a sandy bank. About fifty feet further ahead, the stream opened back up into the ocean on the other side of the island. They didn't want to come out that far.

Max and Renee pushed their Jet Skis up onto the bank, beaching them. They removed their vests, hanging them on the handlebars, and waded the rest of the way through the stream, soft sand under their feet.

Max couldn't help but noticing that he was right about Renee in her bikini. She kept in good shape, and the years had been kind.

"There it is," Renee said.

She had lowered herself into the deep middle section of the stream and peeked out around the corner where it emptied into the ocean. About half a mile to the north, just past the sandbar, Max could see Pavel Morozov's yacht.

"Wow. That is an incredible piece of work."

He took the pair of waterproof binoculars from around his neck and scanned the vessel. It was even more impressive in person. Sleek and aerodynamic, it looked more like a modern warship than a private yacht—although the three tall metallic masts made it more like a work of art than a warship.

On the upper aft deck, he could see private security. Big, thick men wearing black vests over white tee shirts. Each wore wraparound sunglasses. Each looked to have a holstered weapon at his waist. Max counted five of them that he could see. Probably three less than there were a few days ago.

On the two decks below that, there were sets of scantily clad women. Some were rubbing oil on each other's backs, bathing in the sun. Others carried tall glasses of champagne. And there in the middle of it all was the man of the hour.

Pavel Morozov.

He was speaking with someone. A woman. Her back was to Max. She wore a long, flowing skirt and a bathing suit top. Max wished he had a long-range microphone, because he knew who it was.

"That's her," Max said.

"Who? The MI-6 agent?"

"Yes. Wish we knew what they were discussing. Hmm."

"What is it?"

"I see something that wasn't in the picture of the yacht,"

Max said. "There are antennae on the fore and aft of the ship. They look like big orbs. Do you see them?"

"Yes, I think so."

"Those look very similar to the datalink antennae on a Navy warship."

"How do you know that?"

"DIA, remember?"

"So why is that significant? The antennae."

"Because Charlotte told me that the Fend 100 was vulnerable through its encrypted datalink. I wonder if those antennae are how they'll hack in to the Fend network this time."

"But it's encrypted. They'd need some type of passcode to get in."

"If Morozov has someone working for Fend Aerospace, they could help them with that."

"If we could get aboard that boat, I might be able to answer some of these questions, Max."

"Renee. No. You see the security guards. They missed us in Georgia. It would be stupid to hand ourselves over to them now."

"But they're throwing a party tonight."

"So?"

"So it'll be somewhat public, right?"

"No. A private party. The *opposite* of public."

"You know what I mean. What if I placed myself on the guest list and snuck on? I would only need a half hour. I could go as a maid."

Max shook his head. "This isn't the movies, Renee. Don't put yourself in a position of weakness. If they get their hands on you—"

"I can handle it, Max."

"I saw you *handle* it in Georgia."

She reddened. "I said I was sorry about that."

Max sighed. "I didn't mean that the way it sounded. It's just that I don't want to risk *you*."

"Max, if I can gain access to the computer network on that boat—"

"I said no. It's not worth it. We'll leave tomorrow and fly to Jacksonville. Then I'll get in touch with my father and use Charlotte's thumb drive to disarm Morozov's virus."

Renee scrunched her lips together. She didn't like it.

"Come on. Let's go back to the Jet Skis and head back. I'll give you cash and let you go shopping. Girls like shopping, right? We need food and clothes. I'll give you a grocery list and then I'll cook you up the most delicious French cuisine you've ever had."

"I'm not sure whether to respond to the good or the bad part of that."

"Always look on the bright side of things, Renee."

She rolled her eyes.

* * *

Pavel Morozov had two qualities that had helped him to attain his level of wealth: cunning and ruthlessness. These qualities had served him well prior to the fall of the Berlin Wall. His rise through the ranks of the KGB had been swift. But one could only go so far in the Soviet Union. The idiocy of the Communist bureaucracy meant that natural talent had its limits. Politics and ideology always got in the way.

But not anymore. The fall of the USSR had been a godsend to men like him. Men who didn't have any scruples about getting their hands dirty. Men who projected strength. Once the politicians were no longer in charge, there was a huge power vacuum. Former KGB members were only too happy to fill the void.

Pavel found that he was quite a talented businessman. There were so many similarities to his work in the KGB. You always had to be one step ahead of the competition. Deception and innovation ruled the day. To Pavel, business was just a new way of playing the same old game.

After the collapse of the USSR, the Red Army had an enormous inventory of weaponry, and very little need for it. The Cold War was over. Where there was confusion, there was great opportunity, Pavel knew.

The first time he walked into a former Soviet weapons cache and demanded to see the commanding officer, he expected to get pushback. But Pavel was surprised to find out that the same methods of influence and persuasion he had used in the KGB worked just as effectively in his new field.

Arms dealer. The bottom rung of the long ladder he would climb.

There were national armies around the world that would pay top dollar for Russia's unused weapons. The Russian military men who oversaw the weapons didn't care where they went. Those men just didn't want to get in trouble. Don't rock the boat. That way of thinking had served them well in the Soviet era. But in the post-Soviet world, there were so many possibilities. The Russian military men were happy to accept cash and black market items in exchange for misplacing crates of weapons.

The first man to question Morozov got shot on the spot. The second man suddenly had no questions.

The money started rolling in after that. Pavel Morozov sold Russian weapons to whoever wanted them, all around the world. If you were looking for an AK-47, go somewhere else. But if you were looking for ten thousand of them—Pavel was your man. Need a tank? How about twenty? The first pallet of shells would be free.

But others were in on the game as well. The mid-90s—that was when the Russian and Ukrainian mob had gotten their legs under them. They were also staffed with former KGB, GRU, and Red Army veterans. The imbalance of supply and demand quickly sorted itself out. Competition got stiff.

Pavel Morozov had made his first pile of cash. It was time for him to think bigger. He began investing. Putting money into companies and nation-states that couldn't get loans from anywhere else. Iran. Iraq. North Korea. African militias. Some of his best customers.

As oil money pumped up Russia's economy, it breathed life back into the sleepy bear. Russian leadership wanted to flex its military muscle once again. But some of the objectives would be seen as questionable on the world stage.

Morozov saw an opportunity.

Why arm militaries around the world when you could get paid more by fighting their battles? The Russian soldier was still one of the best in the world. So he founded Bear Security Group. Soon, ex-Spetsnaz commandos were training troops and even doing some fighting in hot spots around the world. Places no one else wanted to go. Places others couldn't go, because the political will wasn't there. When Russia wanted to invade Crimea, they first sent in teams from Bear Security Group. When Russia wanted to help anti-American forces in Syria, Morozov's mercenaries were flown in.

Eventually, Pavel's men would fight right alongside Russian special forces soldiers. It often became hard to distinguish between them. Such was the beauty of the private sector. For the right price, one could get the best quality.

Morozov didn't stop with creating a private military. Anyone could do that, although surely not as well as he. But what very few other firms could do to his level was espionage. A private security contractor was nothing without a good intelligence network.

Private spies. Perhaps his greatest idea.

Morozov supplied critical intelligence field agents and information to the highest bidder, around the world. Often times he had opposing national intelligence organizations bidding against each other to gain access to his information. They *had* to, lest it fall into their competitor's hands. Even the CIA had paid to access some of his dossiers. Although they would never admit to it in a million years.

Now, having conquered the world one bullet at a time, Pavel Morozov sat on his yacht, basking in the glorious sunlight off the coast of a nation that had once considered him an enemy. He was too rich and powerful for that now. As long as he kept himself separated enough from the many private wars his companies fought, he was untouchable. Besides, as a master spy, he knew how to keep clean.

Life was good. Especially when it gave him gifts. Like it had last year, when his men had stumbled onto Max Fend in the South of France.

"Mr. Morozov, we will be lifting anchor and heading back into Key West."

He looked up at Charlotte. "Very well. Thank you, dear."

"Is there anything else I can get you?"

"You still haven't told me about last night. You went out into town—how did it go?"

"It was fine," Charlotte said.

"Any details you need to tell me about?"

"No."

Pavel looked at the topless girls next to him. Oiling each other up so they would tan better. Drunk off expensive champagne.

One of them said, "Mr. Morozov, what happened to that other girl who was always with you? The blonde?"

"Her? I think she went for a swim." He laughed to himself.

They looked at each other and didn't ask any more questions.

He turned back to Charlotte and quietly asked, "Are we all set for next week?"

"We're all set to head up the Florida coast tomorrow morning, sir. We'll be in St. Augustine by Wednesday, just as you requested."

He nodded. "Good."

"Anything else?"

He shook his head and waved her away. She left without saying another word. He looked at one of the girls next to him and snapped his fingers. "Hey. Go get me a champagne. Make sure it is cold."

The girl hurried off, not wanting to take a swim.

* * *

Jake Flynn knew that his investigation was high-priority now. The FBI had sent one of their Gulfstreams down to Brunswick to get him. That was a first. He'd briefed the director and deputy director via conference call on the way back up to D.C. While the Bureau leadership was interested, Flynn still got the impression that there was more to Max Fend than they were letting on.

He had just been dropped off at his car in the Reagan International Airport parking lot when his phone rang.

"Special Agent Flynn."

"Jake, it's Steve Brava. Can you meet for coffee again today?"

"Definitely. Same place?"

"Yeah. Seven p.m. work?"

"See you there, thanks."

Flynn drove his G-car with the blue light on the dash. The light wasn't flashing, but most people driving in the left lane of the highway got out of the way once they saw it. They figured him for an undercover cop. The worst was when people didn't get out of the way. They just slowed down to the speed limit, while everyone else zoomed by. But he didn't get any of those on this trip, thank God.

He arrived at the coffee shop in Springfield a few minutes before seven and ordered a cup of decaf. Damn caffeine would keep him up all night if he had one now. He sighed, realizing he would probably be up all night anyway, working on the Fend case.

After the killings on Jekyll Island, the FBI had thrown a lot more agents his way. But he still hadn't turned up many new leads. The CIA was "helping them out" now that they thought the Russians might be involved.

That was a joke.

The CIA expected to get all the information that Flynn's investigation turned up, but offered little in return. It was just more of the same bullshit that he had dealt with when he had driven out to the Farm.

Steve walked in a few minutes late, apologizing. "Traffic was a mess on 66."

"No sweat, man, have a seat. You want anything?"

"Nah. Thanks, though. I can only stay for a moment."

They sat in the far corner of the coffee shop. It was dark and there were no customers at the adjacent tables.

Flynn said, "What have you got?"

Steve had that same concerned look on his face. Disclaimer time, Flynn figured. Steve said, "Now let me just reiterate how much trouble I could get in if they found out I was sharing this. I'm doing this as a personal favor. Capiche?"

"Of course. I swear to God, Steve. This stays between us. I just need a little help on this. You heard about Jekyll Island, right?"

He nodded. "Yeah."

"Well, the CIA's involved now. And they're still stonewalling me."

"Who from the CIA? Is it that guy Wilkes you talked to?"

"No. Someone else. Why?"

"I got more on Max Fend," Steve said. "I told you the classification level on his personnel file was unusually high. Codeword level. But his personnel file was flagged in a particular way."

"Yeah, you said that."

"I asked my friend at DNI what it meant when a personnel file is flagged like that. He knows about these sorts of things. My friend told me it was something he's only seen a few times."

"When?"

"Once was for a guy who was a member of the Army's Delta Force, and then went into some even more spooky black ops unit. Some task force they use to track down terrorist leaders."

"And the other time?"

"The other time he saw that classification level on a personnel file was for an active CIA field agent. But not just any agent. A very high-profile agent. Someone a lot of people know."

"I don't understand."

Steve looked around the coffee shop. "Okay. We never had this conversation."

"I get it. What do you have?"

"There is a certain *subset* of NOC agents."

"NOC—you mean nonofficial cover."

"Yes. But not just any NOCs. Sometimes...well, this is going to sound silly. But—celebrities or famous businessmen get recruited by the CIA. They get special access and trust that would be very useful to the US intelligence services."

"You're kidding."

"No. I'm serious."

"So what are you saying, the CIA has Oprah working for them?"

"I doubt it. But, yes, that's what I'm saying, essentially."

"Come on. Give me a break."

"Jake, there are plenty of famous celebrity spies in history. Julia Child, Frank Sinatra, Cary Grant..."

"Those people are all dead," Flynn said. "It was a different time back then. Hollywood was more patriotic then."

Steve sighed. "Ever hear the expression that there are no new ideas? Well—supposedly the CIA is still using high-profile public figures as spies."

"Come on."

"Don't believe me? Well, maybe *this* will interest you. My friend gave me one name—the CIA guy in charge of the current program. Do you know what name he gave me?"

"Who?" Flynn asked, and then he answered for himself. "Wilkes?"

Steve nodded.

"That lying bastard."

"You asked me to help you. I'm just trying to tell you what I know."

Flynn said, "Okay. So Max Fend is pretty well known. Well, at least his father is. Let's say it's true. What are you thinking?"

"So, hypothetically—if Max Fend was involved in the Clandestine Operations side of the house, they might have realized that he had the potential to someday inherit his father's company. He would qualify for that program—he's rich and famous. I mean, who doesn't know Charles Fend? He's like Howard Hughes and Richard Branson rolled into one. So if Max Fend is going to inherit the throne someday, maybe they have enrolled him. I can tell you one thing, his DNI personnel file certainly fits the bill."

"Can you tell me what's inside it?"

"Not without going to jail. And I like you, but not that much."

"Got it. Okay. Sounds like I need to pay Wilkes another visit."

* * *

When Jake Flynn called the contact number the CIA had given him and asked to be connected with Caleb Wilkes, he was told that Wilkes was unavailable.

Two minutes later, Flynn's phone rang.

"Special Agent Flynn, I hear that you are trying to reach me."

"Mr. Wilkes, I was hoping that we could sit down and have another chat."

"Concerning?"

"Our mutual friend."

The phone went silent for a moment, and then Wilkes said, "I'm heading to Jacksonville, Florida, right now. Would you be able to meet me there?"

Who did this guy think he was? "I'm in the middle of an investigation. No, I can't go to—" Besides, he had just come from there.

"Mr. Flynn, I know all about your investigation. And I know that you've been getting information from someone at the DNI's office. Looking into our mutual friend."

How the hell did he know that?

"Relax," Wilkes said. "I have no reason to inform your superiors. But I think the best thing you and I can do now is lay all our cards on the table. And my table is located in Jax. So do what you need to do, and catch a flight down here. This isn't a conversation you'll want to miss. Besides, if you're doing your investigation well, it'll lead you there anyway."

* * *

By evening, Morozov's yacht had tied up to the pier just off Mallory Square. Normally reserved for commercial cruise liners, Renee had found out that it cost him an extra $150,000 to dock there.

The party that night was for some of Morozov's wealthiest investors and business associates. Renee had been able to access the guest list and add her name. The security guard didn't know any better. All he knew was that her name was on the list.

As she walked up the gangway, Renee was on edge. Max was going to be furious when she didn't come home from the grocery store.

Renee was struck by the beauty of the vessel's design. Everywhere she looked, the ship was a work of art. Dual circular staircases on both sides of the ship. Titanium tables of modern construction. Light-colored hardwood flooring.

Beautiful women in skimpy outfits served refreshing cocktails and delectable hors d'oeuvres. The guests wore a mix of attire. Some were in suits. Others wore expensive-looking marine-themed clothing. A few Arab men wore traditional white robes.

Renee was worried that she would be overdressed, but she wasn't. She had purchased a long, flowing satin gown, like something you'd see at the Oscars, at one of the high-end Key West shops.

She tried to act natural. Standing out on the deck in the midst of the crowd. Looking around and wondering where she should start. Perhaps she had made a mistake in coming here.

Her pulse began racing as an older man in a suit walked toward her. His skin was flecked with the discolorations of age, his oddly colored hair thrown in a pitiful combover. He looked at her like she was his prey—he must know that she was an impostor. What had she been thinking, coming here like this? She should leave.

"What are you doing here?" he said.

"I'm sorry?"

"A woman as beautiful as you shouldn't be standing without a date or a drink. Allow me to provide either that you choose." Russian accent.

She forced a smile. "I'll take a drink. Thank you." Anything was better than raising suspicion.

"Of course." The older man caught the eye of one of the waitresses. He took two flutes of champagne from her, handing one to Renee.

"My name is Vasily. And you are?"

"Renee."

"It is very nice to meet you, Renee. Come—this area is getting crowded. Let's go up here, away from the noise."

He took her arm and led her up three steps to the elevated aft section of the open-air deck. It was only fifteen feet from where they had been standing, but there were considerably fewer guests up there. And the view of the ocean was better.

A waitress headed toward them with coconut shrimp. Vasily grabbed a few, fitting an impossible quantity all onto his tiny white napkin. The waitress left, and the two of them were alone and out of earshot.

"My God, these are delicious." He examined one of the coconut shrimp before stuffing it in his mouth. He used the back of his hand to wipe off some of the sauce that was dribbling down his chin. "Have you tried these?"

"Not yet."

"Here. Would you like one of mine?"

"I'm not hungry, thank you."

"What do you do, Renee? Why are you here?"

Renee had gone over this in her mind a dozen times on the ride over. It felt so inadequate now. "I'm an IT security consultant. I hope to work with Mr. Morozov in the future."

"Really?" He stopped eating the shrimp and looked at her with new interest.

She spoke before he could get off another question. "What do you do, Vasily?" All men liked to speak about themselves, if given the opportunity. Keep it about him.

"I work at the Russian Embassy."

"Really? That's very interesting." She managed an impressed look.

A gong went off. A sharp staccato sound, silencing the party.

Each of the heads turned to the entrance on the top deck. Two glass doors slid apart and Pavel Morozov walked out, a nameless blonde bombshell at each arm. The guests clapped. Several raised glasses in admiration. Pavel smiled, scanning the crowd.

His eyes settled on Renee and Vasily, and his smile faded.

* * *

Max chopped three cloves of garlic on his wooden cutting board, sliding them onto the knife and then into the pan of sizzling olive oil. The garlic crackled, its pleasant scent wafting through the room.

Max had decided on Italian instead of French food. He threw a sprinkle of crushed red pepper and minced onion onto the now-browned garlic. Once the onions were soft, he added two cans of crushed tomatoes, some salt and pepper. He dipped in his wooden spoon and gave it a taste. Not bad.

Turning the heat to low, he was almost ready to place the eggplant into the oven. Eggplant parmesan was one of his specialties. The key was to use salt to dry out the eggplant before breading it. This gave it a nice crunch.

But one couldn't enjoy an Italian dinner without red wine. And Renee had forgotten the wine—so she had run back out to get a few bottles.

He checked his watch. She had been gone for over an hour. How long did it take to get wine?

Max breathed through his nose, slowly stirring the sauce. A feeling of dread grew in his chest.

He placed the spoon down on the counter and stormed into her empty room, looking among her things.

Max and she had agreed that she should do the shopping alone that afternoon. Max needed to keep his face out of public view. It was a gift that he wasn't already in the news, and they shouldn't push their luck.

So Renee had gone out on her own after lunch. She'd said she wanted to check out a few of the shops. Then she'd finished up at one of the few grocery stores on Key West—an overpriced market a few blocks from their rental.

Max had seen the clothing store bags when she came in. She had held them up with a look of defiance in her eyes. It had been his money she was spending. Max had figured that the purchases were a playful way of getting back at him for what he considered a sexist remark about women and shopping.

He was wrong.

That wasn't why she had made the purchases. He was looking through the bags. Empty but for a receipt. *What did you buy, Renee?*

A dress. A pair of shoes. Platinum-and-diamond drop earrings and a necklace. Holy shit, those were expensive. But that wasn't what upset him. He looked around the room. In the closet and in the drawers. Then he checked the bathroom, just to be sure.

None of the clothing or jewelry she had purchased was there. And she sure as hell hadn't been wearing it when she'd left.

He closed his eyes, shaking his head. *Renee, Renee, Renee. Why would you do this?*

He knew exactly where she was. He just couldn't believe it. He ran into the kitchen and turned off the stove, then checked that the oven was off as well.

Back in his room, he opened his travel bag, grabbing a pair of binoculars, his pistol, and a silencer and placing them all in a fanny pack. He threw on his sunglasses and ball cap and hurried out the door.

It would take him a good fifteen minutes to reach the yacht, and he had no idea what he would do once there. It was getting dark. He needed to come up with a plan.

* * *

Morozov walked directly over to them. A strongman's walk, confident and showy, with just a touch of what Renee's brothers liked to call ILS—Imaginary Lat Syndrome. The way some guys held out their arms like their lat muscles were bigger than they really were.

Pavel Morozov had walked past his guests and stood uncomfortably close to Vasily. His hand was extended.

"Good evening, Vasily. I hear we have business to discuss."

Vasily shook Morozov's hand, replying in Russian.

"And who is your guest?" Morozov looked at Renee, an eyebrow arched.

After an uncomfortable silence, Renee said, "We only just met. Please excuse me, I'll let you two talk."

Morozov turned back to Vasily and spoke to him in Russian. Renee walked away, trying not to rush. She didn't want to draw any more attention than she already had. Renee could see two of Morozov's security team holding their earpieces across the room. One of them began heading her way. Renee again began to wonder if she had made a mistake in coming here. But then the security man walked past her and she exhaled.

She traveled along the outer walkway of the yacht. It was time to get to work.

* * *

Renee stepped out onto a forward observation deck. She was alone. The first twinkle of stars began to overcome the fading sunlight. She could hear the noise of the boozy party coming from the opposite end of the yacht.

There were seats and couches in various places. It took her a moment to find what she was looking for. A docking station near the armrest of one of the built-in seats. Luxury yacht owners wanted to be able to charge their phones while they lay out in the sun, right?

She looked around to make sure no security guards were near. Seeing no one, she sat down and removed her laptop from her shoulder bag. She didn't know how long she would have. She checked the docking station. It was equipped with a USB Type C port. That would get her speeds of at least 5 Gbps as long as there were no bottlenecks in the network.

Her fingers danced over the keyboard. Each keystroke was a moment closer toward solving the riddle—or being discovered.

There.

She had accessed a part of the ship's network that showed an enormous number of data transfers over the past week. It was a treasure trove of information. More than she could analyze right now. But she didn't need to. She just needed to send it off the ship so that she could look at it later.

While the data was transferring, she decided to dig into any communications between anyone at Fend Aerospace and the ship.

There were two account IDs listed at Fend. She couldn't trace them to a name right now. But if she could get into the Fend database later, she would be able to match them up. She added those files to the transfer.

Her eyes darted up at the sound of two security men walking out onto the observation deck. One of them held a silenced pistol, pointed at Renee.

"If you'll come with us, please."

It occurred to Renee that perhaps her tour of the ship should have stuck to places visible to potential witnesses. She hit a series of keystrokes that locked her computer and wiped her hard drive, then closed the laptop.

Renee said, "I'm a guest of Mr. Morozov—"

"We just received instructions from Mr. Morozov. He wants you *below deck*—now."

* * *

They threw Renee in a small bedroom deep in the bowels of the ship. They had taken her computer, but it was useless now anyway.

The room looked like it was meant for the crew. Bunk beds pressed up against the curved wall. Very little storage. There was a guard outside. At least one, by the sound of it.

She waited in the small room, cursing herself for not listening to Max. She'd just wanted to help. To make up for almost getting them killed in Georgia. And to prove that she was worthy. It was a colossally stupid motivation.

During hour one, Renee convinced herself that Morozov wouldn't kill her. She was an American. And people had seen her.

During hour two, the door opened up and a towering

man entered. The look in his eyes told her everything she needed to know.

He watched her for a moment before speaking, his eyes examining every inch of her. "My name is Mikhail. What is yours?"

She didn't respond.

He said, "They want me to find out what you were doing with your computer. They say that you erase everything on it. I say, no problem. You will be good to Mikhail. You will tell me what you were doing, and then maybe we let you go?"

Her lip began to quiver, so she bit into it. Her voice was hushed and hopeful. "I was just sending my husband an email. I forgot to bring my phone and..."

He slapped her hard across the face.

The force of the impact sent her onto the floor. Her left ear rang. She placed her hand against her cheek. She could feel it swelling up. Involuntary tears streamed out of her left eye.

Mikhail spoke in a casual manner. "So we will try this again. You tell me truth this time, yes? Then I don't hit you. Or, you can lie to me again, and I hit you. That is how we do this. Yes?"

Renee began to cry.

Mikhail clicked his tongue. "Oh, my pretty little girl. Do not cry. Mikhail will take good care of you."

The large man knelt down over her. She was still in a crumpled heap on the cold floor. Mikhail's thick fingers stroked her cheek and then wandered downward. Caressing her satin dress. His thumb and fingers cupping her breast as he looked into her eyes. She could smell the stench of his breath.

The movement was so fast. He gripped her by the arms

and brought her back to a standing position. Then he tore her dress at the seam, pulling it down so that it began to reveal her body.

Mikhail smiled, nodding his approval. "Yes. You will tell Mikhail everything. Yes?"

She looked away and nodded. Tears streaming down her face. "Okay."

A knock at the door.

Mikhail yelled in Russian, a clear annoyance in his tone. No reply. He frowned and went over to the door, cursing.

He opened the door and found himself staring at Max Fend's silenced pistol. The unconscious body of a guard on the floor behind him.

Max eyed Renee, her cheek red and swollen, her dress torn and half hanging off her. Max turned back toward Mikhail and fired two shots into his chest. The big Russian fell backwards into the lower bunk and then collapsed on the floor, a shocked expression of pain on his face.

Max turned and grabbed the other Russian in the hallway, dragging him into the room.

Renee began sobbing and started hugging Max.

"I'm so sorry, Max."

Max closed the door almost all the way and held a finger over his mouth. "It's okay. It's okay. Calm down. We need to get out of here."

She wiped her tears away with her arm and tried to pull her dress back up over herself. "Any ideas?"

A single, prolonged horn sounded throughout the ship.

Renee said out loud, "What was that?"

"One long horn blast—it means the ship is departing the port. The yacht is leaving."

Renee felt a rumble in her feet, and the sway of the deck as it began motoring away from the pier.

"Let's go. Follow me, and be quick about it. Don't make a sound."

Renee did as instructed, walking down the carpeted hallway. They wound through the ship's passageways, and she began to wonder where he was taking them. Then Max opened a watertight doorway and motioned for them to go in.

The two of them entered into a cave-like room at the aft end of the ship. Renee realized they were in some kind of boat-launching chamber. A pool of dark water took up most of the center of the room. Two small Sea-Doo watercraft were tied up on either side of the pool.

Max smacked his fist against a red button on the wall, and a spinning yellow light came on. The huge aft wall separated, revealing the dark ocean outside. The lights of Key West were in the distance.

As the rear doors opened up, the pool water began whirling and sloshing around, the ocean water now seeping in.

Max spoke quickly as he untied one of the Sea-Doos. "Get in, they'll find those two guards soon."

Max and Renee jumped in. As Max started up the Sea-Doo watercraft, Renee said, "How were you able to—"

"Charlotte."

"She let you on board?"

"She wasn't here. I called her. But she's in Jacksonville— she did, however, tell me the name of the company that was catering here tonight."

"So you snuck on with the caterers?"

Max put the Sea-Doo in reverse and they began drifting backward. "There isn't a lot that five thousand dollars in cash won't solve."

"How did you know where I was?"

"I found one of the guards and persuaded him to tell me."

They backed up into the black ocean, rolling on the wake of the yacht. When the Sea-Doo was about fifty feet behind the yacht, in open water, Max took the throttle out of reverse and put it into neutral. They floated there for a moment, Renee's hand on his shoulder. She stood in back of him, watching the massive vessel sail away.

"They have my computer and purse," she said.

"Was your ID in there?"

"No. And I wiped the hard drive—but they'll still be able to tell what information I was accessing from their own network. If they're any good, they'll probably figure out what we were up to."

"It won't matter. We got what we needed, right?"

"I think so, yes." She placed her body close to him as he ramped up the throttle, speeding over the waves and back toward the shore. She was shivering.

Max and Renee made it to a quiet dock and tied up the Sea-Doo. They walked to the street and hailed a cab back to their rental place. They quickly grabbed their personal items and then had the driver take them to the airport. The cabbie was happy to take a break from ferrying around the drunks who stayed until close.

Max started up the Cirrus while Renee paid for the FBO fees. He kept looking around. It was a dumb idea to leave the Cirrus at the Key West airport. And it might have been dumber to go back to it. Morozov's men had seen them fly away in Georgia, so they knew that they used a small plane. There weren't very many general aviation aircraft at Key West, relatively speaking. Not when compared to cars.

But he wanted to get away quick, and Morozov's goons were all out on that yacht. He hoped.

16

One Day Before the Fend 100 Flight...

The sun rose shortly after they took off from Key West. Max decided they would land in St. Augustine. It had a small airport, and it was close to his father's home in Ponte Vedra.

They flew north along the beach. Lots of heavily trafficked airspace, but a pretty view.

"Are those sharks?" Renee asked through her headset, looking down at the turquoise waters near Miami.

He did an S-turn in the aircraft so they could get a better view. They were only at five hundred feet, and some surfers waved up to them. There was a school of sharks swimming a mere fifty feet away.

Max said, "Yeah. Pretty wild, huh?"

"Oh my God. Should we warn those people?"

"Nah. They'll be fine."

"Are they always that close?"

"A lot of the time, yes. Usually people don't realize it, but sharks are always around." He looked at her.

"I'm sorry that I didn't tell you where I was going. I was only trying to help. I thought that I could…"

He shook his head. "I appreciate what you were trying to do. Just promise me that you won't keep secrets from me anymore."

She pursed her lips and nodded. "You saved me. I don't know what that man would have done."

Max glanced at her and then looked back ahead, flying the plane. "It's done now."

She didn't say anything else about it while they flew. She put her head down on the seat and fell asleep.

Renee slept most of the way. They were passing Daytona when she awoke.

"You okay?"

"Yes. I'm fine."

"So you were able to tap into the yacht's computer network?"

"I was. I transferred a lot of data off the ship. But I'll need time to analyze it."

"How much time?"

"A day at least."

Max said, "We'll find a place to lay low near St. Augustine. You can work there. But the Fend 100 flight is tomorrow. You'll have to work quick."

Renee nodded. "You said you were going to warn your father. What did you intend to do?"

"I'll need to set up a private meeting with him. My guess is that he's being watched closely by law enforcement, in case I show up. I won't be able to contact him through normal means."

"I may be able to help," Renee said.

"How?"

"Think of a way to get him alone. Is there anyone he

would meet by himself? Someone he hasn't seen in a while? Someone who, if they called, it would be unusual?"

Max thought about it for a moment. "Yeah. My aunt."

"Now, is there anywhere that this person and your father would go by themselves?"

Max said, "Yeah. Yeah, I think I have an idea. But you'll have to make the call. Do you have a way to make it look like it's from a different number or location?"

"Come on. Challenge me."

He laughed.

They landed at St. Augustine, and Max pulled his hood over his head, waiting out in the parking lot until Renee finished paying and then pulled up with the rental car. They were getting into a routine.

He again waited in the car while she paid for their motel, making sure to get a first-floor exterior entrance. Max was exhausted once again after flying all night. But he couldn't sleep. They flipped on the news, and the coverage was a mix of stories about the upcoming G-7 conference and the Fend 100 flight.

Renee had started the shower. The door to the bathroom was open. Max tried to give her privacy, concentrating on the TV as articles of her clothing began to grace the floor of the hotel room.

"Do you want me to leave the shower on?"

"Sure," Max said, biting his lip as he stole a glance of naked flesh.

She walked out of the bathroom with a white hotel towel wrapped tightly around her, and a look in her eye that he hadn't seen in some time. Renee slowly walked over to where Max sat on the bed.

Renee never said a word. She just reached down, her

soft fingers curling around his neck and pulling his head close to hers. She kissed him. A long, wet, deep kiss.

Max could feel his heart beating harder in his chest. She reached for the remote and shut off the TV, her towel loosening around her.

The hot shower continued running, steam filling the room.

* * *

They met at the Seven Bridges restaurant in Jacksonville and sat at a secluded strip of the bar. It was 1 p.m. on a weekday. Not many people were in the restaurant.

Wilkes bought a round of IPAs. That got their tongues loosened up enough that it didn't take long to get into the meat of the discussion.

"You said Max Fend wasn't in the CIA."

Wilkes sipped his beer. "He *wasn't*."

Flynn tilted his head, a skeptical look on his face.

"What? He's not," repeated Wilkes. "He was in the *DIA*."

Flynn frowned. "The Defense Intelligence Agency?"

Wilkes nodded.

"Is that really your excuse for lying to me? You purposefully misled me."

"I didn't."

Flynn thought about getting up and walking out. This guy had some nerve. Instead he took another drink of his beer. "Then what's your interest with Max Fend?"

"The DIA and the CIA often work closely together on things. We actually train our clandestine operatives at many of the same schools. Sometimes we transfer folks between agencies. Sometimes we *recruit* folks from the other agency for a specific program."

"So you were recruiting Max Fend for a program?"

"Maybe. It's not something that I can talk about," Wilkes said.

"What *can* you talk about?"

"I think you're barking up the wrong tree."

"What's that supposed to mean?"

"I don't think Max Fend is working with the Russians. And I don't think he allowed anyone to intrude on the Fend computer network."

"Then why did he run away from us last week?"

"Don't know."

"Did you break him out?"

"No. I'm looking into what's happened as well. It wasn't my people who helped Max escape Washington, D.C. We obviously wouldn't have done that. We would have talked to the FBI about it and resolved it quietly."

"Who was it, then?"

Wilkes shrugged. "I have a few ideas, but I'm not at liberty to discuss them."

"So is Fend still working for the DIA, then?"

Wilkes sighed. "He's out of the DIA now."

"As of when?"

"It's a recent development."

"What was the reason?"

"I can't discuss it."

"Look, you called me. Do I need to speak with someone at the DIA?"

"My guess is that *they* won't discuss it either, unless you get someone very high up to pull some strings."

Flynn tried to stay calm. "Do you know where Max Fend is right now?"

"No. But I think I know where he's headed."

* * *

Charles Fend hated reading the news on smartphones. He liked the feel of a good old-fashioned Sunday newspaper in his hands. Heavy and thick. The smell of the ink. No click-bait articles on the bottom of the page, trying to distract him with some meaningless pursuit.

He sat reading the *Florida Times-Union* on the beachfront patio of his Ponte Vedra beach home. A few palm trees, nestled next to the stucco exterior, provided shade. His gaze occasionally switched between the sand dunes on the beach and the article he was reading.

FEND AEROSPACE SET TO MAKE HISTORY

The article was kind. It painted Charles in the best light possible. It could have been much worse had the controversy with his son made headlines.

Charles was sick with worry about Max.

The FBI was saying that Max was linked to the hacking, and that there were possible ties to a terror-linked group in Syria.

Charles knew that couldn't be true. But he still didn't understand why Max had run from the FBI. Seeing the footage of those motorcycles racing across the bridge out of Washington, D.C., was shocking. He wished he could have talked some sense into his son. Whatever the trouble he was in, there was nothing worth the risk that he was taking. And there was nothing his father wouldn't forgive. Charles just didn't want something awful to happen to Max.

He wondered if this all wasn't his fault somehow.

Perhaps he had pampered Max too much. He had shown so much promise as a boy. Max had buried himself in his studies and athletics at his elite prep school. Princeton had introduced him to a great group of friends, and a world of opportunities. But college also introduced young men to a world of temptation. Charles worried about the choices his son had made as an adult. This generation today...

After Max graduated college, he had worked for the Department of Defense for a few years in Washington. Charles hadn't understood why he had chosen that path. His father could have helped Max get into the best business or law school, if that was what he wanted to pursue. He could have helped him get a job at one of the Big Three consulting firms, or something on Wall Street. Charles's network was world-class.

But Max hadn't wanted any of that. He'd wanted to try something on his own. Charles admired that spirit, in a way. He'd given his son the benefit of the doubt. But then Max had abruptly left the Department of Defense and traveled to Europe to work as a freelance consultant. He had taken money from his trust fund and bought a home in the South of France, sparing no expense. Charles should have objected, but hadn't. He still didn't know why.

That's when the stories had started rolling in about Max's wild parties and behavior. He sounded like he was out of control. It got bad enough that board members had mentioned it to Charles. They didn't want to see Max someday inherit the company if he was really as wild as depicted.

So Charles had flown to France, hoping to stage an intervention. The father and son had spent a week together, hiking along the Nietzsche Path near the medieval village of

Eze. Walking along the path, seven hundred feet over the Mediterranean Sea, they spoke candidly about their lives.

Charles watched his son easily navigate the steep path, shaded by olive trees and tall oaks. Max looked tan, fit, and in good spirits. Healthy and in control. It didn't match up with the persona that was being portrayed in the media. But he seemed down about something. Bothered.

Later that day, they sat at an outdoor restaurant near the seaside town square, sharing a bowl of steamed mussels and fries. Charles confronted his son about the stories he had heard. He told him that he was worried that Max would end up wasting his life here in France. He didn't want him to succumb to the temptation wealthy children often faced. Max was better than that.

Max had told his father that he had expected the talk, but not to worry. Max assured him that things would change. He was thinking about leaving France and was interested in taking a more stable job in the States.

Charles had been incredibly relieved. He offered his son a job on the spot. Max told him that he thought he needed a business degree first. He didn't want to walk into a company without the requisite knowledge and skill to do the job. While Charles wanted to ask him what the hell he had been doing out here if he wasn't gaining any business skills, he let it go. Charles told his son he could join Fend Aerospace whenever he was ready. And if he wanted to earn another degree to help him prepare, that was absolutely fine.

Now Charles wondered just what it was that had triggered Max to make such a dramatic life change. While the direction was opposite, it was very similar to the way he'd suddenly dropped his DoD job. It was almost like someone else had instructed him to make the move. *Like it was out of Max's control...*

"Mr. Fend, you have a phone call. Your sister, sir."

Dolores? At this hour? Perhaps she was calling about the news article.

His assistant walked over and handed Charles his phone.

"Hello?"

"Hello, Charles. It's Dolores. I would like to visit Mom's grave today. I was wondering if you would join me?"

It wasn't Dolores. It wasn't her voice. He overcame the urge to ask who it was, because he was pretty sure that he knew.

"Of course. What time shall I meet you?"

"How about half past three? Will that work?"

"Sure thing."

"Wonderful. And, Charles, I would really like to spend the time together, just the two of us. Please be a dear and come by yourself."

"Will do."

He hung up the phone and called to his assistant to have his car ready in the driveway.

"Which car, sir?"

"I'll take the Mercedes."

"Very well, sir."

Charles looked at his wristwatch and thought carefully about what to do next. He knew what he *wanted* to do, and what he had *agreed* to do.

Duty won out.

He dialed the number from memory. The voice on the other end answered immediately.

"It's me," Charles said.

"What is it?"

"You were right. He called."

* * *

Max and Renee pulled into the empty parking lot of a small private school. The kids were out for the summer, so no one would see them walk through the property.

Max looked at Renee. "You stay here. If you don't hear from me in twenty minutes, leave and go back to the hotel. I'll call you tonight."

"Be careful," she told him, affection in her voice.

Max smiled. "I'm always careful. That being said, if I don't call..."

"You don't need to tell me what to do in that situation. I'll know."

Max squeezed her shoulder and turned, closing the car door behind him. He walked through the school playground, ducking under a bright blue-and-red jungle gym. Fresh mulch covered the ground.

He hopped the white picket fence to the rear of the playground and walked through a grove of trees until he came to a flat open field.

The graveyard. His mother's graveyard.

Max visited it about once per year, although normally he entered through the main drive. The entire cemetery was the size of four football fields put together. A few trees provided occasional shade, but most of it was wide-open field.

Max's mother had died when he was very young, but he tried to keep her memory a meaningful part of his life. The grave markers were all flush with the ground. Simple granite, mostly. Max walked towards hers. A location he knew well.

The blistering hot Florida sun beat down on him from above. Her grave was just to the east of a large oak tree. He could see a figure standing over the spot. His father's black Mercedes-Benz sedan was parked nearby.

Max didn't see anyone else.

The figure was a man. That much was for sure. But he was facing away from Max. Max reached into his fanny pack and gripped his pistol with both hands. His eyes scanned the Mercedes, and the trees. Still no sign of anyone else.

The man turned to face him when Max was about thirty feet away. Max smiled.

For a moment.

The door of the Mercedes opened, about twenty-five yards away.

"Dad?"

"It's alright, Max."

Max stood his ground, still holding his concealed weapon. He shook his head. "Dad. Who else is here?"

"Trust me, son. It will be alright."

"Dad, I didn't do what they say I did."

"I know, son."

A man got out of the rear of the Mercedes. Max knew the face. Where did he know him from? He searched his memory. At last it came to him.

He had met him down at the Farm once. He was a CIA agent—Caleb Wilkes.

* * *

Charles drove them back to his home in Ponte Vedra. He had called ahead and asked his staff to leave. They needed privacy for the evening.

Wilkes had assured Max that he would be free to go after their meeting. No one knew that the three of them were speaking. When they sat down at the house, Wilkes set a small device on the center of the table. It looked like an old walkie-talkie.

"What's that?"

"It's a device that'll make it near impossible for someone to listen in on our conversation through one of our phones or some other electronics in the house," Wilkes said.

"Does it work?"

"Oh, yes."

Max said, "I assume you've told my father a little bit about my work in Europe?"

"I gave him a rundown, yes. But I think you'll find that you both have a thing or two to learn about each other."

Max looked at his dad inquisitively. Charles nodded. "It's time we let you in on some family history."

Max knew enough to stay quiet.

Charles turned to face him, leaning back in his swivel chair. "In the late 1970s, I met your mother while traveling through the UK. Her father, as you know, was from Poland. Her mother was English." His father's face looked strained.

"That's where you were married," Max said.

"Correct. We married near Cambridge. It was shortly after our wedding that a man named Hoopengardner approached me in London. Hoopengardner knew that Fend Aerospace was about to get contracts with the US government. Military contracts. This was a few years before you were born. Hoopengardner said it would be in my best interests if we could have a cup of tea. Somewhere secluded, where we could speak about a quiet business proposal.

"As it turned out, Hoopengardner's business proposal was nothing short of extortion. He was a KGB agent. You know him by a different name—Pavel Morozov. His proposal was for me to provide him with information on the military aircraft we were developing. If I didn't, he had access to your mother's family in Poland. By that time, your grandmother had passed away, and your grandfather had moved back to Poland to live."

Max looked at Wilkes, who stayed quiet. He thought about what type of man Morozov was. He could see where this was going. "What did you do?" Max asked his father.

"I'm a patriot, Max. And I wasn't about to let some Soviet bastard blackmail me. When we got back to the States, I quietly contacted the FBI. I had thought they might be able to help me get your mother's family out of Poland. I was naive."

Now it was Max's father who looked at Wilkes, anger in his eyes.

Charles said, "The FBI handed me over to the CIA. The CIA did not want me to break off contact with Morozov. To my surprise, they *wanted* me to give the KGB information on Fend Aerospace's military contracts. But they wanted to control exactly *what* information was sent out. They turned me into a double agent."

Max knew how it went. The counterintelligence types rarely wanted to just solve a problem and make it go away. They wanted to turn agents and provide corrupt data. To manipulate the other side's network of spies.

"How long did you do it for?"

Now Wilkes spoke up. "Your father worked for us for over ten years, Max."

Max looked at his father. "Why ten years?"

"Because after ten years of providing secrets to the KGB —secrets that the CIA was providing me—things began to change," Charles said.

"How so?"

"For one, Morozov got suspicious. It was 1987 when it happened. Reagan was president. The Soviets were getting their asses handed to them by the CIA-armed Mujahedeen in Afghanistan. Morozov was growing desperate. Threatening me more and more every time I saw him."

"Why?"

"He had other sources in the US who were providing him information that conflicted with mine. But my information had made Morozov a star in the KGB. When his star began to fall, he blamed me."

"So what happened?"

"He approached your mother."

Max felt a chill run through his body. His mother had died in a car accident when he was a boy. He had only vague memories of her, along with a few cherished home videos and pictures.

"Your mother came to me one night and said that Morozov had told her everything. That I'd been spying for the Russians. And that he wasn't happy with the information I was providing. Morozov wanted her to put pressure on me to step up my contributions. Or else."

"Or else what?"

"He threatened to harm *you*, Max. You were young—six years old at the time. Your mother became a wreck."

"I see." Max shifted his weight, suddenly uncomfortable.

"I went to the CIA. I told them that we needed protection. Your mother was brought in to meet my CIA handlers. She agreed to participate with me in the counterintelligence operation, despite the threat to her family. She said that her father hated the Soviets, and that he would never want to be used as leverage by them. She demanded one thing—protection for you. The CIA agreed and stationed a security detail at our home, around the clock. They were disguised as butlers. But I was to continue to play the game with Morozov for a little longer."

Max shook his head. "Dad, I had no idea about any of this. What happened?"

"The next time I met with him, Morozov told me he wanted the raw data on the new stealth jets that Fend Aerospace was designing for the Air Force out in Nevada."

"I didn't know Fend Aerospace was involved in that type of work back then."

"They weren't," Wilkes said. "It was part of a charade. A disinformation campaign."

"This was all happening right around the time that Mom got into her car accident."

His father had a grave look in his eye. "Yes. *Exactly* that time."

"Dad..."

His father looked out over the water.

"Did my mother die in a car accident?"

Wilkes said nothing, just watching the exchange between father and son.

His father looked down at the table while he spoke. "No."

"So then how did she die?"

"Morozov."

Max clenched his fists. "How?"

His father was having trouble getting the story out. "The Cold War was ending. Everything was coming to a head. Morozov had finally had enough. The information I'd supplied him on the stealth jets was obviously false. He stopped taking my calls. That's when we got scared. As it turned out, our fears were warranted. Your mother left you with the nanny and one of the security men that day. Then she drove to the store with the other security man to pick up some things. She was found dead in the vehicle. They made it look like the car ran off the road, but I knew the truth."

"What do you mean?"

"The autopsy showed that your mother had died from the impact of the car driving off the cliff. But the security guard had been shot. That part was never reported to authorities. The CIA took care of that. Morozov contacted me the day of the funeral and asked how she was, delight in his voice."

Max's mouth was wide. "Why didn't you...?"

"What? Seek revenge? He threatened to kill you if we went after him. And during the Cold War, the CIA and KGB would kill each other's spies all the time. At the end of the Cold War, no one wanted any errant sparks to ignite a fire. Your mother's death was covered up, just like many others. For the good of the nation, and for your safety."

Max sat in silence for a few moments, taking it all in. *Leaving a single family member alive was a sort of calling card.*

"I'm sorry, Max," his father said. "I should have told you that story a long time ago. It isn't something I like to discuss. Not really something that I was allowed to discuss."

Max spoke quietly. "What happened after that? With you and the CIA?"

"I told the CIA I was done." Charles turned to face Wilkes. "But one is never truly done with them. I realize that now. When I told them that I was finished, the CIA was unhappy. But they didn't push it. They gave me protection, and I've helped them from time to time."

Wilkes said, "As far as we know, Morozov never told anyone else that your father was working with us."

"He knew and he never told the Soviets about my father working for the CIA? Why not?"

Wilkes said, "In a word? Pride. And maybe fear. Morozov didn't want to look bad. You have to remember the way the Soviets worked back then. Your father was feeding the KGB false information for years. Military secrets. Their government made major decisions to increase military spending based on the information that we provided. It was all part of a huge misinformation campaign. We wanted the USSR to spend itself into oblivion. We knew their economic engine couldn't sustain it. It couldn't keep up with the United States' manufacturing power. But why stop there? Why have them think they needed to keep up with reality, when we could provide them an alternate reality that was even more grave?"

"What did you tell them?"

"We gave them information about a classified stealth aircraft program—claiming that they were in development out in the Nevada desert."

"Didn't we actually have something like that?" Max asked.

"Yes. Lockheed's Skunkworks program was very similar. They developed the F-117, the B2, etc...."

"So what did they think *you* were doing?"

"They thought Fend Aerospace was developing a set of supersonic stealth fighters. We made it look like we were decades ahead of where we really were. We even created cardboard cutouts and placed them in the desert. We had an entire base filled with fake aircraft. Hundreds of personnel were involved. Only a few knew that it was a deception, however."

"But Morozov found out."

"Yes."

"And he never told anyone."

"It would have ruined him. He might have even been executed, for not catching that it was all fake."

Max was incredulous. "So he just let the Russians think that it was real?"

Charles shrugged. "Why not?"

"By the time he found out, it was 1989. The Soviet Union was in decline. The Red Army was getting slaughtered in Afghanistan. Bread lines in Moscow. He saw the writing on the wall. Why hurt his reputation? It was better for him if he kept the failure quiet. I have to admit, considering his position today, he was right about that."

"Why didn't you tell me any of this before? About my mother..."

"You were too young to understand. And much of it was classified at the highest levels."

"Still is," Wilkes said.

Max frowned. "Who cares, now?"

Charles looked at Wilkes.

"Because as you now know, Pavel Morozov still presents a threat to national security," Wilkes said. "And the CIA wants to bring him down."

* * *

They ordered an early dinner delivered from a local seafood restaurant. Max ate a grilled mahi-mahi sandwich while he filled them in on what he had witnessed over the past few days.

Wilkes had a lot of questions. "So you think it was MI-6 that helped you escape?"

"I do."

"Why do you think it was them?"

"British accents, mainly."

Wilkes said, "That's great detective work."

"Because they were *good*. And I recognized one of them, from an op a few years ago. I *know* that he was MI-6."

"Fine. Tell me about your interactions with them again. MI-6 had you meet with their woman in Morozov's outfit?"

"Yes. Down in Key West. Morozov had his yacht docked there until recently."

"How'd you know Morozov was there?"

"The MI-6 woman told me to meet her there."

Wilkes looked bothered. "Why didn't they go through normal channels to resolve this?"

"They said they *did*," Max said. "They said the CIA didn't want to halt the Fend 100 passenger qualification flight. They said you wanted to let Morozov keep going so that you could catch him red-handed or something like that. Is that true?"

Wilkes clenched his jaw. "Not entirely."

"Now what the hell are you playing at, Caleb? If that Russian lunatic is putting people in danger, then we need to do something about it," Charles said.

Wilkes didn't answer. He was distracted, looking off into the distance. Like he was trying to sort something out in his head.

"You're right about Morozov's being a threat," Max said. "He's planning to steal all of your company's data—he's going to launch another cyberattack. He'll have the technology for the Fend 100 and be able to sell it on the black market."

Wilkes and Max's father looked at each other. "We know," Wilkes said. "I told your father about it last week. After you made your escape from D.C. What we don't know is how he's going to do it."

"Well, I might be able to help with that part."

"How?"

"The MI-6 woman I met—Charlotte Capri. She told me

that Morozov's hackers have a way to get access to the secure servers where the Fend 100's data is stored."

Max told them what he'd learned from Charlotte, and what Renee and he had figured out on their own. When he was finished, both Charles and Caleb Wilkes looked impressed.

"You were actually on his yacht?"

"That's right."

"You're lucky to be alive."

"Agreed."

"She's supposed to meet with me again. She says MI-6 is working on software that will be able to defend against Morozov's hackers."

"Where and when is she meeting you?" Wilkes said.

"Somewhere in Jacksonville, tonight. Morozov is sailing his yacht up the Florida coast today. Which continues to bother me. Morozov must know that we're on to him. Especially now that I've gotten away. Why isn't he more frightened of US law enforcement or counterintelligence taking him into custody?"

"He's a pro," Wilkes said.

"So what?"

"He's been at this a long time, and he knows the rules. We can't touch him right now. We don't have evidence that he's done anything wrong, other than your word. Which is tainted, at the moment—thanks to him. Like I said. A pro."

"What about the forensics that the FBI had?"

"It's been tampered with, obviously. It links to you. So if we want to go after Morozov, we'll also be using the same forensic evidence that implicates you. Does that sound like it would hold up?"

"No. But this isn't court..." Max decided it was time to bring up Renee. "I have someone I've been working with. A

Canadian woman that I know, Renee. She's former CSE. A real black hat ninja."

"A what?"

"A hacker, Dad. Renee has been able to uncover a lot about Morozov. He has an outfit called Maljab Tactical. They're a group of Uzbek defense consultants, and they operate mostly out of Syria. They specialize in working with Jihadi extremist groups. They also have some pretty good hackers. Our working theory is that this group was involved in the Fend cyber intrusion. They probably linked the network breach to me."

"Why is Morozov interested in Max?" Charles asked.

Max turned to his father. "Whatever he does, Morozov is planning to hang the blame on me. He laid the groundwork with the hacking incident. He'll finish the job by seizing control of the Fend 100 during the passenger qualification flight, and the cyber forensics will point to yours truly." Max paused. "I'm beginning to think you should just postpone the flight. Use whatever excuse you need—including the false evidence that ties me to the Russians. If it's what we need to do..."

"No, Max," Wilkes said. "There's a better way forward. Do you know why we pulled you out of Europe last year?"

"The DIA pulled me out. They said my cover was blown, after the incident with the two Russian arms dealers."

"Not exactly. Max, Charles, it's time that we discussed a long-term relationship between the Fend family and the CIA."

"I've heard this talk before," said Charles.

"Charles, your son was working for the intelligence community, just as I told you. Specifically, he worked under the purview of the Defense Intelligence Agency."

Charles looked at Max as if seeing him for the first time, a mix of fear and pride in his eyes.

Wilkes went on, "The CIA has a network of high-profile agents. Wealthy businessmen. CEOs. Celebrities. Heads of state. People with *access*. They have various levels of training. Some are little more than informants, but the network is one of our most valuable."

"What does this have to do with your reason for not wanting to cancel the Fend 100 test flight? And for pulling me out of Europe?" Max said.

"The Agency doesn't like to shut down potential sources of information. It sort of goes against our mission," Wilkes said. "If there's a way to keep a valuable asset in play, we'll take it. Charles will be retiring from the Fend Aerospace Company soon. We recognize that, and have planned for it. Max, ironically, the best place the US government can place you is in your father's company."

"So what are you saying? That me leaving the DIA was intentional? But I thought my cover was blown."

"A partial truth. *Morozov* knows. But few others, if any. The CIA would like you to continue to serve. When your father retires, your position with the Fend Aerospace Company, as well as your family name and status, will create many opportunities for us."

Max nodded. He didn't completely trust Wilkes, but as much as he hated to admit it, he wanted to get back in the game.

"So the two Russian men in France—that was Morozov?"

"We believe so, yes. We think he set up the deal to test you. He wanted to see for himself whether you were really working as a spy. But he didn't tell anyone else. Just like he never told anyone that your father was working for the CIA."

"So then why did he test me? And if he thinks I work for US intelligence—why did he keep it to himself?"

Wilkes said, "Who knows? Maybe he wanted to finish what he started with your mother. The one thing that keeps KGB agents warm during the cold Russian winters. Revenge."

"Why would he do this now?" Charles asked.

Wilkes continued offering ideas. "Maybe seeing Max in France reminded him of you, Charles. And don't forget Sergei —Max's asset in France. We think he was planning this cyber-attack with one of his Eastern European cyber ransom gangs. Morozov must have caught wind of it. He's well connected to the Russian mafia. Hell, it might not even be about revenge as much as it is an opportunity that he stumbled into."

Max rubbed his chin. "Maybe." That seemed like too much of a coincidence for Max, but he didn't say it. "Whatever the reason, it seems as though Morozov plans to launch another cyberattack during the Fend 100 flight."

Charles shook his head. "Wonderful. If I don't proceed with the Fend 100 flight, Morozov may start selling bits of the Fend technology on the open market, which will spook the investors and threaten to cancel our government contract before it's finalized. But if I do proceed with the Fend 100 flight, we risk another, more effective cyberattack. Is that about it?"

"In a nutshell."

Charles said, "We have to go on with the flight. If we don't, the company will be devastated. We'll have to ensure that we protect ourselves from this next cyberattack. That is the only satisfactory answer from my end."

"Good. That's exactly what I want as well." said Wilkes.

"Why?"

"Proof. The forensic evidence we capture will provide us with leverage against Morozov and the Russians. But there's another reason. Something I haven't told you yet."

Both Fends stood in suspense.

"I think Morozov has a man on the inside of Fend Aerospace. And I don't want to change any of our plans until we find out who that is, lest we tip him off."

"Why do you think that?"

"The FBI told me. I've been speaking to the man who's investigating the Fend cyberattack. The FBI forensics team tells him that the only way someone could have penetrated the network the first time—however limited its success—was with inside knowledge."

"You're working with the FBI?"

"Yes."

Charles frowned. "You think there's someone who works for me that is helping Morozov?"

"Possibly. I think we should bring the FBI investigator into the fold here tonight. Special Agent Flynn. I would like him to provide his theories on the matter."

Charles clasped his hands together. "We need a way to protect ourselves against this."

Max said, "Like I said, the British agent I met—Charlotte Capri—said she'd give me a software program designed by MI-6. MI-6 is designing this software program to protect the Fend 100 from being hacked by Morozov's cyberoperators."

Charles said, "Caleb?"

Wilkes nodded. "They mentioned something to me about this. But we weren't ready to commit."

"Why?"

"At the time, we weren't convinced that Morozov was

going to be able to break through the Fend network. And we were hoping that his initial attempt would give us enough evidence to connect it to him."

"But?"

"But so far, the cyber trail just leads to a Syrian group. If we allow them one more attempt, the gentlemen at Fort Meade will be ready. We'll be able to prove that Morozov's group is responsible for the cyberattacks. Our government can't move on Morozov until that point. When we're done here, I'll call my counterparts at MI-6 and find out about their progress with the thumb drive option. They need to work through me from now on."

Max watched Wilkes when he said it. He looked anxious, a hint of worry in his voice. *Like something wasn't going according to plan.*

Wilkes said, "I realize that I'm asking a lot of you both here. But I would like to keep pressing on with the Fend 100 flight."

"It's something I want as well. But I want to talk to some of my people about this," Charles said. "If there's a vulnerability in our system, I want them to know."

Wilkes said, "Let's keep this information among a small group. Pick one person that you trust implicitly on your team."

He thought for a moment. "Maria Blount. She's the program manager. But she has an engineering background. She would be able to find out if we have a problem."

"Is there a way that Maria can provide another layer of security, to make sure that the Russians can't hack into the aircraft controls?" Max asked.

Charles said, "We'll meet with her and find out. I won't allow the flight to go on unless she can guarantee it will be safe."

Wilkes held up his hand. "Let's run her name by the FBI first. I want to make sure that they approve. I'm going to call the FBI agent I've been working with. He's already in Jacksonville. We'll fill him in and run this Maria Blount name by him. As long as he approves, we'll bring her into the fold as well."

"Make sure that the FBI knows this rubbish about Max being complicit in the crime is not true."

"Yes. Please do that," Max said, his brow arched.

Wilkes smirked. "Of course. I'll make my call."

* * *

An hour later, Special Agent Jake Flynn showed up at Charles Fend's home in Ponte Vedra. Max had thought about inviting Renee but decided against it. He preferred to keep her behind the curtain for now.

Flynn stood in the doorway, greeted by Wilkes and Max Fend. He didn't look happy.

Max was half-expecting a load of FBI agents to come storming in behind him. Instead, he got a disgruntled nod. "Mr. Fend."

"Hello again."

Max assumed that Wilkes had prepped Flynn and decided not to press it any further for now.

Wilkes summarized the earlier conversations for Flynn.

"So this Pavel Morozov is former KGB, and is responsible for the cyberattacks on Fend Aerospace."

"We think so, yes."

Flynn looked at Wilkes. "How do you want to play this?"

Wilkes filled him in on what they were thinking.

As promised, Wilkes made sure to get his superiors at the CIA involved. Wilkes and Flynn jumped on a secure conference call with the bigwigs at the CIA and FBI for the next fifteen minutes. Wilkes smoothed things over and let them know that Max Fend was working with the CIA and should not be considered a suspect in the Fend cybercrime. From the short duration of the call, Max got the impression that the FBI and CIA leadership had already discussed the matter.

When the two men emerged, Wilkes said, "Special Agent Flynn, would you be able to share with the Fends what you were telling me yesterday? Your suspicions about an insider at Fend Aerospace."

Flynn looked uncomfortable. "We're looking closely at a few employees there."

Wilkes nodded. "Could you say who?"

"I would rather not. No offense."

Charles said, "Agent Flynn, with respect, it appears to be in our collective best interests to proceed with the Fend 100 flight tomorrow. The CIA and FBI both want to collect more cyber evidence on Pavel Morozov during that time. We'll need at least one of my experts at Fend Aerospace to help us reduce the risk of Morozov actually succeeding and stealing all of the Fend 100's artificial intelligence technology. But if you won't share your suspects with us, then I don't know who to trust."

Flynn looked thoughtful. "How about you give me a name, and I help you pick who I think would be best suited for the job?"

Wilkes said, "Charles, who was the person that you mentioned earlier?"

"Maria Blount."

Flynn looked at Wilkes. "She should be fine. She was actually the one who first contacted the FBI about the cyber intrusion on the Fend network."

"Alright, let's get her over here."

Maria came thirty minutes later, and they quickly brought her up to speed.

Maria said, "So let me see if I understand. Max, I think what I hear you saying is that this Russian is planning to remotely tap into the Fend 100, and use the datalink connection between the Fend 100 and the Fend 100 control center to steal our most precious AI technology. Is that right?"

"Exactly."

"Okay...and someone who you all trust is going to give you some sort of software that will act as an antivirus—to neutralize any threat that the Russians could actually do this." They hadn't told her that MI-6 would be providing the thumb drive. She didn't need to know who it was, just what it would do.

"Correct."

Maria paused. She frowned and said, "Well, this means they've already infected the aircraft or our control room software. If that's true, they must have done it the first time they hacked in. I find that highly doubtful. But it's possible that we overlooked something. If...and that's a *big* if...they really have a worm in our system, I don't know if it will be enough to just trust that this magical thumb drive software will inoculate us from another attack. Especially with as much as we have riding on this Fend 100 flight. I mean, this is everything to the company, Charles."

"I know, Maria. I understand the importance."

"Sorry. It's just...I know this means a lot to our bottom line."

Max knew it too. While he tried not to let that influence his decision-making, he realized that if the Fend 100 test flight didn't pass with flying colors, his father's company would take a pummeling on Wall Street. His father still owned a controlling share of the stock, but a failed test flight could ruin his life's work. It could mean massive layoffs, not to mention the effect it might have on the whole aviation sector. If the first autonomous commercial airline flight were hacked, no one would want to fly on them. There was already enough fear about riding in one of these things.

Max said, "Maria, do you see any other way that we could provide a fail-safe? Some way of preventing the flight from getting hacked?"

Her eyes glanced up, twitching back and forth as she thought. She started nodding to herself. "Yes. I think I know what we can do. I can go on the flight."

Charles said, "You want to go on the flight?"

"Yes. I'll rewrite some of the remote override code tonight. It will take a while, but I can do it. If anyone *does* hack into the flight, like last time, I'll be able to override it from inside the aircraft." She smiled, pleased with her solution. "It's the safest way."

"What about the thumb drive with the antivirus software?" Max said.

Wilkes eyed Max. "Let's consider Maria going on the plane as a fail-safe. But we should also continue to plan to get the thumb drive from your contact, Max. And I'll check on that solution with my contacts."

Charles said, "Okay—do we feel like there are enough controls in place that this will be a safe event?"

They all nodded slowly.

"And we'll be watching Morozov's yacht," Wilkes said. "If he tries anything, we'll finally have the evidence we need to prosecute him. Mr. Flynn, would you be able to help with a takedown, if we need it?"

Flynn nodded. "The FBI can handle that. Let me talk to my superiors."

They spoke for a few more minutes, and then Maria left to go get to work. Flynn did as well.

Wilkes said to Max, "You need a ride?"

"Sure. Thanks."

Max asked to be dropped off at a gas station near his father's home. He had texted Renee a few minutes before, asking her to pick him up there.

Wilkes smiled. "What's the matter? You don't want me to know where you're staying?"

"Sorry."

Max's ride pulled up. Renee looked at both Caleb Wilkes and Max through her window.

"Is that your Canadian hacker?"

"It is."

Wilkes nodded his approval. They then traded phone numbers. Before getting out of the car, Max said, "Let me ask you something. Why didn't you tell me you were going to recruit me after I began working for my father's company? I mean, why did the DIA—and you—let me think that I was done?"

"Isn't that obvious? Your father is the owner of Fend Aerospace. We received intelligence that Morozov was planning something big, and it involved Fend. I couldn't be certain that you *weren't* part of it."

"You really thought I might be compromised?"

"No. But I'm not paid to get it right *most* of the time. I'm supposed to get it right *all* of the time. So I quarantined you. I couldn't let you in on my operation until you were cleared."

"Are you sure now?"

"One hundred percent."

Max thought something still didn't fit. Wilkes wasn't giving him everything, and both of them knew it. But a good intelligence operative knew when to stop asking questions.

"Alright, thanks. I'll let you know what I hear from Charlotte."

"Max."

"Yeah?"

"Relax. I'm from the government, and I'm here to help."

Max gave a small smile. "That's what I'm afraid of."

He got in Renee's car and they drove away, careful to check that they weren't being followed.

17

When they got back to their hotel, Max and Renee took a quick walk on the nearby beach to talk and go over their plans. Their hands brushed together a few times as they walked, and Max caught Renee glancing at him when it happened, an unmistakable look of affection on her face.

Neither had said much about the rekindling of their old flame. There hadn't been time. Was it just a byproduct of the fear and adrenaline that was pumping through both of them after nearly being killed twice in one week? When this was over, would they go their separate ways? Or would it grow into something more?

All Max knew was that he loved the feel of her smooth bare skin on his body. And he loved seeing her smile at him in that special way.

But he was glad they hadn't spoken about it. He wasn't exactly the kind of guy that liked to talk about relationships or feelings. And they had plenty of other things to discuss.

"You don't trust Wilkes, do you?" Renee said.

"Not really, no."

"Why?"

"There's just something bothering me about the whole thing."

"About what Wilkes wants you to do?"

"More than that. Why would MI-6 go out on their own within the United States? Why does Wilkes want Morozov to hack into Fend Aerospace for a second time? It's all highly unusual."

"Didn't Wilkes say—"

"I know what he said, but it just doesn't feel right."

"There will be passengers on the flight?"

"There will be tomorrow. They have a few dozen aviation and tech writers sitting on the aircraft. And some company executives."

Max stopped and picked up a stone, throwing it out towards the water. It skipped a few times before it plunged beneath the surface.

He said, "I'm letting things influence me that I shouldn't, in this situation. The well-being of my father and his company. And my desire to hurt Morozov. I'm still wrapping my mind around everything that they told me yesterday."

She placed her hand on his shoulder. "You mean about your mother?"

He nodded. Her hand dropped and they continued walking. The sun reflected off the water. A light breeze kicked up a whitish haze of fine sand.

"What if Wilkes has another motive?" Renee said.

"Like what?"

"You said MI-6 disagreed with him, right?"

"Yes."

"Think about it from his position. What actions has he taken? Ignore what he's *said* his objectives are. What has he actually *done*?"

"He has been working with the FBI. He contacted my father and convinced him to help bring me in to him. And he had a disagreement with MI-6."

"What did he say about Georgia, when you told him we were attacked there? Did he seem surprised?"

"No. But I wouldn't expect him to be. Our fingerprints were all over that place. The FBI knew about us being there, so he must have."

Renee looked troubled. "I'm worried that Wilkes is playing you."

"To what end?"

"What if he *wants* Morozov to succeed in stealing the Fend 100 data tomorrow?"

Max stopped walking and turned to face her. "Why would Wilkes want that?"

"What if Wilkes wants you to take the fall for it? Maybe both you and your father?"

"I don't see what he has to gain."

"He's saying he's working to entrap Morozov. But what if he's not? What if he's working *with* Morozov?"

* * *

The call came at eight p.m. sharp.

Renee and Max were both in the hotel room. Renee analyzed the data she had stolen from Morozov's yacht, while Max worked out on the floor beside the bed.

Max picked up the phone with a sweaty hand.

"Hello, Max."

"Hello, Charlotte. Are we still on?"

"Can you join me for a drink?"

"Where?"

"The Lemon Bar. Do you know it?"

"Yes. When?"

"One hour."

"I'll see you then."

The Lemon Bar was situated right on the shore of Atlantic Beach—one of the great bars in a great bar district of Jacksonville Beach.

A group of tall blue tables on an outdoor patio, umbrellas over some of them. The smell of the ocean to the east. A long outdoor bar to one side. The nearby street was lined with palm trees, and the shallow dunes to the east didn't quite hide the magnificent ocean view.

The bar was packed with people. A mix of local twenty-somethings and off-duty Naval personnel from the nearby base at Mayport. The atmosphere was lively. Mixed drinks garnished with slices of fruit. Live music. Everyone smiling.

Max saw her standing alone as he walked towards the bar from the beach.

She looked stunning in a tight black dress that hugged every curve on her body. Not much left to the imagination. But Max had a lazy imagination anyway.

"Hello, Max." She smiled and kissed him on the cheek, then sipped a pink concoction through a straw.

He smiled. "Drinking on the job again? You seem much happier than when I last saw you."

"Well, you aren't disobeying me this time. That was some stunt you pulled on the yacht."

"I don't know what you're talking about."

"There is video, Max."

He raised his hands, palms up. "Sometimes you need to break the rules."

"Well, Morozov was furious. But if you can pull this off tonight, we'll have him—and my job will be over, thank God."

"Where is it?" Max asked.

"Up in my room."

She thumbed behind her. Max followed her gaze over to a tall resort hotel. She finished her drink. "Come on. I'll take you up."

The playful look in her eye was not something Max expected. But it was familiar. There were competing voices in his head. The quiet and reasonable voice of a professional intelligence agent, and the loud shout of her dress, clinging to her derrière.

Max felt his phone vibrating in his pocket. He silenced it. "Okay, I'll follow you."

Charlotte held his arm as they walked out the same way Max had come in. Once on the beach, she removed her shoes and strode barefoot on the sand.

"I'm ready to be done with this dreadful assignment. Things were a little rough after your shenanigans in Key West."

"I was wondering if you would suffer any repercussions."

"It wasn't bad. I know how to cover my tracks."

Max felt the phone going off in his pocket again. They stopped outside her hotel. She was wiping off her sandy feet and putting her flats on again before they walked inside.

"I'm sorry," Max said. "I need to make a phone call. Can I meet you up there?"

"I can wait."

"No, really. It's okay. Just tell me the room number."

She gave him the room number, and he held his phone until she was through the door and into the lobby of the hotel. He looked down at his missed calls.

Wilkes.

He turned to make sure no one was around him and called him back. Charlotte was out of sight now.

The phone rang as Max opened the door to the hotel stairway. She was on the fourth floor, but the stairway would give him both privacy and time. He was making his way past the second floor when he finally got an answer.

"Max."

"Wilkes."

"Why haven't you been answering my damn calls?"

"I'm busy. Did you hear from MI-6 and confirm their thumb drive approach?"

He was up onto the third floor now, trying not to sound strained as he took several steps at a time.

"Now listen up, Max. I've got something urgent to tell you. There's a problem."

Fourth floor. He pushed open the door and began walking down the hotel hallway, reading the room numbers as he went.

"What is it?"

Max found her room. Two more doors down. He walked slower, wanting to hear what Wilkes had to say.

"*I just spoke with MI-6.* I replayed everything you told me about Charlotte Capri. It wasn't her, Max."

The door opened.

"What do you mean?"

Charlotte stood there. She smiled, holding a drink in her hand. That same flirtatious look in her eyes. Max could feel his blood pressure rising.

Max had his phone pressed up against his ear.

"*Charlotte Capri was found dead in Key West several days ago.*" Wilkes's voice was frantic.

"Get off the phone and come in." Charlotte smiled.

Max held up his finger. He mouthed to Charlotte, "One minute."

"*Did you hear what I just said?*"

"I'm sorry. Could you say that one more time?" Max said into the phone.

"Charlotte Capri. The MI-6 agent. *Is. Dead*," Wilkes said. "Her body was found by some snorkelers in Key West. MI-6 thinks Morozov found out about her and had her killed. The estimated time of death was several days ago. Right when you were down there."

How was that possible? Max was looking at Charlotte in the flesh.

Max's voice was quiet. "Any thoughts about that?"

Charlotte twirled her hair, her head tilted. Her eyes staring at Max's own. Studying him.

Wilkes's voice whispered through the phone receiver. "Whoever you've been talking to, it *isn't* Charlotte Capri."

18

"Got time for one quick drink before you leave me?" Charlotte said.

Max pressed the end call button on his phone and slid it into his pocket. He smiled. "Sounds lovely."

She closed the door behind him. "Hope you don't mind coming up here?"

She walked across the room. Max's eyes followed her closely.

"Before I forget, here's the thumb drive. The flight is tomorrow, so you'll need to do this tonight."

"Sure thing," Max said, taking it from her hand and placing it in his other pocket.

She approached him, looking into his eyes, and kissed him. Her chest pressed up against his polo shirt. Then she pulled away and said, "I'm excited. I hope you will forgive me being forward. I always get this way near the end of an assignment."

Max didn't react. He hadn't kissed her back. He just stood there like a stone, his heart pounding in his chest. Thinking about what to do next.

Charlotte gripped his arm, her bright red fingernails digging in ever so slightly. "How rude of me. Let me get you a drink."

She walked over to the minibar.

"What's your poison?"

Did she have to use that choice of words?

"Scotch if you've got it."

He cursed himself for not bringing his gun. He hadn't expected to be up here with her, alone.

"So where did you tell our friend you were today?" Max asked.

"Morozov? He lets me do my own thing when we're ashore. For the most part. Do you want ice?"

"Neat, please."

She ducked down into the minibar and brought up a few tiny bottles of scotch whiskey, pouring them into a hotel glass, which she handed to him. "To finishing the job."

They clinked glasses and she took a sip. He refrained. She placed her glass on the table.

"Anything wrong?" she asked.

"Yes, actually. Hopefully you can help me understand something. Morozov tried to kill me in Georgia. But in Key West, he decided to let me live."

"He did?" A change of tone. The first crack in her mask.

"I know that you're not MI-6. So you must be working for him, right? Which means that he had me located in Key West. You could have easily killed me that night when we first met, but you didn't. Why?"

She kept staring into his eyes. Her face lacked expression, even as she pulled a small pistol from the purse next to her and aimed it at Max.

"Who was that on the phone?"

"Are you going to answer my question? Why did

Morozov let me live? You work for him. You must have killed the real Charlotte at some point when I was in Key West."

"I didn't kill her. That was all Pavel. He stabbed her and threw her off the yacht."

Max saw a flicker of distaste as she said it. Maybe he had an opening.

"Why work for a man that would do that?"

She smiled. "Max. Come now. Don't bother trying to drive a wedge between Pavel and me. The bitch deserved it. Pretending to be one of his whores was a stupid idea. Sunbathing with the others all day. Did MI-6 really think that was the best cover? My issue with it was the matter of the location of the body. If I had known he was going to throw her over there, I wouldn't have let him do it. That area was much too close to all the touristy spots. But the girl had to be killed."

The door behind her opened. Two large men, whom Max assumed were part of Morozov's team, entered the hotel room. One of them made a comment to Charlotte in Russian. She said something back in Russian and the man grunted.

The two security men both pointed silenced pistols at Max.

"Max, if you would please come with us," she said. "Mr. Morozov would like a word."

They took the freight elevator down to the ground floor and then walked in an unusually tight grouping out to the parking lot. Max was shoved into the back of the SUV, sandwiched between Charlotte and one of the thugs.

Max had flashbacks to the similar situation he'd been in

with the FBI, only a few days ago. Ah, to be in the custody of the FBI again. The good old days.

"Charlotte—I've got to ask you, just to be clear—I take it that you really weren't interested in me?"

She rubbed his stubbled cheek with her soft hand. "Oh, Max. Maybe in another life, darling."

The thug in the driver's seat eyed him in the rearview mirror.

Max winked back. The man gave him the finger.

"So what's Pavel want to discuss?"

"You'll see when you get there," Charlotte said.

Max watched as the vehicle turned right on Mayport Road, and then veered left onto A1A. He knew the area well, having spent many summers down here in his youth. He used to go surfing near the Naval Station at Mayport. The waves fell just right, and there was a nice point break.

To his right he could see Navy helicopters taking off and landing at the runway on the base. Their car drove past the area where they could view the runway and turned left into a short line of cars. They waited in line for a moment and then drove right up onto the ferry.

"You stay here."

Thug One got out and headed to pay for the ferry across the St. John's River.

Max turned back to Charlotte. "So why the ruse about the thumb drive? And why let me live?"

Charlotte turned to him. "The thumb drive idea wasn't a ruse. It was real. MI-6's idea."

Max frowned. "But why...?"

She petted his knee. "Just be patient, my dear. If Pavel wants to tell you, he will."

Max searched the vehicle for a way out but didn't see one. He could try to overpower Charlotte and the Russian security man right here. It might be his best chance. Before the other goon returned. But truth be told, Max wasn't sure he could take him. The man was a monster. And an alert one. He was staring right at Max, the veins in his neck bulging. No expression. Maybe no brains. Just thick shoulders and arms. This guy was on steroids, no question. If Max tried to fight him in close combat, it would end badly.

There was another reason Max didn't want to try and escape just yet. He wanted to hear what Pavel Morozov might have to say. Max needed to find out what he was up to. But as the ferry began to rumble ahead, Max realized that the Russians likely did not plan to release him.

* * *

Renee looked at Max and cursed. Men could be such *idiots*. That slut shows up wearing a tight dress and he just follows her up to his room. Didn't he realize people were trying to kill him? Why was he so trusting? Max Fend had to be the worst spy in the world.

She took a deep breath. "*Merde.*"

Renee had been in her car in the parking lot outside the Lemon Bar and watched Max and Charlotte leave via the beach exit.

She had wanted to run up into the hotel and start beating the hell out of both of them. Max was hers. Maybe he didn't realize that yet, but she would tell him. Hell hath no fury like a French Canadian whose man was being seduced away by another woman.

A few minutes later, when Renee saw the two large men accompanying Max and Charlotte back out to the lit parking lot, she was glad she had remained in the car. It was no seduction. She realized that something was terribly wrong.

Now the SUV was several vehicles ahead, driving onto the ferry. Renee needed to decide whether she should risk getting on the same ferry. If she did, they might spot her. The question was whether the men who had apprehended Max would know who she was. Were they the same men who'd manhandled her on Morozov's yacht?

It wasn't a choice. If she didn't drive onto the ferry, she would lose them.

Renee pulled her hoodie over her head. It was dark out. Hopefully they wouldn't be able to see her. One of the Russians got out of the driver's seat of their SUV to pay for the ferry passage. Renee didn't get out of her car to pay. She waited for the man collecting the fees to come to her, and she rolled down her window.

It took about ten minutes before all the cars were on board and the ramp was raised, and another five minutes for the ferry to cross the St. John's River. Renee kept her head down the entire time, pretending to be lost in her phone. Praying for a solution.

* * *

Pavel Morozov was finishing up his round of golf with the counselor to the Russian ambassador to the United States. That was his official title. Unofficially, he was the head of the FSB in Washington. The Federal Security Service was the successor to the KGB.

They were playing at the Amelia Island Golf Club. Pavel noted that while his partner was old and out of shape, he still swung a mean iron.

"Vasily, I think your golf game has improved over the years."

"The Americans love to play this game. Who am I to disagree? I find that playing with them helps with the job." He walked over to the golf cart and removed his putter. Morozov was already on the green, taking a practice swing with his own putter.

One of Morozov's security guards approached and whispered something to him. He nodded and waved the man off. Then he sunk his putt. A five-footer, which drifted from right to left. Morozov watched Vasily take three putts on the green before he was able to get his ball in the cup.

"Well done, Vasily."

"Ah. I may not be the young man I once was, but at least we can enjoy the fresh air."

Fresh wouldn't be the way Morozov would describe it. The air was thick and humid. Much warmer than he preferred.

"Let us go enjoy a few drinks. Have you stayed at this Ritz-Carlton before? I've had them send up a bar directly to the suite. They do a nice job," Morozov said. "I hear that all the Americans are drinking Moscow mules these days. It seems that our country has finally succeeded in influencing the West."

Vasily laughed heartily. The two men rode their golf carts to the exit. One of Morozov's assistants took care of returning everything. Another assistant showed the two Russian men to their car. In a few moments, they were sitting at an outdoor patio table, situated on a private balcony.

The hotel had laid out the finest spread of appetizers. A private bartender prepared cocktails for both men. Morozov's regular harem of imported women were already enjoying their drinks. Two of them began making their way over to Morozov and the FSB man, but Morozov waved them off.

"In a few moments, ladies. We need to speak alone."

Vasily looked at the women and said, "Now that is something the Americans I do business with don't often provide. Are they Russian?"

"I source my talent from all over the globe," Morozov replied. "But to be honest, I can't remember where these two are from."

The two Russian men sipped their drinks. Vasily was admiring the ocean view. The sky was getting dark, but it was still peaceful. Morozov didn't pay the view any attention. He was focused on Vasily.

"When will they arrive?" Morozov asked.

"Tomorrow. Midmorning, Eastern time."

"Flying into Washington, D.C?"

"Yes." Vasily paused. "How will you—"

Morozov clicked his tongue, shaking his head. "This we cannot discuss. But suffice it to say that we have very good targeting information on his plane."

Vasily flushed.

Morozov took a deep breath. "I can see that you are uncomfortable with this."

"If it goes wrong, Pavel..."

"I know."

"*He* is not a man to be trifled with," Vasily whispered.

Morozov's face darkened. "Neither am I."

"And what of the Fend boy? Is he still out on the loose? I told you that I wouldn't give my approval unless he was taken care of."

"He's on his way."

"What? You're bringing him here? Is that wise?"

"You wanted confirmation. I'm giving it to you."

* * *

Max was escorted into a luxury hotel on the coast. He was guessing it was Amelia Island, based on the time it had taken them to get here.

The Russian henchmen led Max to a small hotel room and sat him on a couch. The Ritz-Carlton. Max saw the words on one of the cupholders. The two Russian guards sat on the beds, watching bad TV. Every few seconds, they would look at him. Charlotte—or whatever her name was—had left them when they came in.

They remained in the room for several hours. Max attempted small talk a few times. If the Russians understood English, they feigned a lack of understanding quite well.

Charlotte came in after midnight. "He's ready for him." The guards shoved Max out the door and down the hallway.

Pavel Morozov was waiting for him with another man. Two women in cocktail dresses were draped over them. Seeing Max, Morozov sent the two women away.

Morozov looked at Max Fend. "It's good to finally meet you, Max. I hope your father is well. Did he tell you about our special relationship? About how he worked for me?"

"He didn't work for you."

Morozov smiled. "Is that what he told you? Let me guess. He told you that the CIA was controlling him. That it was all part of a ploy to feed me false information. The almighty American intelligence agency—the saviors of the Cold War. Are those the lies that he told you?"

Max didn't say anything. Charlotte stood in back of them over a rolling bar. She plucked an olive with a toothpick and began chewing it, watching Max. The older man next to Morozov sat quietly in his chair.

"Your father was a traitor to his country," Morozov said. "The only reason he switched sides was because he wanted to save his own skin. He got caught. He was bad at it. He didn't follow the proper precautions like I had taught him. Once the CIA and FBI knew that they could use him, your father cut a deal with them. Before that, I had been giving him everything. His aerospace company would not have been nearly as successful without the documents that I provided him."

"Come on, Pavel. We both know that the Russians stole everything from the US military back then. Not the other way around."

Morozov smiled. "Tsk-tsk. Revisionist history. Of course that is what the American textbooks say. But the truth is malleable. And the CIA, along with your own press, has changed the story of what really happened at the end of the Cold War. Your father wasn't a hero, Max. He was a traitor. And he was responsible for your mother's death."

Max's face reddened.

"He probably told you that it was me, right? *Of course.* Then why didn't he ever come after me? Hmm? Why didn't he go to the authorities? That is what any reasonable person would have done. What any *real* man would have done. But your father? He kept quiet. He covered it up, along with the CIA. Ask yourself—why?"

Max clenched his fists but stayed silent.

Pavel smirked. "The real reason your mother died? Because your father betrayed me. He knew the penalty for crossing me. And he didn't care. Your father only wanted to protect his baby. Not you, Max. His precious Fend Aerospace. That was what he really cared about. He was willing to sacrifice anything to grow that business. Even your mother."

He spoke with conviction. Like he'd had years of practice manipulating others. He had, Max reminded himself. As a KGB operative during the Cold War, Morozov's two main jobs had been to squeeze information out of people, and to insert false information.

Max couldn't play the game anymore. He couldn't stomach it. "You're a sad little man," he said.

"Nothing hurts like the truth. I don't need you to believe me. I have gotten you and your father to do exactly what I want. Now it's just a matter of executing."

"So you're still planning on stealing the Fend 100 technology? Are you an imbecile, Pavel? Everyone knows what you're planning. It's not going to happen. There are probably US law enforcement officers listening to us right now."

"I doubt it. They think I'm on my yacht, which is docked south of St. Augustine, quite a ways from here."

"How do you know what law enforcement believes?"

"The information is all out there, if you know the right people." Pavel turned to the older man sitting next to him. "Enough of this. Vasily, are you satisfied? You heard him, correct? He said *steal* the technology. That is what they think I am going to do. May I dispose of him now?"

The old man studied Max and nodded. "*Da.*"

Pavel made a whistling noise and gestured to his security guards.

"*Wait,*" Max said. His mind was racing. Pavel and this other Russian were planning something else. They didn't intend to steal the Fend 100 technology. "You let me live because you wanted to mislead MI-6? The CIA?"

Morozov smirked. "And you just confirmed that we were successful."

The guards stood over him now. "But you must have intended for me to upload your software into the Fend 100 with the thumb drive. If you're going to kill me, then how are you planning to access the Fend data?"

Pavel Morozov's expression darkened. "Now, Max, there's no reason for you to know that."

"You're pathetic. My father beat you at your own game back during the Cold War. He humiliated you. He let you provide false information to the USSR on his defense projects. And you believed him, you Commie bastard. Now you're trying to get revenge on him by sabotaging his company. They know what you're doing, Pavel. No wonder the Soviet Union collapsed. It was filled with morons like you."

Pavel looked at Charlotte. "Miss Capri?"

"Yes?"

"I am ready for you to take our guest away."

"Very well."

Pavel breathed in deeply and exhaled. "Max, I bid you farewell. Rest assured that your death and subsequent blame for what happens tomorrow will allow you to live on in infamy."

Morozov nodded to his security men, and they grabbed his arms.

Max struggled against the guard's grip. He needed to create options. He kept trying to dig. He wanted Morozov to get emotional and slip up. To give him some tidbit of information that he might find useful.

"You're walking into a trap, Morozov."

Pavel smiled, but didn't say anything.

"This is reckless, even for you. Revenge on my father isn't worth spending your life in an American prison. Think about that. They'll know what you did. They'll know you killed me." Max didn't see any reaction from Morozov.

The men began dragging him away. "You think this will make you feel better about losing the Cold War for your country? This won't change anything for you. You'll still be just another stooge for your president."

At that, Morozov's face went red, and he held up his hand. "Wait."

Morozov walked over to Max. The guards held him tight. Pavel shot a leathery hand out and seized Max by the jaw.

"Say that again."

Max tried to seem as insolent as possible as he choked out his words, staring down Morozov. "That's right, Pavel. There's only one leader in Russia, and it ain't you."

Morozov nodded slowly. "Okay."

He let out a weird snort. Then he unleashed a furious blow into Max's stomach. His eyes nearly burst out of their sockets, and all the air shot from his lungs. The pain was excruciating. Max couldn't breathe.

Pavel whispered in his ear as Max's mouth remained open, empty gasps trying to suck in air.

"I know that I may be vain, young man. But I am not stupid. And you don't have enough respect for me, or where I came from. Yes, the Soviet Union collapsed. But *I didn't*. My people are everywhere. My plans are often years in the making. For this operation, you were just my personal cherry on top, as they say. But I'm happy to exclude you if it means that everything else will flow smoothly. Tomorrow your father's life's work will be destroyed, and you'll take the fall. But a man like me wouldn't go through all this trouble *just* to exact revenge upon your father. I have a much grander vision than that."

Destroyed?

Max's thoughts were a swirl of activity. The way Morozov was talking—it didn't fit with what they knew. Something was wrong, and it was staring him in the face.

They started to drag Max away, and then it clicked. Max's eyes widened. He finally knew what they were really up to. Holy shit. *Of course...*

"You aren't trying to steal the data at all, are you, Pavel? That was just a ploy..."

Vasily looked uncomfortable. "*Pavel.*"

Morozov waved him off. "Relax. He'll be dead soon."

"It won't work. We know who your insider is."

Morozov scoffed. "Who, then?"

Max thought about guessing, but in truth, he hadn't a clue.

A wide smile formed on Morozov's face. "The desperate words of a condemned man, I think."

Then he said something in Russian to his men, and they took Max away.

19

Renee had seen the Russians' SUV pull into the parking lot of the Amelia Island Ritz-Carlton. Renee had parked about one hundred yards away, near the resort's tennis courts. There were lots of cars. She was pretty sure she wasn't noticed.

Renee had seen the Russians leave their SUV in the parking lot and walk with Max into the hotel. She'd thought about calling the police. But Max had specifically forbidden that. He couldn't have foreseen this circumstance, however. She had to get help somehow. Why hadn't she gotten Wilkes's number from Max?

Calm down. Give Max some time. Maybe he had gone here on purpose. Maybe this was part of some plan. He would be okay. He did this for a living. Right?

She needed a weapon. If she went fast and came back here, she could be ready for when Max reappeared.

Five minutes later, Renee walked into a local sporting goods store and scanned the rows for what she needed. Football. Golf. Pool equipment. *There.*

Hunting and fishing.

The department was back of the store. Renee practically ran there. An overweight man in his early twenties stood behind the counter. He wore a red shirt with the words "Go Dawgs" on the front, a toothpick in his mouth.

"Can I help you, ma'am?"

She tried to act normal. Behind him, rifles and bows lined the wall. Under the glass counter he was leaning on were dozens of models of handguns.

"I need a weapon."

The man stared back at her. "Mmm. Okay. Well, it appears that you've come to the right place."

"It's for self-defense. But I prefer not to use a gun."

The man eyed her. "Right. We've got this little sucker over here. Ain't had nobody interested in it before. But there's always a first, I guess."

"What is it?"

"It's kind of like a paintball gun. But these little plastic balls are made special. They're filled with some sort of pepper spray mix that stings the eyes something awful. Blinds you for a few seconds and then you just go down until you can wash it out. Never tried it myself, but—"

"I'll take it."

The store clerk looked at her. "You alright, miss? You sound like you're in some trouble."

"I'm fine. Just in a hurry. Can I pay here?"

"Sure."

"Do you have flashlights?"

"Yes, ma'am. Right over there."

"Good. And one more thing...do you have any field hockey sticks?"

She paid and hustled to her car, then drove back to where she had seen the Russians park their SUV. She waited in the parking lot of the Amelia Island Ritz-Carlton for several hours. As the night went on, she drove herself insane wondering if she hadn't made a mistake. What if he was already gone? What if they had killed him?

All she had to hold on to was the car they had arrived in. She watched it to see if Max would reappear.

* * *

Max was once again in the backseat of the Russians' SUV. They drove south along A1A, back the way they came. It was dark now, and no one spoke. Max could hear the rhythmic thumping of the tires against the slabs of highway.

They turned left off the highway and onto a single-lane road, driving deeper into the darkness. The headlights briefly illuminated a sign for Little Talbot Island State Park. Palms and swampy trees hugged both sides of the road.

Max tried to remain calm, but his mind was racing with what he had just learned. Morozov wasn't trying to just steal the Fend 100 technology. He was trying to do something far worse. And he was going to blame it on Max somehow. Maybe that's why he had decided to let him live, when they could have killed him in Key West.

No. It was more than that.

They had misled Max and used him to feed bad information to...who? To Wilkes? To his father? What was the bad information he had given them?

The thumb drive solution? Max had told them of MI-6's plan to defend against another one of Morozov's cyber-attacks.

But Wilkes and the people at Fend Aerospace weren't even going to use that now. They had a backup plan in Maria. None of this made any sense...

Max needed to get out of here and warn them. They couldn't let the Fend 100 get airborne.

He examined his driving companions. Two large Russian men. Ex-special forces, likely. Both armed and deadly. Driving along a deserted street at night. Max would only have one chance. He would have to make it count.

The car came to a halt in a large open parking lot. Max thought he could make out a few other cars there, on the other side of the lot. But it was hard to tell in the darkness.

The Russians were talking to each other, but they were speaking in their native tongue. Max couldn't understand a word. The one in the backseat kept his weapon out, pointing it at Max. The one in the driver's seat got out and walked around to Max's door, opening it. The man sitting next to Max in the backseat started pushing him forward, weapon trained on Max's back.

Max had been hoping to have an opportunity to take on just one of them at a time during the transition out of the vehicle. But they had obviously done this before. He would wait. Maybe try falling in the sand and...

"This way," Thug One said, pointing with his silenced pistol.

They marched him along the dunes, parallel to the beach. It was slow going, their feet sinking into the sand. Lots of brush. Crabs scattering as they trudged through.

Waves crashed on his left side. Slow rhythmic bursts of white noise. Max made calculations in his head. They were getting farther from the parking lot. It was now or never. He gave himself about a ten percent chance.

Someone called out from behind them.

"Hey! Excuse me?" came the female voice. "Can you help me out?" A flashlight cut through the night behind them, shining on the sand and illuminating the ground between the Russians and a woman walking towards them.

The men said something to each other in Russian. Max imagined that they were wondering whether Morozov would get mad if they killed her too.

The flashlight changed direction and reflected the body of the woman approaching them. Her white shirt was unbuttoned and wide open, revealing a bright-pink-and-white bikini top and tight jean shorts. Seeing that, one of the Russians whispered something to the other, which was followed by snickering.

The way the light was pointed, her face wasn't visible. One of the Russians grumbled to Max, "You stay quiet or we shoot you both right here."

He didn't reply.

The flashlight moved erratically, shining towards them and then back towards the woman. Both Russians clumsily hid their weapons from the woman behind their legs. If she was looking carefully, she would probably notice.

"I'm so sorry," the woman said, "I'm lost. Would you gentlemen be able to help me find..." Max recognized the voice.

The light flashed back in their eyes. Max and the two Russians instinctively winced. What they didn't realize was that the flashlight was connected just under the barrel of Renee's pepper spray gun.

It had the look and feel of a large plastic 9mm Beretta, but it fired paintball-type rounds, filled with a combination of tear gas and pepper spray.

Renee fired multiple times into both of the Russians' chests and faces. Quick clicks and pops, and the sound of high-speed plastic pellets bursting into the muscle-bound men.

Renee then turned out the light and ran towards them. She dropped the pepper spray gun and gripped the field hockey stick, which she had been holding under her left armpit.

She headed towards the sound of Russian cries and cursing. Renee had made the field hockey team at Princeton University many years ago for her athleticism and speed. But once there, she had been known for the power of her shot.

Renee's vision was barely adjusted to the low light level, but it was enough. She bent her knees as she approached, twisted her hips for maximum velocity, and drove the heavy wooden stick forward and up into the head of the first Russian.

The crack she heard was at once frightening and satisfying. The man collapsed into the sand. Renee tried not to think about whether she might have killed him. She just moved on.

But during the swing, she had become disoriented. When she looked up, she was no longer sure which of the dark figures before her was the other Russian.

All three of them had been pelted by the pepper spray bullets, she realized. Unsure of what to do, she looked back to where she had dropped the pepper spray gun. There. She snatched it up from the ground and listened, trying to discern who was who.

* * *

Max, blinded and in pain from just being near the pepper spray bursts, ran away toward the beach. He tripped several times, falling into the sand and beach grass.

"Max!" Renee shouted as loudly as she dared.

Max felt his feet enter the surf. He knelt down and splashed saltwater up into his face. It helped. The pain subsided as he kept washing the saltwater in and around his eyes.

"Max." He could feel her holding on to his shoulder. "Are you alright?"

"What the hell was that stuff?"

"It's a self-defense gun. Pepper spray and mace."

"God, it stings. Why didn't you bring a real gun?"

"I don't like guns. I told you."

"Holy shit, Renee. This hurts. Next time just shoot me with a real gun."

"Men are so ungrateful."

Max squinted up at the dunes. Between his blurred vision and how dark it was outside, he could barely see a thing. "Where are they?"

"They're still up there, but I hit one pretty hard with this field hockey stick," Renee said. "Here. Hold the stick and come on. We should get to my car before they make it back to the parking lot."

"I'm not sure that's such a good idea. Look."

A set of headlights was visible in the parking lot. Renee cursed.

"You think it's more of them?" Over the sound of the waves, they could hear car doors opening and closing. Anxious shouting in Russian.

"Come on. We're not going to be able to go back to your car. Let's jog. This way."

They ran away from the parking lot, south along the beach. It took about five minutes for the Russians to get smart and start driving along the beach in their SUVs. With the headlights on, it was easy for Max and Renee to see them coming. But that also meant that there weren't many good hiding places.

"It's into the brush or into the water, which one?"

Renee said, "I…"

"Water, then." Max pulled her arm. They waded into the ocean. The waves were only a foot or two. When they got neck-deep, Max began to second-guess his choice of hiding in the water. He wondered if they would have night vision. Or infrared. Dammit.

They were pretty far out. "Alright, let's hold our breath and try to stay under for a bit, until they drive by."

Both Max and Renee took a deep breath and went under. Thank God the sea was warm. Max hated cold water. He went up for air about thirty seconds later, and then went back down underneath. He had gotten a glimpse of the SUV, motoring along the beach at five miles per hour.

Max tried to think about their options. A1A was the main highway that ran north-south, parallel to the beach. Anyone with common sense would have headed for the road. But the Russians would know that. So they would keep one team at the beach, searching for him, the other team patrolling the road, waiting for Max and Renee to pop up.

When they came up for air again, he said to Renee, "I say we keep heading south along the beach. It'll be a few miles, but we'll get to the end of Talbot Island. Then we can swim across the inlet. We'll end up at Huguenot Park, right across from Mayport."

"Then what?"

"Then we'll be far enough away from them that we can go try and find a ride," Max said.

"How far is that?"

"A few miles."

"It sounds like it's going to take us all night. It's already three a.m. The Fend 100 flight launches at seven. Do you have a phone?"

"Of course not. Don't you?"

"I'm sorry—I needed to carry a few things to *rescue you*."

They waded back towards the beach and walked along the shore. She was right. This was going to take all night. But he didn't see what choice he had.

*   *   *

Flynn was in his hotel room, fielding calls from Washington and scanning the news about the Fend 100. Many aviation news sources were calling it the dawn of a new era in automated flight.

But the big story that most people cared about was the human element. The *Washington Post* was the first to the punch. They had a source saying that Max Fend was under investigation for a cyberattack on Fend Aerospace. The news channels had fallen all over themselves when they'd heard about it. Even Flynn had to admit that it was a great story. On the eve of one of the biggest moments in aviation history, Max Fend attempts to sabotage his own father's achievement.

The FBI sent out a press release shortly after. Now, they were talking just as much about him, but proclaiming his newfound innocence.

BILLIONAIRE PLAYBOY NOT A SUSPECT, SAYS FEDS

Wonderful. Flynn was reading one such article when he heard the knock at his door.

He looked through the peephole and saw Wilkes staring back at him, still wearing a suit and tie. Flynn checked his watch. It was close to midnight.

Flynn removed the chain. "Come on in."

"Sorry to disturb you, but I thought you'd want me to fill you in."

"Of course. Excuse the clutter." Flynn tried to clean up the remnants of his room service. A twenty-three-dollar burger and fries. Pretty good, but you could get a lot better at Five Guys for a lot less.

The two men sat down. "What's up?" said Flynn.

"We have a problem. Max Fend has gone missing."

"Missing?"

"I told you he might be in contact with a foreign agent," Wilkes said.

"Yes."

"Well, he made contact earlier this evening, and now he's off the grid. I'm worried. I may need your help."

"What did you have in mind?"

"I need backup plans in case this thing goes sideways," Wilkes said. "I think the FBI might be best equipped to respond."

"Caleb, just say what you need."

"How soon could you get HRT down here?"

* * *

The FBI's Hostage Rescue Team is one of the premier counterterrorism units in the world. Made up mostly of ex-special operations personnel, they function as the elite national tactical response unit for the FBI. Based in Quantico, Virginia, HRT has over one hundred operators assigned to its team.

HRT operators conduct training with many of the other Tier One special forces units in the United States military, including the Army's Delta Force and the Navy's DEVGRU —commonly known as SEAL Team Six.

HRT trains in maritime and airborne assault techniques, and also has its own sniper teams and regularly responds to the most dangerous incidents around the world.

Because they need to be ready to go at a moment's notice, HRT always rotates its members on a deployable watch bill. They are required to be on base and ready to deploy within thirty minutes of being called.

Twenty of them got the call tonight.

Within an hour, all twenty men were on a plane to Florida. An hour after that, two US Air Force transport aircraft flew to the same destination. Those aircraft contained members and equipment of the Tactical Helicopter Unit. These were the HRT's elite aviators. Helicopter pilots and aircrew who trained and operated with the HRT and were ready for anything.

Before takeoff, the group's leader made the call to Jake Flynn. "We're headed to Naval Air Station Jacksonville. Where do you want us after that?"

"Have your aircrews set up shop there. The Jacksonville SAC will send vehicles for your team as soon as you arrive. We'll bring you to where we need you."

"Roger. We'll be there in a few hours. I'll call you back in a few minutes. We'll need you to brief us on the plane so that we can mission-plan on the way down."

* * *

Max and Renee had switched from wading along in the

water to trudging along through the beach grass, up on the small dunes.

"I should probably say thanks for coming to rescue me," Max said.

"Hmm. Now you say it." She punched his arm.

"How were you able to find me?"

"I followed you after you left the Lemon Bar. With Charlotte Capri."

"That's not her real name, you know. The woman I met with was an impostor. Working for Morozov. Wilkes called me and warned me about it."

"You're kidding." Renee was shaking her head. "But I don't understand. They tried to kill you in Georgia, then this impostor meets with you in Key West and lets you go. Now they're trying to kill you again? Why do they keep changing their minds?"

"I'm their scapegoat. They aren't just trying to hack into the Fend system to steal the technology."

"*What?*"

Max told her about what he had learned, and what he thought Morozov was planning.

"If I'm dead or in captivity, I can't screw up their plans."

"But why leave you alive in Key West?"

"That must have been when they found out about MI-6's agent. The real Charlotte. By leaving me alive, thinking I had met Charlotte, I helped Morozov deceive someone."

"Who?"

"I don't know exactly. MI-6. The CIA. Both? But whoever it was, it worked."

"How do you know?"

"Morozov told me as much. And now he's decided to kill me again. So I've served my purpose."

"But why bring you up to Amelia Island to see Morozov?

They could have just shot you in the hotel in Jacksonville, right?"

Max shook his head. "That's one thing I'm still trying to figure out. There was another man there with Morozov. What name did he use...? Vasily, I believe."

"Vasily? I met a Vasily. An older Russian man?"

"Yes."

"When I was on the yacht, I spoke to him. Morozov came over and interrupted, and they began talking."

"What did they say?"

"I don't know. They were speaking in Russian, and I left."

Max frowned. "Morozov wanted him to see me. He said something like 'Now are you satisfied?' to Vasily. But why? Why would seeing me alive mean anything to Vasily?"

"Maybe it wasn't seeing you alive. Maybe it was knowing that you would be dead..."

Their eyes met, and they kept walking.

A bright white moon began to rise over the ocean horizon. Max thought how pretty it was, and how much he would enjoy this night, were he not also watching the headlights about two miles down the beach. Headlights that were searching for him so they could put a bullet in his head.

Renee shook her head. "Why does he want you dead so bad?"

"I told you, I'm his scapegoat for what he's planning."

"No, I mean, why you? Why couldn't he make someone else the scapegoat? It would be more believable."

"He hates my father, and he's responsible for my mother's death."

Renee gasped. "So it's all about revenge, then?"

"I think that's why I'm involved. But now I'm not so sure revenge is his only objective."

"What do you mean?"

"I was trying to dig at him. To get him emotional and see what he would say. He made one comment that stuck with me. I said something about revenge, and he responded that his plans are much grander than that. Something to that effect."

"What if he's trying to mislead you again?"

"That's possible. Never trust an ex-KGB agent. That's always been my motto. Well, that and never fall off a barstool."

"Both good pieces of advice."

"Here comes the truck again. Better get down." They lay flat against the sand, hiding behind a large clump of grass.

While they were waiting, Max whispered, "I'll tell you another thing that bothers me. He's too confident. Like he knows he won't be caught."

"You told me the FBI thinks he has someone on the inside."

"Yes, but wouldn't you still be worried if you were him? It's pretty ballsy of him to be here in America."

Max thought about the cryptic way Morozov had said it. *My people are everywhere. My plans are often years in the making.*

The SUV rumbled slowly past them. Only fifty feet away.

Then it stopped. Brakes squealing.

The lights went out, and the doors opened. Two men got out from either side. The doors slammed shut.

Max could make out a faint green glow near their heads. Night vision goggles.

* * *

Flynn hung up the phone and looked at Wilkes. It was

almost 3 a.m. now, and he was still in his room. They had ordered coffee and set up shop. There would be little sleep tonight.

"HRT is on the way to Jacksonville now. I've finished briefing them, and they'll be doing scenario planning the whole way down. The Jacksonville SAC will meet us at the Fend Aerospace headquarters tomorrow. Are you sure we shouldn't just call this thing off?"

Wilkes shook his head. "We can't. I need Morozov to make his move tomorrow. It'll allow us to snare him and his agent working for Fend."

"Okay. We'll get the HRT team ready to go in with an air assault on his yacht when ready."

"Let's walk through what we think will happen tomorrow," Wilkes said. "The Fend 100 will take off at seven a.m. It's roughly a three-hour flight. They do a bunch of circles over Florida and then land back at the Fend Aerospace headquarters near Jacksonville."

"I'm with you so far."

"Morozov will, at some point, initiate a cyberattack on the Fend 100. That electronic signal is expected to come from the yacht. I have a team of experts at the NSA who are ready and waiting for that electronic signal. Once it occurs, we'll have what we need. The HRT team can then move in and take control of the ship. We have surveillance teams that will be monitoring communications from our suspects within Fend Aerospace."

"You still think its Karpinsky or Hutson?"

"Honestly? I don't know. But we'll be watching them both closely."

"We'll need a cyber expert on the yacht."

"I got a guy who'll be here," Flynn said. "HRT can take

him when they go assault the yacht. If there are any problems with the aircraft link, he'll solve them."

"What about Charles Fend's employee that he's got on the plane—what's her name?"

Flynn said, "Maria Blount. She's plan A now. Once we get the signal that Morozov's hackers are trying to steal the Fend 100 data, she'll be able to shut them down."

"Good. Without Max Fend, we'll need to rely on her."

"Is Max going to show back up before the Fend 100 gets airborne?"

"I hope so."

* * *

Max watched one of the Russians head their way, scanning the beach with his night vision goggles in a side-to-side sweeping motion. The other Russian was doing the same thing, but walking along the beach in the opposite direction. The moonlight would make his night vision much more effective. And the moon was rising.

Max touched Renee's hand. Then he made his fingers into a gun. She gave a barely perceptible nod. She carefully raised the pepper spray gun. Max still held her field hockey stick. What he wouldn't give for his Sig right now.

The Russian security man was only a few steps away now. Renee raised her plastic pepper spray gun and fired. Three pops in the night air.

The plastic pellets filled with caustic gas burst after impacting his chest. The Russian screamed in pain as the gas hit his eyes, then swore loudly. Max was already sprinting forward. He tackled the big Russian by jamming his shoulder into his chest, knocking him off of his feet and into the sand. The Russian crouched on the ground, trying to regain his balance while holding on to his weapon. Max chopped down with the field hockey stick, knocking the gun out of the man's hands. He then wound up and slammed the stick into the Russian's face as hard as he could. Lights out. The night vision goggles shattered, and his neck snapped back. He fell limp to the ground, unconscious.

Max heard the other Russian security man calling out from fifty feet away. Renee was now standing next to Max.

Max frantically searched around in the sand for the Russian's fallen pistol. It was so dark he could barely see. He felt among the clumps of sand and grass, desperate to find the weapon.

There.

He clutched it in his hands. Cold metal, his fingers fitting neatly around the grip and trigger. He kneeled down and aimed at the Russian, who was running towards them.

Max fired three times.

At least one of the rounds must have found its mark, because the man spun around and fell to the ground.

"Come on!" Max called back to Renee as he headed for the empty SUV. He pressed the keyless start button, but nothing happened. He cursed and turned back to Renee.

"Check their pockets for a key fob," Max said to Renee.

She ran to the unconscious man, found the keyless remote, and headed back towards the SUV.

Headlights lit up the dunes in the distance.

"That's the other set of Morozov's security men. It's got to be. These guys must have radioed them."

"Hurry, then."

Max pressed the ignition button and the engine rumbled to life. He cursed as the headlights came on automatically, alerting the incoming vehicle to their presence. The headlights also illuminated the second Russian, the one who'd been spun around when Max had shot him. He was still on the ground, but now he was sitting up, aiming his weapon at Max and Renee from thirty feet away.

The windshield of their vehicle filled with holes as a barrage of bullets whizzed through the glass.

Max instinctively crouched down, put the SUV in drive, and slammed on the gas, turning the wheel hard left. The vehicle accelerated to near fifty miles per hour, moving through the beach sand.

Glancing up in the rearview mirror, Max saw that the other vehicle had stopped to pick up the wounded Russians.

"Where are you going?"

"If we keep following the beach, I think it connects with the road again."

"I thought this was an island."

He glanced at her. "Why do women have to question everything?"

She muttered something in French.

"You know I spent several years in France, right? I know the word for stupid."

Renee began playing with the car's center display.

"What are you doing?"

"Checking the GPS. I want to see if I can find out where they've been."

Smart, Max thought.

In the rearview mirror, Max could see the other SUV catching up now, its headlights springing up and down as it raced over the mounds of sand. The beach ended just ahead. But as he suspected, the road met with the beach at that point.

"I'm going to turn over the dunes and try to make it to the road. Once we get there, we can try and outrun them or get to a police station. They wouldn't risk making a scene there...I don't think."

Their SUV launched itself over the dunes, bouncing hard against the suspension. Renee yelped as they went.

"They're gaining on us," she said.

As they reached the road, Max accelerated and turned hard left onto the pavement.

Loud metallic bangs emanated from the rear of the vehicle, and both Max and Renee ducked. *Gunshots.*

They heard a huge pop as one of the tires burst. Streetlights lit up the road as Max held his foot down on the accelerator and they began crossing the bridge. Bright white light revealed dozens of bullet holes throughout the vehicle. Their vehicle was slumping to one side, and the flat tire was making rhythmic slapping noises as they drove.

"What's that? Someone's at the other end of the bridge —*who is that*?"

Max saw it too. There was a sedan parked across both lanes of traffic near the end of the bridge they were trying to cross.

In front of the sedan stood a woman. She was aiming a large semiautomatic rifle at them.

"I think that's *Charlotte.*"

Max looked in his rearview mirror at the SUV behind them, which was just coming onto the bridge.

"You need to ram her or go around her," Renee said.

"There doesn't look to be enough room to get around her," Max said. "And if we ram her, they'll catch up." He glanced outside, trying to see where they were. Darkness lay on either side of the bridge. Nothing but a small bay.

"You're a good swimmer, right?"

"I'm sorry?" She sounded afraid.

"Okay, lower your window and hold on. This is probably going to hurt."

He swerved hard left and the tires slammed into the short concrete barrier. At the speed they were traveling, the barrier served as a ramp. The SUV left the ground and launched over the metal bridge rail. Max and Renee went weightless as they fell, the engine's RPMs spooling up without the resistance of the road.

The front of the vehicle impacted the water, and both of them were jolted forward, their seat belts restraining them. The airbags burst open on impact, pounding them both in the face, but minimizing the whiplash.

The vehicle began sinking into the shallow inlet. Max and Renee had lowered their windows several inches before he'd made the jump. The SUV began to fill with rushing water.

The water rose above their heads and they sank, fast and quiet. The vehicle hit the seafloor seconds later, at a depth of about fifteen feet.

Max and Renee both unstrapped and swam out and away from the bridge. They were disoriented, but still aware enough to stay underwater as long as possible. After about fifty feet of swimming, Renee tapped Max on the back and signaled that she needed to come up for air.

They broke the surface, for just a moment, gasping for air as quietly as they could, and then went back under, continuing to swim away from the crash scene. Max had taken a snapshot of the bridge in his mind.

Charlotte had been standing near the edge of the bridge, where they had broken through the barrier. She was looking down at the wreckage. The Russian security team was in their SUV behind her.

His instincts told him that Charlotte hadn't seen them.

The streetlights shined bright white light onto the bridge, and the water was quite dark.

Max and Renee continued to swim underwater, both doing a sort of submarine breaststroke. Max's shoes and clothes were slowing him down, but he didn't want to take the time to remove them. Renee was indeed a good swimmer. She was keeping up with him no problem. She tapped him on the back again, and they came up for air.

Now they were substantially closer to an uninhabited section of shoreline. In the darkness, it looked like nothing more than a large sandbar with a swath of beach grass on top. They were far enough away from the Russians that they were treading water now, slowly sidestroking their way towards the shore.

"Do you think they saw us?" Renee panted.

"They would have fired at us if they did. It looks like they're leaving now. They probably don't want to be around when the police come to investigate the crash."

He felt his toes scrape the slimy bottom of the bay. "We can stand."

They swam a little further and soon enough both of them were wading, then walking along the beach, their clothes heavy and drenched with seawater.

"Where are we?"

"I'm not sure. I think we're on the opposite side of Mayport."

Max checked his watch. It was almost 6 a.m. The eastern horizon was starting to lighten up. The Fend 100 was scheduled to take off in less than an hour.

"We need to hurry."

20

The morning had not yet risen over the Atlantic horizon, but the sky was already a fiery red over the shore. The day had arrived. Charles Fend had not slept much. Partly due to his age—sleep was getting harder to come by—and partly due to his anxiety over the day's events.

His personal assistant and chef were waiting in the kitchen. The news played on a small TV in the corner.

"Sir, can we get you anything?"

"Earl Grey tea, please. And perhaps a grapefruit."

"Right away, Mr. Fend," the chef said.

His assistant had laid out the usual clippings and daily schedule on Charles's outdoor table, where he liked to eat during the nicer weather. Small metal weights in the shape of Fend airplanes rested on top of the paper stacks so that an errant sea breeze wouldn't blow them away.

His assistant had tried to convince Charles to switch to an iPad or some other electronic device to get his morning briefing, but Charles couldn't do it. He liked the feel of paper. It was real. And it wasn't trying to sell him something half the bloody time. Well...it wasn't trying to sell him *products*, anyway. Just ideas.

He ate his grapefruit and sipped his tea, reading over the news clippings that mentioned him and his company. There were quite a lot of them today. The kinder headlines hailed him as a champion in technology and aviation progress. The less friendly news stories were all gossip about his son. One of them showed a picture of Max with women in lingerie, dancing at his French villa.

Charles wondered how much of that was real and how much of it had been for show. Now that he knew Max had been working undercover for the DIA in France, things made much more sense. These wild parties didn't fit with the son he knew. Max was too driven to get caught up in that nonsense.

"Have I any messages?"

"Dozens, sir."

"Any from a Caleb Wilkes? Or from Max?"

Charles knew that his assistant wouldn't have simply taken a message if Max had called, but he asked anyway. The assistant was a loyal man, but Charles had yet to tell him everything about Max. And he had no doubt seen all the headlines. He would naturally be curious. It was even possible that reporters had called to try and fish out details. Charles laughed at the thought. They would have more success breaking into a bank vault.

"Just Mr. Wilkes, sir. He asked to speak with you when you woke."

"Please dial him for me."

A moment later, the assistant handed Charles the phone, already ringing. Charles looked at his watch. He needed to be on the road. The Fend 100 team had already been working for hours today, and Charles would be in high demand the moment he walked in to the building.

"Good morning, Mr. Fend."

"Morning, Caleb. What's the good word today?"

"I'm afraid we've had a few setbacks."

"Oh? Is Max alright? Anything I need to do?"

There was no answer.

"Caleb?"

Charles checked the phone, but the call had gone dead. After trying to call him back for a minute, he gave up. He tried calling in to work, but his phone wasn't connecting to the network.

Charles pointed it out to his assistant, who offered his own phone. But Charles suggested that they just go in to the office. Everyone he needed to see would be there.

His assistant briefed him as they drove.

"You'll be speaking with the *Today Show* again—live at eight oh five a.m.—followed by two other morning shows later in the morning. Reporters for the *Times* and the *Post* both wanted to speak with you, if you could give them a few minutes. And *60 Minutes* will be doing a profile on you."

"Again?"

His assistant was diplomatic. "I think they feel that they have more material."

Charles grunted. "They're probably right."

The drive from Ponte Vedra to Cecil Field took slightly under an hour. Their car entered the private drive to his headquarters and saw several large dark vehicles parked in a column along the curb. Government vehicles.

Wilkes and another man stood next to the lead SUV.

"We were disconnected."

Wilkes said, "Good morning Mr. Fend. I'm sorry about

that. Several of us have been having phone trouble this morning." He gestured to Flynn, who was standing beside him. "You know Special Agent Flynn."

Charles eyed the man. "Hello again. What are all these vehicles for?"

Flynn cleared his throat, looking between Wilkes and Charles. "Mr. Fend, we want to make sure we're ready for anything. So we have a special team of FBI agents ready to step in if anything should go wrong today."

"Well, they can't be seen by the press. That would look suspicious. It'll ruin the whole event. I know that we need security, but I have a business objective here as well."

"I understand, sir. We'll keep them out here, in your private parking area. Only some of your employees will see them."

Charles raised an eyebrow, looking back and forth between the CIA and FBI men. He wondered how much the FBI knew. Did Flynn know everything about Morozov? About Charles's own history with him? Unlikely. Wilkes played things too close to the vest. Just like all the other handlers Charles had worked with over the years. The CIA was filled with boys who had never learned to share.

Charles looked at his watch. "Takeoff is coming up. I need to head inside, but I've asked my team to set up an office space for you to work out of—have they shown it to you?"

"Yes. Thank you."

"Of course. It will be right next to the Fend 100 mission control center, so you'll be able to monitor the flight"—he shot them a knowing look—"and the personnel involved."

"Thank you, Charles. We'll try to stay out of your way. Have you heard from Max?"

"No. You were telling me something before we got disconnected—something about setbacks?"

Wilkes's face darkened. "I'm concerned that Max might be in trouble."

"What kind of trouble?"

"Morozov. Max never came back from his meeting yesterday afternoon. Listen, we'll do everything we can to find out where Max is. You just focus on the Fend 100 this morning. I promise you that we'll let you know the moment we hear anything on Max. I'm sure it will turn out okay." He didn't sound convincing.

Charles stood on the steps of his building entrance, looking into Caleb Wilkes's eyes. Through gritted teeth, he said, "Please do let me know when you have more."

With that, the CEO of Fend Aerospace turned and walked up the steps and through the large revolving door of his building. Several employees were waiting for him inside.

"Congratulations, Mr. Fend. You're about to make aviation history. Do you have a minute?"

Charles looked up at his chief marketing officer. "Yes. Thanks. I'll be there momentarily." The other employees took the hint and sauntered off.

He strode into the open atrium, surrounded by the excited crowd noise and flashes of professional cameras.

This section of the Fend Aerospace building was of modern architecture. Open floor plans. Lots of high ceilings, stone, and clear glass walls. An upper-deck observation level with a glass barrier.

Hundreds of aviation reporters and industry analysts were gathered around the Fend mission control center—observing through thirty-foot glass walls. Those walls encapsulated the Fend engineers and scientists, clicking and typing as they monitored today's flight from their rows of computers.

The Fend mission control center reminded most onlookers of the NASA space shuttle mission control. That was intentional. But there was a major difference—this space was specifically designed to be observed by an audience.

Ever the marketer, Charles had made sure that his team of industrial designers and advertising gurus had taken part in the creation of the facility. He wanted the building to provide a home court advantage at these sorts of press and media gatherings. Events like these would help feed the frenzy in the technology blogosphere. These test flights were a show. He was the Steve Jobs of flight. And this was his iPhone presentation. Charles would need the positive buzz if he was to succeed in having people begin using his new product.

As the CEO of Fend Aerospace, he wasn't just asking people to try a new way of communicating. He was asking them to put their lives in the hands of a robot.

Fend Aerospace was about to become a pioneer in commercial aviation. The crowd had gathered to witness the first passenger flight of their brand-new aircraft, the Fend 100. The FAA had certified the aircraft type a few months before. A seismic government contract for the technology was in the works. But human acceptance of the technology remained an issue. The FAA and other key stakeholders were watching closely.

The Fend 100 was the first fully automated airliner. No pilots required. The pilots were there, of course. Three of them, in fact. All test pilots. They would oversee the flight from the cockpit and be ready to take the controls if anything went wrong.

While the FAA had approved the flight after seeing dozens of demonstrations, most people still weren't comfortable flying without a human being behind the controls. Charles figured it would take five to ten more years, and many millions of lobbying dollars, before the airlines were allowed to take full advantage of the technology.

Baby steps.

Charles's vision was that, over time, the FAA would allow commercial airliners to become single-piloted, with one Fend 100 AI machine taking the place of the copilot. Eventually, the AI machine would operate all of the controls and execute all communications. At that point, the pilot would be nothing more than a safety observer. It wouldn't take long until the pilot stayed on the ground, overseeing multiple automated commercial airliners, similar to the way an air traffic controller was able to guide multiple aircraft simultaneously. This would provide cost savings and improve efficiency. It really would be the dawn of a new era.

That was, as long as nothing went wrong.

Charles looked at the office adjacent to the Fend 100 mission control room. Through the open door, he could see the government men in there, trying to look inconspicuous as they observed his team doing their jobs. Wilkes and Flynn looked worried. And they had good reason to be.

Charles had already been nervous about today's flight going smoothly. But now—with Max in possible danger, and a counterespionage operation underway, today's flight had taken on a whole new importance.

As Charles walked the floor, he could overhear the CMO giving a TV interview with the local news channel.

The reporter said, "So they'll be flying up and down the coast of Florida..."

"That's right, they'll be flying up the east coast of Florida —and returning to land here at our headquarters near Jacksonville."

"And how many on board?"

The man smiled. "We've got a full flight. As you can imagine, a lot of folks wanted to join. Many are reporters and aviation writers. A few are employees of Fend Aerospace that we wanted to recognize for their hard work on the project."

And our lead program manager, who has been placed on board to help protect against a former KGB operative, Charles thought to himself.

The reporter said, "Well, I'm a little sad that I didn't get an invite."

The CMO laughed. "I'm sorry—but hopefully you'll get to fly with the technology soon! We want to begin putting this on all airliners in the US within the next few years."

"Now what makes this different than autopilot?"

"We get that question a lot. Our Fend 100 Artificial Intelligence Pilot System is *way* more advanced than a simple autopilot function that you see today. The Fend 100 aircraft can communicate with air traffic controllers, set up on the approach, complete the landing, and even taxi into the terminal without anyone on board. It's going to revolutionize the way we travel."

Charles hoped so. While drone flight was becoming more and more prevalent in military and commercial use, it had yet to be approved by any major global aviation agency. If things went well today, that could all change.

He entered the mission control room. The Fend 100 mission control team had twenty workers, all sitting at neatly spaced-out computer monitors. Forty-foot ceilings.

Giant screens at the front of the room showed the aircraft's location and status. The floor was a glossy stone.

Even within the glass walls, Charles could hear the crowd noise outside. Some were posing for pictures. Many wore press or other VIP badges around their necks. The aviation media had been plastering this story on the front pages of their websites and magazines for the past few years. This was their first real taste of the Fend 100 aircraft.

"How's it coming, Bradley?"

Bradley Karpinsky said, "She's taxiing for takeoff now, sir. Just another minute or so."

Claps and cheers outside as the Fend 100 taxied by.

Wilkes walked through the door and gestured for Charles to follow him. Wilkes said, "Can you join us outside for a moment?" Flynn stood next to him, dread in his eyes.

"Takeoff is in two minutes. Can't this wait?"

"Afraid not. Flynn just got a message from the FBI—a man claiming to be Max Fend contacted the Jacksonville field office. They weren't sure if it was a hoax or not. They said the guy wants us to halt the flight. He said not to let the Fend 100 take off."

Charles looked incredulous. "What? Why? And why wouldn't Max contact me or you?"

Wilkes shook his head. "I don't know, Charles. But the FBI said that Max was on his way here now. If the timing is right, he should be in the parking lot any minute. We're going to check."

"Should we still have them take off?"

The two government men looked at each other.

Flynn lowered his voice so that only the two others would hear him. "We have Maria on board. We have a backup plan—nothing that we have seen suggests that

Morozov will be successful in hacking into the network, let alone getting past Maria's new security measures."

Wilkes said, "I would hate to ruin all of our plans unless we know for sure that this is Max."

Charles nodded. "I'll come out with you." He looked back at his chief engineer. "No need to wait for me, Bradley. Stick to the schedule." They walked outside.

* * *

As the three of them walked down the concrete stairs and into the parking lot, the quiet morning air filled with the loud noise of a commercial jetliner throttling up its engines. The men looked through the chain-link fence and witnessed the Fend 100 starting down the runway.

Charles looked at his watch. "Seven a.m. Right on time."

The giant white aircraft pitched up and began climbing, its landing gear folding up into its belly. The airliner became a slow-moving silhouette against sunlit clouds. As it rose over the Jacksonville skyline, the jet noise gave way to a honking horn.

All three men turned around to see a taxi racing towards them and skidding to a halt.

Max sprang out of the door, panicked. He and the woman with him looked like hell – clothes damp and sandy.

"It took off? Shit. Come on, we need to get to the control room and contact the pilots. You have to recall them."

"Don't be absurd. Why?" Charles asked.

"Hold on now, Max," Wilkes said.

Max pointed up at the departing aircraft. "Listen to me. Morozov isn't planning to steal the Fend 100 technology."

"What are you talking about? What is he trying to do, then?"

The group stared at Max as he spoke.

"Morozov is going to crash it."

* * *

A drink cart made its way down the aisle of the Fend 100. The passengers were a mix of company employees being rewarded for their hard work, aviation enthusiasts who had won contests to go on the first flight, and members of the media.

In seat B13, Betsy Sivers ordered a mimosa and looked out in awe at the beach below. She had worked for Fend Aerospace for almost thirty years. She'd started off in manufacturing at the original plant in Texas, then made her way to Florida when they'd expanded in the early 2000s. This flight was a great reward for her hard work.

Rick Powell sat in G23. He wrote for *Plane and Pilot* magazine and was eagerly typing up everything he experienced so that he could publish it on his blog when they landed. His wife and twelve-year-old son had made the trip up from Daytona and were waiting back at the airport. He couldn't wait to tell his son about the ride.

In seat F57, Bobby Turell thanked the flight attendant for his apple juice and smiled to himself. He had turned thirty-two last week. He was one of the ten contest winners. A self-proclaimed aviation nut, Bobby had been to every SUN 'n FUN air show since he was a boy. Getting to ride in the first passenger flight of the Fend 100 was the thrill of a lifetime for him. Right up there with riding in a Ford Tri-motor at Oshkosh. He couldn't wait to tell his girlfriend about it. In a moment of pure euphoria, he decided right then and there that it was time to go ring shopping. Life couldn't get any better than this.

As the aircraft banked right to head south over the Florida shoreline, beams of electromagnetic energy began to illuminate the Fend 100's data link antenna. The energy beams originated from a large yacht just south of St. Augustine and rapidly intensified in magnitude.

The Fend 100 was being hijacked.

21

While the group marched into the Fend 100 headquarters building, Max did his best to fill them in on what he knew. Renee followed him in, listening.

"Come on," Charles said. "I've had them set up a special office space for you. You'll be able to monitor the flight from there."

"We need to recall the flight, Dad. *Now*."

Charles said, "We can talk inside."

They walked through the revolving doors and past a throng of reporters who were setting up for their morning interviews. The group watched as Max and his father led the others into an office right next to the Fend 100 control room.

One of the reporters said, "Is that...?"

"No, he's taller," another one said.

A few flashes erupted as cameramen snapped pictures.

Once in the office space, they closed the door. Flynn said, "Okay, spill it, Max. What's going on?"

"Morozov tried to have me killed last night. We barely escaped. You were right, Caleb. Charlotte Capri was working for him. By the time we escaped, it was almost dawn—it took us longer to get a phone and a vehicle. We kept trying to call, but the Fend Aerospace phone network and my father's phone weren't connecting. Neither were the local police. We finally tried the FBI."

"Could be Morozov's hackers trying to prevent you from reaching us."

"Well, it appears to have worked. Can we recall the Fend 100?"

Max was scanning the room, looking to see who was in there.

Wilkes said, "We have fail-safes in place. You know what we need here, Max. I need the Russians to make their move so that we have verifiable electronic data. Leverage to use against Morozov."

"That was back when the risk was a simple cyberattack —stealing a few terabytes of data from my father's company. Now we're talking about people's lives, Caleb."

Agent Flynn grimaced. "Dammit. We shouldn't have let them take off. I agree with Max."

Charles said, "So do I. I'm going to see what I can do." Charles marched back into the Fend 100 control room.

Max looked at Flynn. "Are you armed?"

"Of course."

Max looked through the window of the office and into the adjacent Fend 100 mission control room. "If Morozov was going to kill me last night, that means that he didn't need me to upload any software. But he's still planning to hijack the Fend 100. I think you were right about him having someone on the inside."

Each of their heads turned to look through the window. They scanned the faces in the Fend 100 control room. The engineers and project team working diligently as the Fend 100 had its big show. Now that Max was silent, they could hear the project engineers and radio controllers speaking to the aircraft through the overhead speakers.

"Fend 100, Control, we have good uplink and downlink. What's your status?"

"Control, Fend 100, everything looks good here. We're along for the ride."

The group could hear the voice of the pilot and the project engineer, Bradley Karpinsky, on the overhead speaker system.

The pilot said, "Cecil Control, Fend 100, things are looking good. We're in fully automated mode and everything is proceeding normally."

"Fend 100, Cecil Control, roger. Nice job, boys. We'll see you in a few."

"I am going to head next door for a moment," Special Agent Flynn said. Wilkes followed him.

Renee sat at one of the computer terminals in their office, looking at all of the displayed information. "What are we looking at?"

"So this map here shows the aircraft track, altitude, airspeed, and heading," Max said.

Renee said, "Where are they now?"

"East of Cape Canaveral. Headed South."

"So nothing unusual yet?"

Max shook his head. "Not yet. Perhaps Maria's security fix is working."

Max could see his father standing over the shoulder of Bradley Karpinsky, a grave expression on both of their faces.

Karpinsky's voice came on the radio again. "Fend 100, Cecil Control, there has been a change of plans. We're being asked to cut the flight short due to unforeseen circumstances here on the ground."

"Say again, Control?"

"We're bringing you back, Fend 100. Sending the aircraft new directions now."

Max could see the engineers in the other room becoming agitated, pointing at their own displays and yelling back to Karpinsky.

Renee said, "What's wrong?"

The overhead speaker relayed Karpinsky's voice. "Fend 100, Control, I just input a return to base command, but I'm not showing the aircraft turning."

"Affirm, we're seeing the same thing here, Control."

"Fend 100, Control, I now show you in a descent of one thousand feet per minute," they heard over the overhead speaker. "Please verify. The flight profile has you maintaining altitude at twenty thousand feet for the next fifteen minutes."

"Roger, Control, we see that. We're in fully automated mode. Not sure why it's descending on us. We're troubleshooting now."

Max could see his father speaking to Wilkes and Flynn. They all looked worried. "I think it's happening."

Renee typed at her desktop computer. "I'm going to see if I can get us some more information."

"Fend 100, we now have you descending at a rate of two thousand feet per minute. Airspeed still three hundred and eighty knots indicated."

"Control, Fend 100, roger. Troubleshooting."

"Fend 100, please have Miss Blount get on the radios."

"Control, Fend 100, say again?"

"Control, Fend 100, no joy on troubleshooting. Sorry, folks, but we're going to conduct a manual override."

A few tense moments went by before they heard from the pilots.

"Cecil Control, Fend 100, we seem to have a problem." The pilot's voice sounded agitated.

Karpinsky said, "Go ahead, Fend 100."

"Control...the manual override doesn't appear to be *working*. The electronic flight controls aren't responding the way they should. They...they aren't responding at all. We can't stop the descent."

"Fend 100, Cecil Control, did you try the backup?"

"Control, Fend 100, that's affirm."

"Did you try pulling the circuit breaker?"

"Control, Fend 100, we've tried everything and are retrying all the steps again. So far we've tried the primary system override, the backup override, and pulling both circuit breakers. We're ready to pull all the AC power in the cockpit and try a full restart."

Max looked at the airplane's statistical readouts. They had just passed below ten thousand feet. The hair on the back of his neck stood up. The altitude kept ticking down.

Renee said, "Where are they now?"

"They're still headed south. Heading towards the Bahamas."

Flynn and Wilkes came in. "Have you guys tried to reach Maria on your radio? They aren't putting her on our radio."

"I'll try," Max said.

They had set up a special communications section on the aircraft for Maria to talk on.

"Maria, this is Max, come in."

"This is the Fend 100 flight engineer, who's this?"

Max spoke into the microphone. "This is Fend Control —we have a separate comms channel set up. Please put Miss Blount on immediately."

"Fend 100, Control, we are initiating the override procedures now. You should be able to take control of the aircraft now."

Max could see flashing green text on the bottom of the aircraft statistics screen. *Remote Aircraft Control Datalink connecting.*

"Control, Fend 100, what's the status? We need you to take control now. Our troubleshooting is nonresponsive."

Karpinsky said, "Roger, Fend 100. Stand by."

"Fend 100, Control, I show you passing through four thousand feet."

Then the radio call came that made everyone turn white.

"Mayday, mayday, mayday, this is Fend 100, forty miles northeast of Bimini Island. Flight controls nonresponsive, in an uncommanded descent...we will be ditching in the water."

In the chamber where the press and aviation enthusiasts were watching, some people started to yell in worry. Max could hear the commotion from their office room.

Max said in a firm voice, "Fend 100, *please place Maria Blount on right now*. She will be able to override the remote control."

"Control, 100, say again?"

"Fend 100, Control, get Maria on the horn. She should be able to help."

"Control, Fend 100, Maria is with you on the ground."

The people in the office shook their heads, annoyed at the confusion of the moment.

Max was almost yelling now. "Negative, Fend 100. Maria Blount is on board with you. Go tell someone to find her and get her on the radio—now!"

"Control, Fend 100." Another pilot speaking, now. "I'm positive she is not on this flight. She told us that there was a change of plans this morning. She was there for preflight, but not for takeoff. She said she would be with you."

Renee said, "They just went below one thousand feet of altitude." People were screaming outside the room now. Some were family members of the passengers on board.

They have someone on the inside.

Max closed his eyes.

"It's Maria. Maria Blount is Morozov's person on the inside."

The altitude now read zero.

The door to the mission control room was being held open by one of the FBI agents. Max could hear his father telling Karpinsky to contact the Coast Guard and start a search and rescue. Outside the room, people were sobbing.

* * *

Maria typed on her computer inside Morozov's yacht. The vessel was sailing fifteen miles off the coast of St. Augustine.

"Sync complete. We now have control." She spoke to Morozov, who was piped in through the speakerphone in the center of the room. Morozov had left the Ritz-Carlton at Amelia Island and gone to their safe house. It would be too risky to bring him back to the yacht. The yacht had served two purposes: to gain initial control over the Fend 100, and to divert any American response.

Morozov sounded in good spirits on the speakerphone. "Excellent work, Maria. Are the men ready?"

The ex-Spetsnaz man standing next to her nodded. "Yes, Mr. Morozov. As soon as you give us the signal, we'll move."

"Maria, you know what to do at this point. I have received the transponder code that we will need. I am sending that to you now."

Maria turned to a dark-haired young man who sat in front of a computer terminal to her left—a very talented hacker, with a very capable mind. Chechen by birth, he worked for one of Morozov's companies—Maljab Tactical. He served as a consultant for many of the extreme militias in the Middle East. Until recently, much of the work he did was in Syria, helping the Islamic State to maintain a solid social networking presence without getting caught by the NSA or other Western cyber agents.

Maria said, "You get it?"

"Yes," the Chechen responded.

"We have what we need, Mr. Morozov."

"Good. Send out our headline news updates. And get moving."

"We will. Goodbye."

Maria ended the call and turned to the Chechen. "Send it."

The boy made several keystrokes in rapid succession and then hit the return key.

"It is done."

"Ms. Blount." It was one of the security men.

"Yes?"

"The helicopter is ready, ma'am."

"Good. Let's be quick."

Maria and the Chechen entered the cabin of the helicopter, which was spinning on the small flight deck of the yacht. As soon as they were on board, it took off and headed north along the coast, remaining far enough out to sea that it wouldn't be visible from the shore.

* * *

The men and women at the Fend headquarters stood in

shocked silence. Some of the engineers were crying. Some were still trying to do their jobs.

The reporters outside the mission control room all wanted to get Charles Fend in front of a microphone.

Max cursed himself for not thinking that Maria could be a part of it. Maria had only been with the company for a few years, but she was one of Charles's most trusted employees. And she had been one of the first to report the cyber intrusion to the authorities. Why would she do that?

But being trusted and being in charge of the Fend 100 program also meant that Maria had access to everything. What would make her do this?

Max turned to Wilkes, who was talking to the FBI agent. "We need to get onto Morozov's boat as fast as possible."

"Already on it. Flynn has the FBI Hostage Rescue Team ready to go outside. They flew in last night."

"Good. We'll need to…" Max stopped talking as he saw a TV outside the glass walls of the control room.

The headline on the news channel read:

ISLAMIC STATE TERRORISTS CLAIM RESPONSIBILITY FOR Fend 100 HIJACKING

The Fend chief marketing officer stormed into the room. "Charles, you've got to see this."

* * *

"Is it true that someone from ISIS has hacked into the Fend 100 aircraft?" A reporter shoved a microphone in front of Charles Fend.

Another said, "Can you confirm that the Fend 100 has actually crashed? Are terrorists responsible?"

Charles held up his hands. "We're just finding things out

in real time, as are you. We're working with our team to establish what—"

"The terrorist organization sent a message saying that there's a Fend defense program that's responsible for the deaths of innocent civilians in the Middle East, and that this is retaliation for that."

The chief marketing officer glared at the reporter. "Was there a question there?"

"Can you comment on whether there's a secret Fend drone program?"

Charles shook his head. "No, I can't comment on that. Ladies and gentlemen, obviously we've just suffered a catastrophic event today. If you'll please depart the building. We need to work with the United States Coast Guard to rescue any survivors. If you will excuse me."

He walked away, ignoring the shouted questions behind him.

Max walked out of the building with Wilkes and Flynn. The column of dark FBI vehicles was in a frenzy of activity. Rough-looking men in tactical gear and sunglasses were gathered around the back of each vehicle, checking weapons and equipment.

One of the HRT men walked up to Special Agent Flynn. "This them?" the HRT man asked.

"Gentlemen, allow me to introduce Special Agent O'Malley." Brief introductions were made.

O'Malley said, "Is everything that you briefed us on last night still relevant?"

"Yes," Wilkes said. "How soon will you be able to take off?"

As if on cue, four MD 530 helicopters flew overhead and landed on the taxiway over the fence. The helicopters were similar to the tiny MH-6 Little Birds that the Army special forces used. In fact, several of the FBI's helicopter pilots were former Army helicopter pilots and had flown for the Army's 160th Special Operations Aviation Regiment.

O'Malley said, "We're ready."

"I need to go," Max said. "Do you have extra gear?"

The HRT man looked skeptically at the three others.

Wilkes said, "Max, why don't you just stay here for now?"

Max was stewing, but he could tell it would be a waste of breath to push further.

A few moments later, sixteen of the HRT men filed into their helicopters, which then buzzed off to the east.

22

The flight of four small black HRT helicopters skimmed the water, two sets of legs hanging out each side, weapons at the ready.

The team leader could see the massive yacht now.

"What the hell *is* that thing?" said the FBI agent next to him.

"That, my friends, is what you buy when you have absolutely more money than you know what to do with. Okay, gents, lock and load. Expect civilians on board. Rules of engagement as briefed."

As the helicopters flew closer, fast ropes slung down from each side. The team leader kept scanning the deck of the yacht. So far, there was almost no movement...

There.

"One o'clock. I have two men, armed, one with a set of binoculars, just aft of the bridge."

Yellow flashes came from several different locations on the yacht.

"Taking fire!" came the call from one of the pilots. The four-ship formation broke off into two sets of two aircraft, flying away from each other. They began evasive maneuvers to reduce the chances of taking on enemy fire. Two of the helicopters did an arc around the ship at high speed, angling their aircraft so that the HRT men could return fire.

A burst of controlled gunfire erupted from the cabin of the helicopters.

"One down. *Two* down. Looks like there's some movement on the aft deck."

When the two helicopters finished their arc around the boat, they peeled off and climbed. The other two helicopters were already on their approach to the flight deck of the ship.

Those HRT team members began sliding down the fast ropes. They landed gracefully on the helipad as the next pair of commandos followed suit. The first helicopter finished dropping off its four men, and the next one did the same.

The HRT men worked with fluid precision. Their movements carefully choreographed through hundreds of hours of repetitive practice. Weapons always trained outward— followed by expert eyes, scanning the ship, quickly entering and clearing the compartments.

A moment later, the other set of helicopters dropped off eight more HRT members. They joined the team already on board, systematically searching every compartment of the ship.

Bursts of machine gun fire could be heard at times, the HRT men communicating on their headsets as they neutralized all threats and secured the vessel.

Within ten minutes, five Russian security personnel were dead, and three were taken prisoner. Another seven civilians were on board, and the FBI agents had placed them in confinement near the flight deck. Two of the agents were working with the ship captain to turn the vessel towards Coast Guard sector Jacksonville.

"This door is locked," said one of the men.

The HRT team leader said, "We need to get in there."

One of the men was an explosives expert.

"Fire in the hole!"

A loud bang, and the door lock was blown. One HRT commando threw in a concussion grenade, and it burst as they waited outside the door. Then four of the HRT team members moved in fast.

The team leader knew this was the room they were looking for. "Get the CIA guy in here!"

Wilkes's man—a computer expert—was escorted down to the room. It was empty, filled with rows of computers and electronics—all unmanned. After a quick evaluation, the CIA man concluded that all of the computers had been zeroed out. None of it was usable, let alone active. He radioed as much back to Wilkes, who was standing by at the Fend headquarters.

* * *

Wilkes and Flynn had just finished telling the group what the HRT team had found—or rather, what they hadn't found. Max, Charles, and Renee listened.

Max said, "So where is Morozov?"

"We're working on it," said Wilkes. Flynn nodded.

The group disbanded, each of them needing to speak with someone on the phone to take next steps.

Renee called Max over. "Something isn't right."

He was only half-paying attention. His father was leaning against a wall, his face in his hands. Max needed to speak with him.

"Max. Listen."

"Renee, it's over."

"I don't think so. Look at this."

She pointed to one of the computer monitors. It showed the aircraft status. Airspeed zero. Altitude zero. The latitude and longitude were static.

Max sighed. "What am I supposed to be looking at?"

Her voice was emphatic. "The plane's pilots made their mayday call and said they were forty-five miles north of Bimini. I just looked up these coordinates that are on the screen here. They don't match up."

"What are you saying?"

"I don't know yet. But when I did research on how one would hack into a drone aircraft, I learned that one of the main ways it could be done is through something called GPS spoofing. Basically, they trick the system into thinking it's somewhere else. If Morozov's hackers made the Fend 100 think it was somewhere it wasn't, who's to say that they couldn't trick us into thinking the same thing?"

Max blinked. "What are you saying?"

"I'm saying, what if we're looking at bad data." She pointed to the aircraft status, which showed that it had impacted the water.

Max turned and yelled, keeping his eyes on Renee. "Bradley! Come here. Now."

Karpinsky walked over, a somber look on his face. "What is it, Max?"

"What GPS coordinates should be on the screen here?"

"The last known location of the aircraft. It should be right where it hit the water. Listen, Max, I have to get ready for the NTSB team to—"

Max and Renee looked at each other. Renee said, "The coordinates on the screen here—the aircraft status screen—

they don't match up with the coordinates the pilots called out when they made their mayday call."

Karpinsky shrugged. "So what? They probably glided a little farther—"

Renee shook her head. "No. They're one hundred miles off."

Karpinsky's eyes narrowed. "Huh. Well, that is a little weird, but..."

Max looked at Wilkes. He stood in the corner, talking on the phone with an intense look in his eyes.

Like he was still in the middle of an operation.

* * *

Max gathered Wilkes, Flynn, Renee, Karpinsky, and his father into an office.

"What if the plane didn't go down?"

Charles shook his head. "Max, what are you saying?"

Flynn said, "That's silly. Look, we need to look into this Islamic State thing. I'm getting calls from D.C. about—"

"Hear me out, Agent Flynn. Please."

Flynn sighed. "Okay. Where would it have gone?"

"You tell me," Max said. "Bradley, Renee, and I just looked at the in-flight statistics—Bradley told us they're programmed to stay on the last known GPS location of the aircraft. That helps them set up for a search and rescue. Right, Bradley?"

"That's right."

"But those coordinates were one hundred miles away from where the pilots claimed to be when they went down."

"What are you saying?" Charles asked.

"What if Maria reprogrammed the system to make it look like they crashed, when they really didn't?"

Flynn said, "Why would they do that?"

Max said, "Think about it."

The blood drained from Flynn's face. "How far could it have flown?"

"It had enough fuel for another fifteen hundred miles at least," Karpinsky said,

"But people would have noticed it, right?" Flynn shook his head, his voice a pitch higher. "I mean, you can't just fly a commercial airliner around without getting noticed. Right?"

Karpinsky shrugged. "It depends."

Flynn said, "On what?"

"It would attract a lot of attention if they tried to land it at just about any airport. And I'm pretty sure some radar controller would notice if it was flying over the continental United States without its transponder on."

Max said, "I would think so. They at least would have noticed it when it first entered US airspace, right?"

Karpinsky nodded. "Yes."

Renee said, "So we're saying it's possible that the Fend 100 is still airborne right now? How would we know that?"

No one immediately responded. Just sideways glances at each other—faces mixed with hope and fear.

Bradley Karpinsky cleared his throat. "According to our aircraft in-flight stats, it has crashed. We aren't getting any signals sent out from the aircraft. The only way we would know is if someone had it on radar."

Max said, "Who can check that?"

"We can look into it here," Karpinsky said. "The Fend 100 mission control center has several people who are trained as radar controllers. And we've got a good relationship with air traffic control in the area. I'll go talk to them and tell them to start searching for anything suspicious. But at this point, I suggest the government get involved."

Renee said, "Aren't they already?"

Flynn shook his head. "He means NORAD. We need the professionals looking for this aircraft."

* * *

Bradley left to go speak with the radar controllers, and the group kept talking. Wilkes excused himself to go make another phone call. Flynn went to call FBI headquarters and make sure that NORAD was updated on the situation.

Charles said, "I can't believe this is happening."

"Relax, Dad. It's not your fault."

"I was a fool to think we could take a risk like that. I just wanted them to get Morozov. It was all I could think about— I wanted to get back at him for what he did to your mother. But now...all those people. I feel responsible. We should have insisted on stopping the flight. We shouldn't have relied upon—"

Max placed his hand on his father's shoulder. "Dad, let's worry about that later. I have a feeling this isn't over yet."

Max glanced at his father's newspaper, which was lying on the office desk. Below the article about him was a feature on the G-7 summit. It was to be held tomorrow at Camp David, but the world leaders were due to arrive today.

Max picked up the paper and scanned the article quickly. After much political posturing, the Russian Federation was reportedly rejoining the group, and it would be renamed the G-8. Several of the member nations were making a big fuss about it.

Wilkes and Flynn walked back in.

Max placed his finger on the article. "Have you guys seen this about the G-7?"

Wilkes watched Max from across the room. "What about it?"

Max stared back at him. "It would make one hell of a target. The news is reporting that the Islamic State has claimed responsibility for the hijacking."

"I know," Flynn said, "but that's impossible. They aren't equipped—"

"Pavel Morozov has a subsidiary that works closely with the Islamic State," Max said. "They actually do defense contracting for them in Syria."

Flynn said, "You're kidding."

"So Morozov is trying to attack the G-7 conference? And blame it on the Islamic State?" Renee said.

"Oh, Jesus. You think that—"

Renee nodded. "If the Fend 100 is really still airborne, and Morozov's got control of it..."

Flynn's phone buzzed, and he quickly answered it. "Special Agent Flynn. Yes. Understood. Use this number." He hung up and looked up at the group. "NORAD and the NSA are both working to locate the aircraft now. If it's airborne, they'll find it."

23

Eastern Air Defense Sector
Rome, NY

Air Force Master Sergeant Krites sipped his coffee out of a paper cup. He liked his coffee plain black. Cream messed with his digestion, and sugar rotted his teeth. But a good cup of black joe was heaven. He always brought his own coffee in. None of this rotten stuff that the kids around here drank. They liked all the big fancy brands. He knew better. If you wanted good coffee, you had to grind the beans yourself, the same day. So he did, every morning. His wife certainly liked it. She was looking forward to him doing a lot more cooking after he retired. And that day was coming up faster than he could believe.

He had been in the US Air Force for twenty-three years. He'd become an expert in modern air defense and air traffic control. For the past ten years, they'd lived in New York state, and Krites liked it just fine. His job with the Eastern Air Defense Sector was meaningful. Especially after September eleventh.

EADS was the US Air Force command that was permanently assigned to detect and defeat an air attack on the United States. It was his job to identify unknown aircraft and vector in fighter jets to intercept them when needed.

In his eight years working at EADS, he was used to two types of these intercepts: knucklehead private pilots who accidentally flew into restricted airspace, and drills.

After September eleventh, his outfit had drilled a lot. And Master Sergeant Krites took it very seriously.

"How'd your shift go?"

"Did you see the news?"

"Down in Jacksonville?"

"Yeah. Airliner went down in the water. ISIS is claiming responsibility."

The two men were silent for a moment. Then Krites said, "It was supposed to be some new type of plane, right?"

"Yeah, like a drone airliner or something."

"Hell, man. I would never let some drone fly me around. How many died?"

"A couple hundred, I heard."

Krites shook his head. "That's just awful."

The two men finished their watch turnover and Krites sat down at his desk, headset on, looking at the information on the screens in front of him. With the news of the Jacksonville terrorist incident, backup duty sections had been called in to the watch floor. Everyone on the floor was on edge, their eyes and ears alert for anything that might be out of the ordinary.

"Krites!" the watch officer called from the platform behind him.

"Yes, sir?"

"You got a call on line three. FASVAC Jacksonville wants to talk to you."

"Got it."

"This is Master Sergeant Krites, Eastern Air Defense Sector."

"Master Sergeant, this is Chief Slade at FASVAC Jacksonville. We just got contacted by Fend Aerospace with an emergency. Have you heard about the accident that just happened down here?"

"Yes, Chief. Very sorry to hear it."

"Yeah, well, I'm a little confused. First, we get word that they had a crash. That was about an hour ago. Now they're contacting us saying that it might not have crashed. They think that the aircraft might be hijacked, and still airborne."

Hijacked. The H-word.

Krites shot a look over to his watch supervisor and waved, eyes wide. The supervisor came running over, and a few other heads turned. Krites switched the audio to the speaker so they could both hear.

Krites said, "Say that again, Chief?"

"The Fend company thinks their drone passenger plane might not have gone down in the ocean after all. They think it might have been hijacked."

"Someone hijacked a drone airliner?"

"That's what they're saying. A remote-control hijacking."

"And where is it now?"

"We aren't sure. We're looking at the tapes, and we had a radar contact about fifty miles east of Jacksonville with no transponder. It was traveling south to north at twenty-five thousand feet. But that was forty minutes ago—and it's not on my scope anymore."

"Understood. Just to be clear, this is not, I repeat, not a drill. Please confirm."

"That's affirmative. This is real-world. The flight profile matched what the Fend guys said their aircraft would probably be doing." A muffled conversation that the Master Sergeant couldn't hear. "Yup. It was almost the exact same speed and altitude that the Fend 100 was doing earlier, before the crash report."

"Where's it heading?"

"Hell if I know. I don't even have it on my radar anymore."

Shit.

"Thanks, Chief."

Krites looked up at his supervisor. "You catch all that?"

A young airman yelled from across the room, a landline phone in his hand. But not just any phone. The red phone.

"Sir, NORAD is on the line—asking for the duty officer."

Krites's boss got on the phone and began a rapid flurry of *yes sirs* to whoever was on the other line. When he came back, he said, "Okay—we've got NORAD feeding us information now—scan in on Warning Area W-122, off the Carolinas. They're tracking something going northeast at over five hundred knots."

"I see it. They tagged it. Okay, I got it now. It's got no IFF. No transponder at all. It's just flying parallel to the coast, staying out of the ADIZ. Boss, I don't like this at all."

"Neither do I."

Krites said, "I recommend we scramble the interceptors."

His supervisor nodded. "Aligned."

24

Captain Jason Easteadt, United States Air Force, would soon be ordered to shoot down a commercial airliner. He realized this while watching the news and eating his dinner from the on-base sub shop.

BREAKING NEWS

Those two words consumed the entire TV screen. Big white lettering over a red background, ensuring that the audience was held captive for whatever came next.

He took a sip of sweet tea from a plastic straw, curious about what they might announce. He munched on baked chips and wiped away a smudge of mayo on the corner of his mouth.

Bzzz. Bzzz.

His phone vibrated in the breast pocket of his flight suit. He clicked the button to silence the phone, not taking his eyes off the TV.

"We interrupt this broadcast to bring you this breaking news alert. NBC News has just learned that a commercial jetliner flying near Jacksonville, Florida, may have been hijacked by Islamic State terrorists. We now bring you live to our expert in Washington..."

Whoa. He stopped chewing as he listened to the newscast.

"Easteadt, you catching this?" asked the other pilot on duty with him. The major was yelling from his office one door down the hallway.

Bzzz. Bzzz.

His phone again. He looked down at the messages. It was from the squadron. An emergency notification, telling him to contact the duty officer for instructions. That message had been sent two minutes ago.

He was going to get launched to intercept this hijacked plane.

Jason couldn't take his eyes off the news. The aircraft was the Fend 100. The newscaster said that it had somehow been hijacked. He tried to think how that would be possible. Jason had just read a magazine article on it the other day— the Fend 100 was fully automated. How would it have been hijacked?

His pulse was racing. He thought about what this meant. About all the people on board. And about what he might have to do.

A circular emergency light protruded from the wall. It was flashing and rotating, covering his shocked face with yellow every few seconds. A bell rang in the hallway. It sounded like a school bell. It was joined by other sounds. Men running, yelling orders, their boots beating against the linoleum flooring.

This was not going to be like the other intercepts Jason had done. This wasn't some off-course Cessna pilot.

A banner scrolled along the bottom of the TV screen.

Fend 100 AIRCRAFT, FIRST AUTONOMOUS COMMERCIAL AIRLINER, REPORTEDLY HIJACKED. ISLAMIC STATE CLAIMS RESPONSIBILITY. CONFLICTING REPORTS AS TO WHETHER AIRCRAFT HAS CRASHED OR IS STILL AIRBORNE.

"Easteadt!"

Jason looked up, beads of sweat forming on his forehead. The major stood in the doorway.

"What the hell are you doing just sitting there? Come on! We have ten minutes to be airborne."

Jason nodded and rose from his seat. His knees wobbled a bit, and his head felt dizzy.

The Air Force major yelling at him to hurry was the flight lead for the two-aircraft interception unit. Easteadt grabbed his gear from his locker and jogged out to the flight line. A golf cart took him and the major out to their aircraft.

The major, noticing his unusual silence, said, "Are you good to fly?"

He hesitated. "Yes." No more conversation. At this point, their training took over.

The major hopped off the golf cart and walked up to their separate aircraft. Their jets were being prepared for launch. Jason climbed up and strapped into his F-16. His hands were shaking as he raced through his checklist.

"Good luck, sir," the plane captain outside said as he removed the ladder, a proud and serious look in his eyes.

Jason waved back, not trusting his voice. The glass canopy descended and enclosed him. He returned a crisp salute from the plane captain.

The engine of the major's F-16 Fighting Falcon started up next to him. His aircraft fired up next.

The major said over the radios, "Angry 509, Angry 515, radio check."

"Lima Charlie, how me?" *Loud and clear*.

The major responded, "Read you the same, 509. You all set?"

Jason said, "Roger."

"Ground, Angry 515 flight of 2, taxi to runway 19 Right."

The ground controller responded, "Angry 515 and flight, clear to taxi to runway 19 Right."

Jason began taxiing his F-16 behind the major's aircraft. The march towards the start of the runway was painfully slow. The sky above was a deep blue, with a few thick puffs of gray, the seeds of summer thunderclouds beginning to form. He could see commercial airliners on final at Reagan International Airport. He noticed that none were taking off. Had they been grounded?

The major's aircraft jerked, and Jason pumped his brakes.

The F-16 in front of Jason's slowed, then unexpectedly came to a full stop about halfway down the taxiway.

Something was wrong.

* * *

Morozov had sent only one man to do the job. Like many of the men working in Bear Security Group, he was ex-Spetsnaz. But unlike the others, this man's expertise was in long-range marksmanship.

The shots would be challenging. The range was almost one thousand meters. The target would be moving at about thirty kilometers per hour, and the sniper must hit it at precisely the right moment. From a suburban rooftop, adjacent to one of the world's most well-protected military bases.

The sniper had scouted out several locations to take the shot. The woods around Joint Base Andrews were out of the question. He was sure that the Secret Service and base security would have cameras and motion sensors. Even just snooping around there to evaluate the area would likely get him unwanted attention from the US government.

He thought about getting access to the military base. Forging a fake identity or stealing one—and gaining entry for any number of reasons. He could pretend to be a soldier stationed there, or a janitor working at one of the buildings. But there were too many unknowns. What if the base security guard was familiar with the unit the sniper claimed to be from? Taking the shot from the base would also make his escape that much more difficult.

So the sniper had decided on a neighborhood just next to the base. Many of the families who lived on the street were away on vacation for the summer. That was something he had noticed after canvassing the street. He picked the home that was closest to the base. The last home in a circular court. Thankfully there were no nosey neighbors nearby and no home alarm system.

He broke in, quick and silent, climbing through a

second-story window in back and onto the rooftop. A small private perch.

He checked his watch. The sniper had been told to expect two pilots to access their fighters. One was a major, the other a captain. He recognized the rank insignia on their flight suits. Through his scope, he watched them enter their aircraft and then waited for the right moment to shoot.

The sniper had been told to fire when they were on the runway, but he thought that to be a stupid idea. What if he missed? Two shots at that range was a tall order. He would fire while they taxied. It was a shorter range to target. And if he missed, he would have several more moments to retry. Great snipers were not just great marksmen. They were smart in their preparation.

He was lucky he'd planned it that way.

Crack.

His first shot missed the front tire of the first F-16. His rifle was bolt-action, and he had another round ready a second later. Sweaty palms. Heart beating fast, but controlled breathing. Trying not to think about neighbors opening their screen doors and looking outside, or dialing the local police department.

Crack.

A hit. The tire of the lead fighter jet burst open, and he saw sparks as the metal of the landing gear drove into the ground. A few seconds later, the jet stopped completely.

He took aim at the second jet, but it was already taxiing around the first. He took aim again and then heard the sound of a siren. He lifted his head up to look but didn't see where it was coming from. When he looked back, the other F-16 was already making its way down the runway. He had missed his chance.

To hell with it. Morozov would still have one less fighter

to deal with. And this part of the mission wasn't worth spending the rest of his life in an American jail. He packed up his rifle and began his escape.

* * *

"509, 515."

"Go."

"You aren't gonna believe this, but I think I just had a tire pop. My front wheel. Can you taxi around me?"

"Affirm."

"Alright, 509, you're gonna have to handle this one on your own for now. I'll radio base and have them get a backup bird ready ASAP. You'll be fine, just go by the book."

"Roger."

Jason taxied his aircraft around the F-16 in front of him and called up the ground controller to change his flight plan from a formation flight to a single aircraft.

He switched up to the tower frequency. "Tower, Angry 509 holding short 19 Right for takeoff."

"Angry 509, Andrews Tower, you are clear for takeoff on runway one-niner right."

"Tower, 509, clear for takeoff one-niner right."

Jason felt the same thrilling rush of adrenaline every time he pointed the nose of an aircraft down the runway, and it was especially exciting when it was an F-16 at Joint Base Andrews.

The thrill wasn't there today, however. Today it was dread. Dread at the thought of what he might be asked to do. He hoped to God he wouldn't have to shoot down a plane full of civilians.

"Angry 509, Tower, please execute your takeoff without further delay. We have inbound aircraft, sir."

"Tower, 509, roger."

Jason pushed the throttle forward. Twenty-five thousand pounds of thrust propelled the aircraft down the runway. As the airspeed reached 120 knots, he pulled back on the stick and lifted up into the air, the ground rapidly falling below him.

25

"Renee." Max touched her shoulder, whispering her name.

She was sitting down in front of her computer. They were in the corner of the room, out of earshot.

"If the Fend 100 is still airborne," Max said, "wouldn't that mean that Morozov's team is still remote-controlling it?"

"Honestly, I don't know enough about it. But it makes sense."

"Would there be a way for you to tell if there's a signal, and where the signal's coming from?"

Renee's eyes grew bright. Sensing that Max didn't want everyone to hear their conversation, she whispered back, "Yes. I think so. Give me a few minutes."

"Hey—keep it just between you and me."

"Why? What's wrong?"

He looked over his shoulder, in the direction of Wilkes and Flynn. "I'm not sure yet."

"Okay." She paused. "I'm surprised Wilkes isn't already working on this."

"Maybe he is."

Renee nodded. She began typing—chatting with someone on her computer.

"Okay. I'll be right back. I'm looking for the best location you can find. Try and get me GPS coordinates."

She didn't look up, still typing. "That may be tricky."

"Just do the best you can."

Max walked through the exit and into the parking lot. A few HRT men were gathered there. These were the backups —the ones who were left behind when the helicopters flew to Morozov's yacht.

Max went up to them and introduced himself as DIA.

"We know who you are," one of them said in a southern drawl.

"Right. I keep forgetting that my mug got sent to every FBI agent."

"That really you, running from the police in D.C.?"

"I'm afraid so."

"If you don't mind my saying so, that was a pretty dumb thing to do."

"Yeah, well. Live and learn, right? Listen, I think I have a lead—but I might need help. You guys interested?"

The HRT members kept their arms crossed and stayed silent.

Max nodded. "Okay—tough crowd. So the man who's responsible for all this goes by the name of Pavel Morozov. Are you familiar with him?"

Nods. "We got a brief, yes."

"And you guys just heard from your team that Morozov wasn't on the boat, right?"

"That's right," one of them answered, sounding curious.

Max said, "What if I told you I might know where he is?"

While they might not have entirely trusted Max yet, he

was familiar with the breed. The type of men in HRT were like golden retrievers. Brought down here to play fetch and then asked to sit and wait instead. To them, nothing was worse. Now they sensed that they might get in the game after all. A glimmer of hope flashed in their eyes.

"That would be mighty interesting," the FBI man said.

Max said, "When will your helicopters be back?"

"Not for a while. The yacht was pretty far south. They just called in. They got fuel at St. Augustine and are about to start bringing people back and forth between the yacht and the airport down there. The local FBI SAC has his men headed down to St. Augustine."

Max nodded. "Okay. Let's say, hypothetically, that I get Morozov's location. How many of you would be able to come with me to nail him?"

The men looked at each other. "Look, man, we'd love nothing more. But we'd have to run that up the chain, you know? Someone in the FBI would have to direct us..."

Max looked back at the Fend Aerospace building. He wasn't sure whom he could trust in there, but he needed the muscle. "Okay. I'll be right back."

Max walked inside and asked Special Agent Jake Flynn to step into the parking lot with him. He explained what he was trying to do.

Flynn peered down at Max over the rims of his sunglasses. "Come on, Max. What are you trying to pull? You should be just sitting back and thanking your lucky stars I don't have you in handcuffs right now."

"Don't you find it odd that Wilkes isn't working on this?" Max asked him.

"On what?"

"On finding out where Morozov is, after you didn't find anyone on the yacht."

Flynn's eyes narrowed. "Well, we just found out about that, so...maybe he just hasn't gotten around to it yet."

Both of them looked inside, through the glass door. Wilkes was in a glass-walled office. They could see him in there, walking around, headphones in his ears, talking to someone on the phone.

"Mr. Flynn, I've been doing this kind of stuff for a while," Max said. "It sure as hell looks to me like Wilkes is right hot in the middle of something. And he isn't involving either of us."

Renee opened the door and came outside, looking at Max with an eager expression. She stayed quiet, eyeing the FBI man.

"It's okay, Renee. Let us both know what you found."

"I pulled some strings with an old friend. Canadian CSE has triangulated the position of a signal that might be what we're looking for. It has all the right electronic characteristics for the Fend 100 remote-control data transfer. And it's been broadcasting for the last hour and a half. I think we've found it."

"Where?"

"I just did a quick check, but it looks like it's near Amelia Island. A mansion up there. Max, do you remember when I looked through the GPS history of Morozov's SUV?"

"Yes."

"I think this is a house that was in that GPS history. I can't be one hundred percent sure. I didn't write it down, but I saw it on the map..."

"Slow down," Flynn said. "Tell me what you think, Max."

"Morozov put his yacht off the coast of St. Augustine. The HRT had a shootout with them. But no one was there, right?"

"Right."

"The yacht is an obvious base of operations. But it would leave Morozov exposed. I think he kept his yacht as a diversion, close enough for him to get somewhere else he needed to be, but far enough for us not to stumble onto him. I think Morozov and Maria Blount are up at this house Renee just uncovered. Near Amelia Island. That's where they're controlling the Fend 100 from."

"What are their intentions?"

"I'm worried it has something to do with the G-7 meeting. Some of the world leaders have already begun to arrive. The conference is supposed to start tomorrow. I think he's planning something devastating there."

Karpinsky came running out. "Special Agent Flynn, I think you need to see this."

The group ran inside.

"This is our radar controller. He's been monitoring everything that's going on," Karpinsky said.

Wilkes walked in. Renee and Max looked at each other.

Wilkes said, "Fill me in, please."

"The EADS folks have scrambled an interceptor," Karpinsky said. "An F-16. And they've diverted and grounded all flights on the Eastern Seaboard. Nothing should be airborne except the Fend 100."

Max could see a TV in the next room. The media was just as far along as they were, it seemed. The headline read:

ALL US-BOUND FLIGHTS DIVERTED. OUTBOUND FLIGHTS GROUNDED. IMMINENT TERRORIST AIR ATTACK POSSIBLE, DEPARTMENT OF HOMELAND SECURITY SAYS.

Max could see the Fend 100 radar track on the screen. It was headed northeast, positioned a few dozen miles east of the Outer Banks.

"Where are they going?"

Flynn said, "I think we should consider the G-7 summit at Camp David a possible target. How long until they get there?"

"Maybe an hour?"

Flynn frowned. "Alright, Max, what are you thinking? Tell me what you want to do."

Max looked at Wilkes, who was listening now. "We may have a location on Morozov," Max said. "Up near Amelia Island. I originally thought we could use the helicopters. But they're going back and forth around St. Augustine...and, frankly I'm not sure we have enough time."

"So what, then?"

Max looked outside, on the flight line. There was a Cirrus SR22T parked out there—just like the one he owned.

"I have an idea. But I need you to lend me some of those HRT guys."

26

"Huntress Control, Angry 509, one hundred miles southeast of Andrews at angels twenty."

"Angry 509, Huntress Control, radar contact, turn right heading 180, maintain altitude and make best speed. We will have a tanker for you up shortly."

"Roger."

"509, your contact of interest is due south at approximately two hundred nautical miles."

"Roger, Huntress Control."

Captain Easteadt had just checked in with the Eastern Air Defense Sector controller, callsign Huntress. They would vector him towards the Fend 100 aircraft.

He tried to compartmentalize his emotions. To block out any fear or apprehension. But he kept thinking about the people and families that might be on board the Fend 100 flight. What if there were children?

He began to go through his air intercept checklist.

* * *

Max, Renee, and two of the FBI HRT men were taxiing for takeoff in the commandeered Cirrus. Max wondered who the owner was. Oh well.

Max thought about what they might face. He wasn't sure how many men would be at Morozov's mansion on Amelia Island. He would have preferred to bring twenty agents instead of two, but they didn't have time.

By his math, they had about forty-five minutes until the Fend 100 reached Camp David. Wilkes had wanted to use the FBI's HRT team and their helicopters, but Max had convinced Agent Flynn that there simply wasn't time. It would take HRT almost the full forty-five minutes for them to get ready and fly from St. Augustine to Morozov's location on Amelia Island.

Max had argued that if he flew the Cirrus parked right outside the Fend Headquarters at Cecil Field, his small team would be able to arrive in less than half the time.

There was only one *minor* problem with Max's plan.

"But it's a fixed-wing aircraft," Flynn had argued.

Max said, "Meaning?"

"With the FBI helicopters, we'll be able to land right outside Morozov's house. With that little plane, you'll have to land at the nearest airport."

Max shook his head. "Not with *that* plane." Then he had explained his plan. "It's the only way to get us there in time to fix this. If there's a way to reprogram the Fend 100, Renee can do it. We just need to get her in there, and stop Morozov and his men from interfering."

Wilkes objected. "That's crazy, Max. I think you should wait for HRT to get there."

Max turned to Flynn. "Special Agent Flynn, it's up to you. But you know the math. With the Cirrus, we'll be there in ten minutes. Those helicopters won't get there for forty-five. That'll be too late. And I need a decision now."

Flynn looked between Max and Wilkes. "I agree with Max. Go. Take two of the HRT men. I take responsibility."

It had taken Max about five minutes to locate the set of keys at the airport's FBO, and another five seconds for the HRT men to persuade the person behind the counter to hand the keys over. FBI commandos in full tactical gear could be quite persuasive when they wanted to be.

Now they were about to take off.

"Everyone ready?"

"Yes."

Max pushed the throttle forward and sped down the runway. The Cirrus was heavy. The FBI men weighed at least two hundred pounds each with their gear. As the end of the runway approached and the airspeed indicator slowly crept up, Max began to feel the cold fingers of fear creeping over his body. He hadn't bothered to do a gross weight calculation. It was a hot summer day, and that could be a fatal mistake. He kept the aircraft nose level for a bit longer than normal, gaining more speed, and slowly pulled back on the stick for the climb out.

He exhaled. A safe takeoff. Once they were up, he banked right and headed northeast.

"Renee, see this screen here?"

"Yes."

"Plug in the GPS coordinates you got for Morozov's mansion. Then press this button." She did as he said. A moment later, the needle on his heading indicator swung a few degrees to the right. Max adjusted his heading to fly directly towards Morozov's location. There was a distance indicator that was ticking down.

Twenty more miles.

At over two hundred miles per hour, they would be there in no time.

Max reached up and ripped off the warning panel on the ceiling of the aircraft, handing it to Renee. Everyone was nervous.

A moment later, he rechecked the distance. Only fifteen miles to go.

"Okay, team, I have to tell you, I'm really not sure what to expect here. The landing might be pretty rough. Renee, can you read the instructions?"

Renee's face was white. "Activation Handle Cover —Remove."

"Done."

"Activation Handle...Both hands...Pull straight down."

Max nearly yelled. "*Don't do that*. Just *read* it for now."

"Okay." She continued, "Approximately forty-five pounds of force is required to activate the Cirrus Airframe Parachute System. Pull the handle with both hands in a chin-up style pull until the handle is fully extended. After deployment, mixture...cut off. Fuel selector...off. Fuel pump...off. Bat-alt master switches...off." She continued reading the checklist, including the part that told them the proper way to position their bodies for impact.

Max said, "Everyone get that?"

One of the FBI agents said, "I was in a helicopter crash in Iraq once. This sounds like it'll be easier."

"Good attitude," said Max.

"Max, this is Fend Control, come in, please." It was Special Agent Flynn's voice.

"Go ahead."

"I need to put you on a conference call. Just keep monitoring this radio frequency. We're going to be talking to NORAD."

* * *

"Huntress Control, Angry 509, I have visual of the Fend 100 aircraft."

"Roger, Angry 509. Attempt to establish comms."

Jason expertly maneuvered his F-16 to the left wing of the Fend 100 aircraft. He could see passengers through the windows. Some were waving frantically.

He switched his radio to the guard frequency. Every aircraft and ship would be monitoring that.

"Fend 100, this is United States Air Force armed F-16, you are approaching restricted airspace, do you require assistance?"

For a moment, he heard nothing. Then a woman's voice came on the radio.

"Air Force F-16, this is Fend 100. We do not require assistance. We are having autopilot problems. We are troubleshooting now."

Jason gripped his yoke tightly. Thank God. Maybe this was all just some misunderstanding. He looked in the cockpit window of the massive airliner, but it was hard to see anything.

Then one of the people in the cockpit held up a sheet of paper to the window. But from this distance, he couldn't read what it said.

"Fend 100, Air Force armed F-16, I understand you are having a flight control emergency. Are you able to regain control?"

The woman responded on the radio. "We're working on it, Air Force F-16. We expect to have it fixed momentarily."

Jason put in a little right stick and tried to get closer to the Fend 100. He could almost make out what the pilots had written on the white paper they were holding up.

Then he heard the voice of the EADS controller. Only Jason could hear that radio call as it was on a discreet frequency. "Angry 509, Huntress Control, the Fend aircraft is approaching a National Defense High Security Zone. They will not be allowed entry into that airspace. Are you able to establish communication?"

They will not be allowed entry into that airspace. He mulled over the phrase. It sounded innocent enough, but what the controller was really saying was that Jason would be ordered to shoot the aircraft down if it tried to enter.

"Huntress Control, affirmative. I now have comms with the Fend 100. They tell me that they have almost fixed the problem."

He looked out the window. He could now read what was written on the white piece of paper.

NO COMMS. NO CONTROLS.

He frowned. That didn't make any sense. He was talking to them right now. Of course they had comms.

What was going on?

* * *

Flynn stood with his hands on the desk. "General, I have you on speakerphone. In the room I have a CIA rep, and via radio we have a DIA agent. Please tell them what you told me."

Wilkes and Flynn had taken control of the office and were speaking with a general at NORAD who was managing the F-16 intercept flight and the air defense for the Eastern Seaboard of the United States.

"As you can see," the general said, "the Fend 100 is headed towards the Air Defense Identification Zone. It looks like it'll enter the restricted airspace soon. We can't let that happen. Is there any way to manage this on your end—this thing is supposed to be remote control, right?"

"General, I'm afraid we've spoken with the personnel at Fend Aerospace, and they insist that they are unable to regain control of the aircraft."

Via his aircraft radio, Max said, "I'm still about ten minutes out from our location of interest. I'll be able to tell you more once I get there."

Flynn looked at the radar picture. "General, a question. You said they diverted and grounded all the other flights."

"That's correct."

"Sir, we're looking at the air traffic screen here at Fend Aerospace. We can see most of the Eastern United States. It looks like there is still one aircraft headed towards the Maryland-Virginia area."

A few hundred miles to the northeast of the Fend 100, there was another aircraft track. It was still several hundred miles away, but the Fend 100 was closing fast.

"Hold on," the general said, "I'm trying to find out which aircraft that is. Everyone should have diverted away from the Baltimore-Washington area."

After a momentary silence, the general said, "They said it's a head of state plane."

"Which country?"

"The Russian Federation."

* * *

Max tried to listen carefully to the conversation over his headset as he flew his plane towards Amelia Island. Had he heard that correctly?

The Russian president's plane?

What was it Morozov had said to Max? *A man like me*

wouldn't go through all this trouble just to exact revenge upon your father. I have a much grander vision than that.

And all at once, Morozov's plans snapped together.

Max said, "The Fend 100 isn't headed to Camp David. Tell the interceptor not to shoot it down."

Flynn sounded irritated. "But you said...what the hell, Max? What are you saying?"

"Gentlemen, I think Pavel Morozov is trying to assassinate the Russian president. I think we're witnessing a coup."

* * *

Max excused himself from Flynn's relayed phone call—he needed to give this his complete attention now. He checked his altitude. One thousand feet. That was as low as he felt he could comfortably go, considering what he was about to do.

He glanced back at his passengers. "Okay, folks. We're two miles out. I'm slowing down. Once I get on airspeed and set up for wind drift, I'm going to pull the chute."

He brought back the throttle, and the engine lowered in pitch and intensity.

"I'm going to try and get us as close to the house as possible. But frankly, I have no idea how this is going to go."

Renee's voice was shaky. "Are you sure this is a good idea? Couldn't we just land at the airport?"

"No time. Now remember the body positions for impact. And while I doubt they'll be expecting anything like this, my guess is they'll probably notice the plane parachuting from the sky. So be ready to fight as soon as we touch down."

One of the FBI men said, "Once we're down, you two follow us. We'll get you in safely and let you take it from there."

Max began sharp S-turns, bleeding off speed until the plane got to below one hundred and forty knots. He moved the stick so that the aircraft was straight and level.

"That's the house, straight ahead, right?"

"I think so, yes," Renee said. The mansion was right next to a beach, and adjacent to a golf course.

"Okay, here goes nothing."

He reached up and pulled down hard on the red metal grip. They heard a loud pop from the rear of the aircraft, and then everyone was jolted forward in their seats. Renee let out a yelp. The two FBI men were grunting and swearing as the aircraft decelerated.

The aircraft pitched down violently, and Max's stomach fluttered as he felt them falling. It took about eight seconds for the plane to slow from one hundred and thirty knots to almost zero.

Max's face was turning red, the blood collecting in his head due to the downward-facing angle. Then the parachute swung them like a pendulum, and the aircraft was once again level with the ground. They were falling, but at a manageable speed. Each of them looked outside.

"Where are we going to land?" Renee said.

"It looks like we'll end up on the golf course. Pretty damn close to the house. Do I get points for that? We'll need to be ready for his security men as soon as we get out." Each of them was armed and wore Kevlar vests.

Max watched the altitude wind down. Five hundred feet. Four hundred. The ground began rushing up to meet them. Three hundred. The descent didn't feel slow anymore. He remembered reading that the impact would feel like they had dropped from four meters in the air.

That sounded a lot higher now that he had pulled the shoot.

"The seats are supposed to take the brunt of the impact," he said aloud, trying to convince himself as much as anything. That was the last thing he said before the big crunch.

They slammed into one of the greens on the golf course. When the plane finally came to a rest, the hole flag stood right in front of them.

"Oh, damn, that was hard. My back..."

"Come on, we need to get out." Max's back was aching too, but he forced himself to open his door and tumble out onto the low-cut grass. The others were doing the same, weapons drawn. Each of them was in pain, but they looked to be okay.

Max looked up at the house. "I don't see any security. Are we sure this was it?"

"As sure as we can be," Renee said.

"Oh my God, are you guys alright?" came the surprised voice of someone in a golf cart several yards away.

None of them answered. The two HRT men began running towards the mansion, their HK416s pointed ahead. Renee and Max were close behind, their pistols aimed at the ground as they ran.

* * *

Flynn looked at Wilkes, exasperated by their continuing conversation with the NORAD general.

The general's voice, coming out of the speakerphone, was also noticeably agitated. "Gentlemen, that is unacceptable. I've got maybe five minutes before I need to give the order to shoot that plane down. Tell those engineers at Fend that they need to turn that plane around now!"

"We're doing the best we can, General. We have multiple potential fixes at work."

"I understand, but I can't be sure that your theory is correct. How am I supposed to know if the target is the Russian president's plane or other VIPs on the ground at Camp David? Hell, it'll fly right over D.C. to get there. Maybe it's headed for the Capitol Building. I have to call SECDEF in one minute. He wants an answer. I'm sorry, gentlemen, but we have that temporary flight restriction up for a reason. It's time to enforce it."

* * *

The FBI men were fast. Even Max, who considered himself to be in excellent shape, had trouble keeping up. They flew along the lawn of the mansion. Max noted several large antennae protruding from the roof. A custom job.

The first Russian security man they saw looked shocked to see them. He poked his head out of the double doors of the basement. He was holding a gun, and it got about halfway up before he took two bullets in the chest from one of the HRT men.

The FBI men didn't break stride. One opened the door and entered, scanning the finished basement with his carbine. The second HRT man followed closely behind. Max and Renee took up the rear. The room was very large. A pool table, rows of couches and a full bar. Two big-screen TVs on the wall.

No one spoke. But the other Russians must have heard the gunshots, because two men came running down the basement stairs. They fired a burst from a small automatic weapon, and the assault team took cover.

Max had one of them in his sights when the Russian

spun around, hit by a burst of gunfire. The other Russian security man met the same fate. Two more down courtesy of the FBI's Hostage Rescue Team. They were *good*.

Max looked to his side. Renee was hunkered behind a couch. "We need to find the room they're controlling the aircraft from," Renee said. She winced as another round of gunfire erupted from the stairway.

Max took Renee by the shoulder. "Listen. You go back outside the door. Get under the back deck and hide under the stairs. I don't want to risk them hitting you. Once we're clear, I'll come right back down and bring you up. Okay?"

She nodded. "Okay." She looked scared. Max didn't want to risk her getting hurt, both for personal and professional reasons. Renee hurried outside the door through which they had entered, then hid off to the right, under the back deck staircase.

Max turned around and scanned the room. The FBI agents had cleared the basement and were now advancing up the staircase.

His pulse racing, Max followed. He looked up the staircase at a closed door, wondering what was on the other side.

The HRT men were fearless. The first man opened the door and fired several rounds, then recoiled as a barrage of bullets ripped through the wall next to him.

The second HRT man grabbed a concussion grenade from his belt, pulled the pin, and tossed it through the open stairway door.

The sound was deafening.

Max felt it in his chest, and his ears rang.

The two HRT operatives disappeared beyond the top of the stairs. The sound of automatic weapons screamed through the stairway.

Max bolted up the stairs, aiming his pistol forward and scanning the room.

There were three bodies on the floor. The first HRT member was on the ground, gasping for air. He'd been hit in the Kevlar vest. The second HRT operative was spread eagle —Max couldn't see where he was hit, but blood was seeping out from under his uniform and onto the tile flooring.

They were in a large open kitchen, but the center table was covered with computers, wires taped down along the floor and running up the wall.

The third body was a dark-haired young man of about twenty. He was slumped over in front of one of the computers, dead.

Maria sat in front of the other computer, looking dazed.

Max pointed his weapon at her. "Fix it, Maria. Give control over to the Fend 100 pilots right now."

She looked like she was trying to focus on his face. Trying to read his lips. He realized she was probably deaf. Wisps of smoke flowed through the air—remnants of the concussion grenade.

Max was about to go downstairs and get Renee when he caught Maria glancing behind him. He turned, weapon raised toward a dark figure in the next room.

The figure moved awkwardly from the second-floor deck through an open screen door. Flowing white curtains partially masked him and his prisoner.

Pavel Morozov stood behind Renee, a gun to her temple. "Stay there, Mr. Fend."

Max wrinkled his brow, making calculations in his head. His gun was aimed at Morozov's forehead, about a fifteen-foot shot. Doable on the gun range. But not with a hostage...especially one that he cared about.

Max sidestepped behind Maria, keeping his pistol trained on Morozov.

Seeing this, Morozov nodded at Maria. "You think I won't shoot her too?"

"She's been working for you."

"Is that what you think?"

Max frowned, confused.

Morozov shrugged. "Fine. More fake CIA propaganda, I think. But whatever you may think of her, she is the only one who will be able to turn the plane around for you."

Maria was looking up at Max. A tear ran down her cheek.

A voice from a radio in front of her said, "Fend 100, Air Force armed F-16. Can you do me a favor? I can't read the sign that the pilots are holding up. Can you tell me what it says?"

Maria glanced at Morozov and then began to reach for the radio transmit button.

"Wait," said Max. Her hand froze. "He thinks you're on the plane. Why?"

* * *

Captain Easteadt couldn't understand it. The woman hadn't answered his radio call. What if she wasn't on the plane?

"Angry 509, Huntress Control, has the aircraft altered course, or does it still appear to be entering into restricted airspace?"

"Huntress Control, Angry 509, no change in the aircraft's course or speed."

"Roger, 509. Have you been able to establish communications?"

Jason thought about that. He wasn't sure what was going

on. "Negative, Control. No joy with the pilots aboard the Fend aircraft."

He looked at the cockpit window of the airliner. The pilots were still waving frantically, holding up their sign. Jason decided to try to raise them one more time.

* * *

"Fend 100, Air Force F-16, come in, please."

Max kept his pistol trained on Morozov's head.

"That's the Air Force intercept aircraft?" He was looking at Maria.

Max looked at one of the flat-screens on the wall. It showed the Fend 100 heading towards a lone air contact.

Max began stepping forward.

"What are you doing? Stay where you are," said Morozov.

Max continued to creep forward, slowly heading towards the table of electronics. He knew what he was after. And it was only another step.

"I said *stop*."

Max said, "Fine. I'll stop. I'll even place my gun down on the table." But he didn't. He just lowered the gun and used the barrel to depress the transmit button on the radio.

* * *

Jason listened in disbelief. It had taken him a moment to recognize what he was hearing, but once he did, everything fell into place.

Over the radio, Jason heard a man say, "Tell me, Pavel, why did you take over the Fend 100? And why have you had Maria here pretending to be on the Fend 100 while she talks to the Air Force fighter? At first, I thought you two were planning to remotely take control of the Fend 100 to attack the G-7 summit. But now I know that isn't true. Pavel, the one thing that really pissed you off was being subservient to the Russian president. You must really envy him. Similar background and all—yet he's in charge, and you're just his little assistant. Must be hard for a man like you."

"There is nothing you can do at this point, Mr. Fend. You should cut your losses and allow me to leave. Put your gun down." A second man's voice. Jason didn't recognize it. Low in tone, with a Russian accent.

"So you don't deny it?"

"I deny nothing."

"What will happen to you after the Russian president's plane goes down? We know it was you. How did you think you were going to escape?"

"You know only what your news media and intelligence agencies agree on. And it seems as though the Islamic State has already claimed responsibility for this hijacking."

The first man's voice. "Courtesy of Maljab Tactical, no doubt. One of your own companies. Your fingerprints will be all over this."

"You are wrong. I have friends *everywhere*. When those planes go down, I will take the reins in Russia."

"So you're going to fly the Fend 100 into the Russian president's plane right now? And then you think America will recognize you as the new Russian president? Come on, Pavel. Even you aren't that dumb. Why would the US ever recognize your legitimacy?"

"When I am in charge, Russia will forge a new partnership with the United States. It will be better for all."

"Morozov, you're assuming that the Fend 100 continues

on its current flight plan and flies into the Russian presidential aircraft. But won't Maria be able to fix that for me?"

Jason couldn't make out the rest of what was said over the radio, except that it sounded like an answer in the negative. He tried to process what that all meant. He looked at the aircraft that was flying next to him. An enormous white airliner, filled with people and fuel. Controlled by computers.

And supposedly heading towards the Russian president's plane...

He had to act. But what could he do?

Jason looked at his air search radar. Sure enough, there was one contact about one hundred miles ahead. At the rate they were closing, they would be there in mere minutes.

Jason pushed forward his thrust lever and hit his afterburner. His F-16 accelerated forward at close to twice the speed of sound. He would be almost out of fuel when he reached it, but he had to try and warn them.

The Russian presidential aircraft was a four-engined beast. A wide-bodied IL-96. Jason buzzed it from the front, passing only two hundred feet away.

That *must* have grabbed their attention. He then pulled and banked hard, arcing his nimble fighter to a position just off the right wing.

Jason flipped a few switches and then fired a burst of machine gun fire well ahead of the Russian aircraft. The tracers were clearly visible against the blue water below.

Now they knew he meant business. He wasn't sure what kind of homing system the other aircraft was using, but he knew enough about dogfighting theory to know that if the Fend aircraft missed the Russian presidential plane on the first pass, that was it. Game over. There wasn't enough of a speed advantage for the Fend aircraft to get a second chance.

Jason was already on the guard radio frequency. Time to make his call.

* * *

Max heard the voice over the radio and smiled.

"Russian aircraft approaching the United States, this is US Air Force armed F-16. You are about to be attacked by an incoming commercial drone aircraft. Begin evasive maneuvers *immediately* to avoid collision."

Maria and Morozov both looked shocked. Then Morozov's face turned to rage as he looked at the radio transmit button, which was depressed into the full detent. He realized that their entire conversation had been played to the American fighter jet. Morozov's wrist muscles flexed as he gripped Renee tighter. She let out a cry.

All of their eyes turned to the radar screen on the wall. The two air tracks were so close, heading right for each other...about to converge.

But they didn't.

The Fend 100 continued on in the opposite direction. The Russian Federation presidential aircraft turned sharply and changed altitude.

Maria could see the aviation stats of each aircraft being displayed on the board. "It didn't hit. The Fend 100 missed it."

"Put down your weapon, Pavel," Max said.

Morozov's eyes were on fire now, his nostrils flaring. "It seems that you have changed my plans. But your aircraft is still at risk. All those people will die if you don't regain control of the Fend 100. So let us bargain, Max Fend."

"Let's."

Morozov pulled Renee up close. "Maria is the only one who can save the people on that aircraft now. If you don't have her, they'll run out of fuel and crash into the ocean."

Max wondered if Renee would be able to analyze and interpret the data on this computer system in time. Unknown. He needed Maria alive.

Morozov began backing away toward a doorway in the corner of the room, holding Renee in front of him. He was heading to the garage.

Max could hear the FBI men on the floor and behind him, a groan from the stairway.

"Leave Renee," Max said, "and I'll let you go."

Pavel Morozov's eyes narrowed. "Done." He pushed Renee towards Max, raised his gun and fired three times.

Max caught Renee and covered her with his body as he returned fire through the closed doorway.

Max ran towards the door, but it was locked. He fired his weapon into the door handle. Wide holes formed and wood splintered. Max kicked the door open and burst through into the garage.

He fired into the fleeing SUV, hearing the sound of an engine revving up and the squeal of tires as Morozov peeled out of view, making his getaway.

But Max didn't have time to worry about him. He ran back towards the computers laid out in the kitchen, glaring at Maria.

She had been shot in the arm.

"Fix this," Max said to her, his weapon trained on her head. Sympathy for her gunshot wound wasn't something he had in him.

Maria nodded and began typing with her good hand, wincing in pain.

He glanced back at Renee. "Are you okay?"

Renee nodded. "Yes, I'm alright."

"I need you to watch her, Renee. Make sure she's really doing what we want her to do."

Renee stood behind Maria, who was typing slowly into one of the terminals.

Max said, "Turn it around now, and give control to the pilots on board."

Maria nodded, flustered and upset. She typed in a command, dragged her mouse, and began clicking a few times. "There. They should be able to control it now."

"Call them on the radio and tell them."

Maria did as requested. "Fend 100, this is..." She paused, not sure what to say. Max grabbed the radio. "Fend 100 on guard, you should have control of your aircraft now. Please respond."

After a moment, the radio came back with, "This is Fend 100 on guard. Flight controls are now responsive. Declaring an emergency and heading to the nearest suitable runway."

* * *

The ambulances and police cars arrived moments later. The EMS crews provided treatment for the FBI men. Both ended up okay.

The one who was hit in the Kevlar vest had two broken ribs. The one who was facedown and bleeding from a gunshot in the kitchen had lost a lot of blood, but was stable.

Max walked up to Maria as she was receiving treatment under police supervision. "What made you do it?"

She didn't answer. Just kept her head down, looking at

the ground. A few minutes later, the FBI arrived and took custody of her.

Special Agent Flynn flew to the scene, courtesy of the FBI HRT helicopters.

Max said, "Have you found Morozov?"

"Not yet. But we have agents and local police scanning the area. Roadblocks are set up all over for fifty miles around. And flights are still grounded. He'll turn up."

The FBI drove Renee and Max back down to Jacksonville. They had a prolonged after-action report to complete with the local FBI office. Then they were cut loose in time for dinner. Max invited Renee to his father's house in Ponte Vedra.

"You think you're ready to take me home to your father?" she said with a wink.

"I'm ready for more than that."

"How about a beach vacation? I know a nice quiet spot in Georgia—near Jekyll Island."

Max grinned. "In all seriousness, you did great. Thanks for all the help." He leaned in and kissed her.

"Thanks. You too." She was blushing.

Dinner that night was a busy affair. Charles Fend, understandably, had to work much of the evening. He had invited many of his company executives to his home. They could manage the public affairs nightmare from there. Max and Renee sat by the pool, sipping on cool drinks and watching the sunset.

When the night finally wrapped up, and the majority of his employees had left, Charles came and sat down with them. He sipped on a glass of scotch and looked at his son.

"Your mother would have been proud."

"Thanks, Dad."

"And you, dear. If there is ever anything I can do to repay

you for saving the lives of all those men and women on my aircraft, you just say the word."

Renee said, "Your son has already promised me a job."

Charles looked at Max. "An excellent hire."

Max said, "What will happen to the automated flight program?"

His father sighed. "I'm sure it will be some time before people feel comfortable enough with the technology. But I think it's safe to say that we won't be moving forward with the contract as soon as we thought we would. It's too early to say what the fallout will be."

"Well, perhaps we can start making parachutes for commercial airliners?"

His father laughed. "Perhaps."

27

Wilkes met Max at the Conch House restaurant in St. Augustine three days later. They sat in one of the secluded grass huts that overlooked the marina. A waitress brought them waters and appetizers.

Wilkes said, "We'd like to retain your services for the future, Max."

"And what will that entail?"

Wilkes took off his glasses, rubbing them with a napkin. "You liked working for the DIA, right?"

"I did."

"Well, we would like to have you serve your country in other ways. Your position in your father's company, and your fame...or infamy, depending on who you ask...will grant you access that few enjoy. You're a patriot, and a skilled operative. Your talent and loyalty were never in question."

"Funny how Special Agent Flynn wasn't made aware of my loyalty when he took me in last week..."

Wilkes sipped his water. "Look, I agree that the entire situation should have been handled differently. But things turned out rather well for us."

"Did they?" Max looked out over the water and said, "There's something I want to know."

Wilkes said, "Go ahead."

"I spoke with Flynn yesterday. Our final chat, I hope. He suggested that Maria Blount might no longer be in the custody of the FBI. He implied that *another* agency had taken her from them. Perhaps for interrogations? Or perhaps not."

Wilkes didn't say anything.

"I seem to recall a few operations from my days in Europe where our assets were retired by similar means. Sent off to rural lands to live out their days on a government pension, their covers ruined, but their mission accomplished."

Wilkes's face remained a blank canvas. Seeing that he wasn't getting a bite, Max said, "Maria wasn't *just* working for Morozov, was she?"

Wilkes stared back at him. "Who else do you think she was working for?"

"You."

"*Me?*"

"I think you knew that Pavel Morozov was going to try and kill the Russian president. And I think you thought that my father's plane, and the lives of everyone aboard, were an acceptable risk to take for a chance at changing the Russian leadership."

"An interesting theory. But very cynical, Max."

Max said, "If I were a man of low moral character, and the only thing that mattered to me was winning or losing the great game of espionage between the Russians and the Americans, I might see this Pavel Morozov situation as an opportunity."

Wilkes grinned. "I hope you aren't referring to me there. But pray tell, how so?"

Max said, "Let's say that I found out Morozov was able to crash the Fend 100 into the Russian president's plane. What would happen then? The Islamic State had already claimed responsibility for it. From my conversation with him, this was part of Morozov's masquerade. *You* might have been tempted to encourage the public belief that terrorists were responsible for the whole thing. The Islamic State is responsible for so many atrocities. Why not this? It takes out a Russian leader who has been a thorn in our side and increases the American desire to pour more resources into fighting terrorism."

"I hope you have more faith in me than that."

Max said, "I do, actually. And I have more faith in the CIA. I can't see them signing off on that."

"Good."

"But I think it was a worst-case scenario for you. A high-magnitude, low-probability risk that you were willing to take. And instead, I think you ended up getting exactly what you wanted."

"Which is?"

"Either way it was a win-win for the CIA. But now, you got rid of Pavel Morozov and have the Russian president in our debt."

Wilkes raised his eyebrow at that. "I hadn't thought of that. I guess he is, isn't he?"

"I noticed on the news yesterday that the Russians have announced they're pulling a large number of their troops out of Syria. Interesting timing."

"Well, I suppose it is, isn't it?" Wilkes sipped his ice water.

"The enemy of my enemy is my friend. If you took out

Pavel Morozov and saved the Russian president's life, I could see how something like that might present you in a very favorable light. Stopping a coup d'état? Maybe that appearance of savior-ship would help influence a deal. Maybe it could start a more peaceful relationship."

Wilkes shrugged. "Maybe."

"I remembered something about one of my Russian mafia contacts in France. Sergei. He was introduced to me by his former handler. But his former handler wasn't DIA— he was CIA. It happened so long ago, and it didn't seem important at the time. Just one agency sharing with another. Now, though—I'm not so sure that wasn't orchestrated more carefully."

Wilkes was chewing his ice cubes. "Alright, Max. I can see that you aren't happy with me."

"You used my father and me as bait, didn't you? You knew that Morozov was working with some of his contacts in Russia to orchestrate a coup. But you wanted to manipulate how it happened. So you dangled a carrot that you knew he couldn't resist. A chance to twist the knife in my father's back, by hurting his company—and by blaming me. That got Morozov's mouth watering. Just like you said... revenge keeps KGB agents warm at night."

Wilkes said, "You have no idea how big this operation was, Max. We didn't just dangle one carrot. We put out hundreds. You and your father weren't the only bait. You just happened to be the bait that Morozov went for. And once he did, we had to keep up appearances."

"That's why MI-6 was used to break me out. There couldn't be any connection to your operation."

Wilkes nodded.

Max continued. "You didn't want any chance of Morozov finding out the CIA was involved in all this. So you called in a favor to your friends at Legoland. But why did you care whether I was in FBI custody or not?"

"Because MI-6 got word that Morozov had ordered a hit on you, so that you couldn't prove your innocence. We preferred that not to occur."

"Why, thank you."

"See? And you say I wasn't looking out for you."

"My guess is that very few people knew the risk you took with the Fend 100 aircraft. That was dangerous. Did the Russian president know what was happening as he flew towards the Atlantic coast of the US? Was it used as leverage while he was in flight?"

Wilkes looked like he was thinking of something to say.

"Don't bother answering. I don't need to know. There's only one more thing I want you to tell me. What happened to Morozov?"

"I'm afraid that isn't something I'm at liberty to discuss, Max."

Max snorted, disappointed.

Then Wilkes said, "But if, hypothetically speaking, of course, I knew where he was, just know that you would probably be quite satisfied with his present condition."

Max's eyes were hard. "Good."

* * *

The unmarked jet touched down at the airstrip near Sevastopol, on the Crimean Peninsula. After the annexation of Crimea, the airport was predominantly used by the Russian military.

It had been a long flight. The aircraft taxied to a stop near the end of the runway. Three black cars waited on the flight line. Security men opened up the door for one of the cars, and the Russian president stepped out.

As the door opened and the CIA men began taking their prisoner down the steps of the aircraft, a broad smile formed on the Russian president's lips.

Wilkes walked up to the Russian president and shook his hand.

"I trust that you finished getting everything you could out of him?" he asked, a smirk on his face.

Wilkes shrugged but didn't say anything. *No more than you must have done working in Berlin many years ago, old man.*

Wilkes's men had to put Morozov through an accelerated interrogation regimen. He would have preferred to take more time, but they had still obtained a great deal of valuable intelligence.

The Russian president looked at the prisoner like he was a precious gift. "Mr. Wilkes, my thanks for this. Even if he is a week overdue."

Pavel Morozov was gagged, bound, and blindfolded. The Russian president walked up and removed the blindfold. Red, bloodshot eyes looked back at him, filled with fear. The president patted Morozov's cheek a little too hard, then gestured for his men to take him away. Then he got in his car, and the motorcade departed.

Wilkes began walking back towards the jet. He shuddered to think what might be in store for Morozov. But the man deserved his fate. Wilkes looked back from the top of the stairs once more, watching the motorcade speed off down the road. He pulled his jacket tight to fight the cold. The winds coming off the Black Sea lent a chilly bite to the air.

<<<< >>>>

ABOUT THE AUTHOR

Andrew Watts is the USA Today bestselling author of The War Planners series. He graduated from the US Naval Academy in 2003 and served as a naval officer and helicopter pilot until 2013. During that time, he flew counternarcotic missions in the Eastern Pacific and counter-piracy missions off the Horn of Africa. He was a flight instructor in Pensacola, FL, and helped to run ship and flight operations while embarked on a nuclear aircraft carrier deployed in the Middle East.

Today, he lives with his family in Ohio.

From Andrew:
Thank you so much for reading. More Max Fend is coming! (And Renee...) Be sure to join my Reader List to find out when the next book launches.

JOIN THE READER LIST at andrewwattsauthor.com

andrewwattsauthor.com

THE WAR PLANNERS SERIES

Now a USA Today Bestseller!

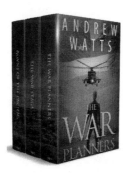

A nation on the brink of war.
A conspiracy that threatens the globe.
And one military family, caught in the middle, fighting for freedom.

From a secretive jungle-covered island in the Pacific, to the sands of the Middle East. From the smog-filled alleyways of China, to the passageways of a US Navy destroyer. The War Planners series follows different members of the military and intelligence community as they uncover a Chinese plot to attack America.

Chinese billionaire Cheng Jinshan and his wicked spy, Lena Chou, are moving their pieces on the board. Deception and misinformation are everywhere.

Now, in order to save America, the leaders in the CIA and Pentagon have set up a secretive task force. Their mission: to thwart Jinshan's plans, and prevent a global war.

Each member of the Manning family has a critical role to play. Technologist David Manning is taken from his family's home and thrown onto a special CIA task force. Ex-SEAL Chase Manning is sent to team up with a Marine Corps special operations unit. Admiral Charles Manning leads a US Carrier Strike Group, filled with America's latest and greatest naval technology. And Lieutenant Commander Victoria Manning is the officer in charge of a helicopter detachment on the navy destroyer, the USS Farragut - the only ship that stands in the way of a Chinese onslaught.

Get your copy at andrewwattsauthor.com

FIND OUT WHAT'S COMING NEXT...

ALSO BY ANDREW WATTS

The War Planners

The War Stage

Pawns of the Pacific

JUL - - 2018

Made in the USA
Middletown, DE
22 May 2018